FEALTY OF THE FALLEN

D.M. SIMMONS

ASIN: B09YGDGMNR
ISBN: 9798807138965

Published by Foggy Day Publishing
Cover Design by RFK Designs

Reader's Note

Fealty of the Fallen is a dark paranormal romantic told in dual POV. It contains enemies to lovers, forbidden love, stuck together, soulmates, found family, and alpha hero tropes.

It is the first book in a planned series. Each book should be read in order. It is intended for mature audiences and contains adult language, sexual scenes, and situations that may trigger some readers. Read at your own risk.

Blurb

After the War in Heaven, they fell.
Stripped of their wings, they divided into sides:
daemons and undecided.
He wants loyalty.
She wants freedom.
When fire fights fire…who burns?

1
DANTE

I take off my helmet and look around as a mild breeze sweeping off the Mediterranean brushes my cheek, welcoming me back. "Well," I turn to Vinny and run a hand through my hair, fingers burning with anticipation. "Are you ready?"

My brawny best friend gets off his bike and grins. "Like you can't believe, brother."

I stretch my arms overhead, easing my back and shoulders from the ride. "Well then, how about we get this show on the road?"

Vinny slings an arm around me as we make our way down the street, curling his free hand into a fist and rubbing it into the top of my head. I push him back and punch him in the arm, and he laughs. We've waited decades for this day, and now that it's here, the feeling of reckless abandon is palpable.

Being in Eden is always a welcome respite in our long and wicked existence. The enigmatic city on a secret island off the coast of Spain was built for debauchery and never disappointed. But we're not just here for pleasure. We're here for a greater purpose. One that has us returning every century for the last five thousand years.

By us, I mean daemons, but if I'm being honest, I hate the name. It suggests fire and brimstone, and it's just not the case. We are more than what folklore and legend have depicted. However, one truth they have gotten correct is our need for desire and corruption. Pursuit of both has driven our existence since The Fall–the day the angels rebelled and divided Heaven. But the reason we are back in Eden also drives us.

After we were stripped of our wings and cast out of Heaven, a schism among the Fallen occurred. Those who pledged allegiance to Luke, leader, and mastermind of the rebellion, became daemons–eternal beings in mortal form with an appetite for satisfaction. With our loyalty came the freedom to do as we pleased in exchange for our service once a century.

But those who refused to swear their loyalty became the undecided–eternal beings, also in mortal form, who wanted to exist free from the legion. Luke accepted their decision, but it came at a cost. He confined them to Eden, where they were to remain in perpetuity or until they swore allegiance to him.

That is why we're here. At the beginning of each century, daemons return to Eden in honor of that promise. For ten days, our focus is to do whatever we can to persuade the undecided to join us. But not just any undecided. The one to whom we are bound. Diablo, the one to whom I was bound, had not wavered in five millennia, and I not only wanted her on our side, but the idea consumed me.

I wasn't always so determined to win her fealty. When we were first bound, she was petulant. She didn't want to be on our side, which was fine. I filled my time in with decadence and immorality, thanks to the lost souls who called it home and whose purpose when we were here was to serve us.

Yet, despite her stubbornness, Diablo intrigued me and started to occupy my every thought over time. She was confident and intelligent and possessed an undeniable charm, and her beauty was almost painful. I was drawn to her and did whatever I could to get her on our side.

Just thinking of her stirred the most delicious thoughts, and now that I'm here, I'm beyond anxious to see how she's

2

changed since the last time we were together.

Vinny and I stride into *Saints*, our favorite place in Eden, and slide into a booth to order a drink. It, too, like the outside world had changed since we were here last. Then, it had a speakeasy vibe. Scant décor, with wood tables and chairs, and filled with cigar smoke, which clung to the walls. Now, however, it was a bar with a club-like vibe, throbbing bassline, and a tap that never ends.

No matter the time, no matter the change, *Saints* was still our place. Only daemons are allowed when we're in Eden, and everything from the alcohol to the music catered to our preferences. Vinny likes metal and beer. Currently, I'm a rock and bourbon guy.

Every daemon was as different in their tastes as they were in looks, but I'd fight alongside any of them until the end of time. Bonds forged in war are unbreakable.

"Are you anxious to see Lila?" I hold up my finger to flag a server. Vinny's undecided was a pixie-sized redhead who had as much personality as he had muscle.

"Are you kidding?" his gold-brown eyes flash. "I can't wait to get started."

Vinny's methods of trying to win Lila's fealty differed from mine, but who was I to judge? He'd made progress with her the last few centuries, and it sounded like he might succeed this time.

A server comes up to our booth and stands in front of us with her hip jutted out. "What'll it be?" she taps her fingernails on the underside of the tray and licks her lips.

Like all the soulless in Eden, she's dressed to please. Her long blonde hair is pulled high on her head in a tight ponytail, and she has on a short leather skirt and fuck me heels.

Having already signed away the most important part of

who they were, anything the soulless did in service to us was child's play. Judging by the way she's looking at me, she'd like to serve me right here.

"Bourbon, neat," I give her the once over, then turn to Vinny. "You?"

"Beer," he thrums his fingers on the table, ignoring the server completely.

"Got it," she flashes a smile that emphasizes her interest in me. "I'll be back."

I watch over my shoulder as the server returns to the bar. She looks like she could be fun for an hour. I'll keep her in mind if things with Diablo turn sour fast–which, given our history, was not only possible but highly likely.

I take a contemplative breath and lean back, looking around. It's hard to believe that humanity was coming out of its first world war and a global pandemic the last time we were here. Given the state of things currently, a lot hasn't changed–same shit show, different century.

The server returns with our drinks, leaning over the table seductively to place Vinny's beer down first, then mine. Once she leaves, he proposes a toast. "To the next ten," he says with enthusiasm and lifts his bottle.

"To the next ten," I raise my glass and tap it against his beer, grinning wide.

After taking a sip, I turn to the mirror behind the booth and check out how I look. The ride was long, but I wasn't disheveled, which is good. This century flatters my appearance, and I want Diablo's jaw to drop when she sees me.

The Fallen may have been stripped of ethereality when we fell, but there was an upside to siding with Luke. As one of the most powerful angels in Heaven, Luke used what power he retained after The Fall to sculpt his legion, and I'd reaped the benefits.

Each of us is attractive. The legion, when together, was an undeniable collection of good looks and strength. But Luke did some of his best work on me, and I knew it. The reflection staring back at me is one of vitality and power. My chiseled jaw is demanding, and my dark brown hair and cobalt eyes are a dangerous combination.

From our looks to our pursuits, daemons enticed to get what we want, and I wanted Diablo. She would be on our side, no matter what it took.

In the mirror's reflection, I see everyone's attention shift to the far side of the room. Whoever is cleaning this place was doing a horrible job because I can't see shit. I turn to see what's causing all the commotion, and my stomach plummets. Diablo saunters up to the booth, smiling at me coolly, emerald eyes flanked by thick, ebony lashes flickering with light.

"Shit," Vinny chokes on his drink and sprays droplets of beer onto the table as I stare at her, stunned. She's changed again, in a big way, and there are no words.

"Good to see you again, Dante." She looks at me over her shoulder, black as night hair cascading down her back in thick, beautiful waves. "Do you like it?"

Like is not the word. Diablo's body ebbs and flows in all the right places, and I can't stop staring. Her legs are no longer coltish, her tiny waist emphasized by curves mortal women would kill for, and her flawless skin is like fine porcelain. If she weren't bound to me, I'd be envious of the daemon to whom she was.

But it's not her appearance that's rendered me speechless. It's what she's wearing. A black, low-cut bra pushes up her round, perfect breasts while matching panties cut high on the hips, and a leather studded waist belt and leg harness pull tight across her stomach and thighs. However, the part that stuns me is the black wings, held in place by leather straps that wind around her torso, over her shoulders, and down her back.

I get up from the booth, shaking the daze from my mind, and grab her by the arm. "Put some clothes on," I growl while yanking her to the back of the bar.

"Nice to see you, too," she looks up at me from under lowered lashes. Her eyes flicker with fire, and my pulse kicks up a notch.

I back her against the wall and place a hand on either side of her head, caging her in. I want no one, and I mean no one, to look at what belongs to me.

"Do you see something you like?" her lips pull into a playful smile.

I roll my lower lip under my teeth and rake my eyes over her. All of it. I like all of it. I want to touch her but equally punish her for showing everyone what only I should see.

I run a thumb along her jaw and lock my eyes on hers. "You're going to pay for this."

"Dante," she lets out an airy laugh and places a hand on my chest. "I've been paying since The Fall."

My muscles flex under her touch, and I take a deep breath, filling my lungs with her. She smells of vanilla and sugar and makes my mouth water. "Are you ready?" I ask, eyes intent on hers.

She swallows and licks her lips, heat stirring in the space between us. "The sooner it starts, the sooner I get back to what I was doing."

"And that was?" I reach for a lock of her hair, rolling it between my fingers.

"Wouldn't you like to know?" she purrs. Her hand flexes, and I wonder if she can feel how I, too, have changed.

I like to run and spar on the mat, increasing my stamina and strengthening and refining my physique. It's not overbearing like Vinny's, who is all brawn, with a build that says, 'stay out of my way, or I'll break your face.'

"Um, not like to know," my eyes narrow as her hair slips through my fingers. "Demand. Diablo, you answer, to me, remember?"

She presses her lips together and studies me. "You don't own me. We are bound. There's a difference."

"Is that so?" I grin, her stubbornness making my fingers twitch.

"Yes," she locks her eyes on mine.

"A mere technicality." I drink her in again, still in shock over what I see. She was beautiful before, but now seeing her makes me ache with longing.

"One that matters," she says with a knowing smile, pulling me back to whatever this is we're doing.

"Oh yeah," I lean in, my eyes drifting to her perfect pink mouth. "And why is that?"

"Because Dante," she reaches up and runs her finger along my lower lip, sending fire through me. "I, too, have power."

"Is that so?" I swallow, and the muscle in my jaw tics in response to her touch.

"It is," she drops her hand.

"And what, pray tell, is this power?" Her willfulness intrigues me, but I also want to erase that smile from her lips in so many ways.

She locks her eyes onto mine, smile growing. "Knowing that the technicality also applies to you."

Her response surprises me. But before I can respond, she

slides out from under my arm and walks away, leaving me speechless for the second time in minutes.

Shock, then anger courses through me as I drink in the exposed skin of her perfect bottom, peeking out from under the lace of her panty. Then the anger gives way to something else entirely. What I'm feeling, I can't describe it. But for the first time since we began, I'm nervous about the next ten days.

2
DIABLO

I know I'm going to pay for what I just did, but as I said to Dante, I've been paying since The Fall. I can handle his anger. Not to mention, the look on his face is worth it.

The consequence of what happened when the angels rebelled may be what binds Dante and me together for eternity, but it's also what led me to do what I did just now. His anger will be my absolution.

"Diablo!" he shouts, footsteps thundering in my ear. "You will answer me when I call you."

He grabs my arm and spins me around, heated eyes locked on mine. He's breathing hard, jaw clenched tight, and his response is just as I imagined.

"It's going to be a long ten days if you don't calm down," I place a hand on my hip and exhale. The determination that fuels Dante is now also alive in me. He doesn't intimidate me. Not anymore.

"Are you testing me?" his eyes flash.

"Testing you?" I shoot back. That's rich, considering all he'd done to win my fealty. For centuries, his time in Eden has felt like the Roman Bacchanalia. Ten days of depravity that hurts to witness.

"What if I am?" I straighten. In the years leading up to today, I've thought of nothing but the need to make him feel as he's made me, and his anger right now is just a drop in the bucket.

He looks me over, lips pulling into a sardonic smile. "Then

those leather straps will come in handy."

"Funny," I lift my chin. "I was thinking the same thing."

His eyes widen, and he leans in. "What did you say?"

"You heard me," I cross my arms.

I'm not the girl I once was. The timid doe Dante preyed on like a wolf. Then again, I never was a girl. My energy was as old as time itself. But my body, the cavity that imprisoned my spirit, took thousands of years to understand.

Now that I did, however, it will be what saves me. I am no longer an ancient being in an unfamiliar body. I know how to use it and will fight with everything in me to win my freedom.

"Now you listen to me," Dante looks over my shoulder, then back to me. We had an audience, but he's told them to find something else to look at with one look. "I will not accept this kind of defiance. You will go home and put some clothes on."

"But Dante," I ignore the intensity of his demand. "I did this for you. Don't you like it?"

"I do not answer your questions," his eyes flash. "You answer mine."

I can see the frustration my resolve is creating, and it sends a rush of satisfaction through me. But I also see the familiar look of hunger in his eyes and remind myself not to back down. Things need to be different this time. They have to be.

"Fine," I sigh and drop my arms to my sides, trying to ignore how stunning he is. If possible, he's even more handsome than before, and I can't deny my body's response. It is as old as my spirit.

"Fine?" his head snaps back, clearly surprised by my acquiescence.

"Yes," I bite my lower lip. "Were you expecting something else?"

"Expecting, no," he shakes his head. "Hoping, yes."

"And why is that?" I ask, not sure I want the answer.

"Because," his voice smolders, "I really want to spank you for disobeying me."

The human body wanted to be touched, and I know how powerful that longing could be. But I also know Dante's cravings are dark and that he draws pleasure from pain. Still, the heat in his eyes both frightens and excites me, the latter, I'll never admit, and sends goosebumps dancing down my arms.

"Stop doing that," his hold on my arm eases.

"Doing what?" I swallow, focusing on anything but the heat his touch is stirring.

He rubs the inside of my wrist with his thumb as his eyes zero in on my mouth. "Biting your lip."

"Is that how it's going to be?" I straighten my shoulders and lift my jaw. "You order, and I obey?"

His grip on my wrist tightens again, and he wraps his other arm around my waist and pulls me to him. "While I'm here, you will do as I say. If I want you to stop biting your lip, you will stop. If I want you to get dressed, you will do it. And if I want to spank you," his eyes focus on my mouth, "you will bend over for me."

My breath hitches. Not out of fear but excitement. "And…if I comply?"

"With which part?" he arches a brow.

"Any of it," I look him in the eye, summoning all my bravado. "All of it."

I need Dante to see he's fighting fire with fire. He's used every trick imaginable to get me to do what he wants. It's why I'm wearing what I am. Why shouldn't I?

His eyes dance, and his lips pull into a suggestive smile as he tightens his hold and crushes me against his chest. "Well then, I think we're in for an interesting ten days."

I look down, avoiding his eyes. Not because of what he said, but the heat in his words and how they made me feel.

"I do," he runs his finger under my jaw and tips my head up, locking his eyes onto mine. "Just, so you know."

"You do, what?" I ask softly, the heat of his touch curling around my neck and warming my cheeks.

"Like the outfit." His compliment fills me with satisfaction, and my chest tightens. "But I don't like everyone staring at you."

"They weren't staring at me," I sigh.

"Angel," he exhales. "They were."

Angel, what he's called me for thousands of years. It shifts the energy between us and stirs memories of all I've felt for him. Frustration, connection, longing. As painful as the last one is, I can't deny it.

"Have you seen the others?" I clear my throat and change the subject.

"The only one I see," his eyes search mine, "is you."

"Lila will give Vinny a run for his money this time," I pull away from his hypnotizing gaze and look at my spirited best friend.

"I'm looking forward to her being on our side," he says confidently.

"I wouldn't get your hopes up," I turn around. But I know my response is in vain. Lila's as smitten with Vinny as he is with her. Being apart from him for another century is the last thing she wants.

Dante strokes the skin on my lower back, sending a rush of heat shooting up my spine. "The only thing I'm hoping for is that you'll be there, too."

"Hope can be futile," I arch into him, bringing us closer while trying to escape his touch.

"Nothing is pointless," his eyes flicker in response to my nearness. "There is a reason for everything."

I bite my lip again–some kind of nervous habit he must incite–and this time, I know I'm doing it because I feel it. I run my finger across my lip to ease the pain, but when I pull my hand away, he reaches for it and licks my finger.

The feel of his tongue grazing my skin is both alarming and electrifying and sends an image flashing in my mind. We're lying together, and he's smiling, with one arm behind his head, and the other, underneath me. What I'm feeling, I can't describe it. But for the first time in centuries, I'm looking forward to the next ten days.

3
DANTE

Diablo gasps and looks up at me as all the delicious thoughts I've had of her slam into my mind. "What do you say we get out of here?"

She steps back, and I let go of her hand, the space between us growing cold. "Is that all you're interested in?"

"What?" I shake my head. "Doing my job?"

She turns her attention to Vinny and Lila again, and my eyes follow. They're all over each other. His mouth is on her neck, and her hands grip his arms in delight.

"That's not what I was thinking," I look back at Diablo.

"Oh," she responds, and I can't tell if it is a relief or disappointment.

I've never kissed Diablo. At least, not the way Vinny is Lila. A sardonic brush of my lips against a cheek or hand, sure. But mouth to mouth, teeth, and tongue, never. But I want to, with everything in me.

"Hey Dante," Vinny calls out as Lila rubs her hand over his cropped, dirty blonde hair. "Get to work, brother."

"He's right, you know." Ten days is only ten days, and I need to focus on what I am here to do. "The clock is ticking, as they say."

She looks at me and exhales. "I'm aware."

One hundred years is a mere blink of an eye to the Fallen. The world around us changes. Cities rise, fall, and build up again. But still, we go on. At least, that's the way it used to feel. This past century, however, I felt the weight of time,

14

which was strange because I hadn't before. I longed to see Diablo again, and now that I'm here, I just want to look at her and stare into those gorgeous eyes.

"I know," she lifts her chin, jaw set. "It is why you're here. But like I said earlier, you don't own me."

"The hell I don't," I cross my arms.

"For ten days, every one hundred years, you can try your best to secure my fealty," she contests. "But what I do outside that time is none of your business."

Diablo is radiant and spirited, and I have to stop myself from the urge to throw her over my shoulder and carry her out of here.

"You are free to exist as you do because of Luke," I push back. "Doesn't that deserve some loyalty?"

"Loyalty?" she bristles. "Why did you ever think I would side with him?"

"Oh, I don't know," I smirk. "Maybe, because it's a good existence."

Diablo knows what I do when I'm not here because I tell her. I enjoy seeing her reaction. The flush in her cheeks. The mix of discomfort and curiosity in her eyes. She thinks I can't see the latter, but I do.

"Is it?" she looks at me, her expression cold.

If only she knew how good it feels to do what satisfies you without guilt. She wouldn't be looking at me with such judgment, that's for sure.

"Beats being a concubine," I shrug.

As soon as the comment leaves my mouth, I regret it because it's not true. Our binding is not like that. I may want Diablo to join me, but she is still one of us and deserves respect. It's why I've never kissed her the way I want to.

I make sure my dark urges are satiated so that I don't do

something I'll regret. The willingness of the soulless allows me to indulge so I can focus on the task at hand, and I take what they offer because they give it freely. But I see the recognition in Diablo's eyes when she smells sex on my skin. It's the same look she's giving me now, and it sends a pang of regret through me.

She snaps back, her eyes filled with tears. "Screw you, Dante."

Damn it, I blow out a heated breath and run a hand through my hair. I didn't want things to start this way.

"Diablo—" I start to apologize, but she pushes past me. I turn to follow, and when I do, I notice that the bartender is watching us. "What are you looking at?" I growl.

He doesn't respond but keeps his eyes on Diablo, which only angers me more. I storm over, press both hands down on the bar, and lean in. "I asked you a fucking question. Are you looking at her?"

The bartender turns his attention to me and smirks. "And what if I was?" he challenges.

I grab the bar, and it cracks with the strain. "Then I'd say you have a death wish."

"Well, that's obvious, isn't it?" he rolls his eyes. "I mean, I'm here. Wish, granted."

"Boy," I laugh and shake my head. "I'm about to make this the longest ten days of your life."

He shrugs and continues wiping. "As long as the other ninety-nine years are free of you, I'm good with that."

Diablo grabs my arm, staring at me with an expression I can't read. "Dante, stop!"

I look from her to the bartender. "Wait, are you..."

"Am I, what?" she narrows her eyes.

I hike my thumb at the dick behind the bar. "Involved

16

with him?"

"It's none of your business what I do," she says for the second time since I got here.

"You know," I let out a heated breath. I am one second away from showing Diablo, who's boss around here. "That response is starting to piss me off."

"I don't care," she shoots back, fire and determination in her response. "You can't go around threatening everyone you don't like."

"If he's looking at you, I sure as shit can."

She places both hands on her hips. "Says whom?"

"Are you kidding me right now?" I was willing to play this game of cat and mouse with her. Today, when she walked in, hell, I was ready to do whatever she wanted. But now I only want one thing. I want her out of Eden and with me. And I'll do whatever it takes to make it happen.

"You just made the worst mistake of your existence," I seethe.

"Ha," she rolls her eyes. "I think falling takes the cake."

"We'll see about that." Without thinking, I pull her to me and crash my lips onto hers. She tenses but doesn't push me off as I thrust my tongue into her mouth and stake my claim.

I just broke the only promise I ever made to her. One I've kept since all of this began. To never take without asking. But I don't care. Her mouth is warm and tempting and tastes like Heaven.

For a moment, I forget everything, and light flashes in my mind, as she holds onto my arm and digs her nails into my skin. Her touch sends a rush of heat through me, and as she opens her mouth and kisses me back, I can only think one thing....more. But as soon as it begins, it ends, and she pushes me away with surprising force.

17

We stand there staring at one another, both of us breathing heavily, then she wipes her mouth with the back of her hand and scowls at me. "How dare you!"

"Oh, relax," I lick my lips, savoring her taste. "It was just a kiss."

She looks at me, eyes blazing. Even angry, she's impossibly stunning. "I hate you."

I know she doesn't mean it. One does not kiss someone the way she just did if they hated you. "If that's what you need to tell yourself, then fine."

"I don't need you to give me permission for how I feel!" she clenches both her fists.

She's worked up. Good. It means the kiss broke through that facade she was putting on and made her feel something real. "I'm not," I grin, enjoying this more by the second.

Fire was better than ice any day. And there is no doubt that kiss filled her with fire. I can see it in her eyes and hear it in her voice. "You're angry, and that's fine. It means you feel something, and it's a start."

"A start to what?" her chest heaves.

I reach out and brush the back of my hand against her cheek. "Our beginning."

4
DIABLO

My heart pounds hard in my ribs, competing with the screaming in my mind. Sometimes, I hate the mortal instrument. "You had no right!" I spit out. I'm so angry with Dante that I could claw his face.

"It was just a kiss," he says for a second time. "Besides, the one that should be mad is me. How dare you!"

"How dare I, what?" I stare at him in disbelief. It's almost as if I were the one who took something from him without asking.

"Come in here dressed like that."

"Like, what?" I press, wondering what insult he'll throw at me next. "You don't like sexy, or don't like dark?"

He looks me up and down and clenches his jaw. "Either way, a tease is a tease."

I pull my hand back and smack his face. He rubs his cheek, and his eyes flicker. "So, you like it rough?"

"I like anything but you," I grit my teeth, fighting back the tears that threaten.

"Why are you so worked up?" he laughs.

"You just called me a tease!" I shout, anger getting the better of me. "And, because you had no right to kiss me!"

"Oh, are you afraid I hurt the feelings of your…whatever he is?" Dante taunts, waving a hand at the bar.

"What?" my head snaps back.

He clenches his jaw, and his eyes narrow. "I saw the way he was looking at you."

I shake my head, not sure what he's getting at. "And?"

"And?" he repeats, incensed. "Who is he?"

"I don't know." My breathing picks up, and I feel my anger building with his insistence on something that hardly matters. "I don't even know him."

"Well, he wants to know you!"

"I don't care what he wants," I raise my voice. "I'm not interested in talking about him!"

"Then why are you so angry?" Dante eyes me, curious.

"I'm angry because I didn't want you to—"

"Didn't want me to do what?" he cuts me off.

I know Dante wants me to fight with him. He likes it. Craves it. But I won't give him the satisfaction. "Not that I owe you an explanation," I take a deep breath, trying to bite back my anger, "but that wasn't necessary."

"Yes, it was. That bartender was looking at you, and everyone knows you are off-limits."

"Off-limits?" I shake my head in bemusement.

"Yes," he nods with vehemence. "The rules are clear. He had no right to interfere in anything related to us. I could destroy him."

The spark that happens when dark and light collide is exciting and terrifying. I feel it in the kinetic energy firing between Dante and me. "Do you think you have the right to control everything I do?"

"Everything, and everyone," he crosses his arms.

"Well, here's a newsflash...you don't. Just because you like to show and tell everything and everyone you do, doesn't mean that I have to do the same."

"Your point?" he asks with fading interest. He's heard this argument from me before. The next part, however, is new.

"There are thousands of days you're not here. And in that

time, you and I don't exist, and I am free to do whatever I want."

"We will always exist," he says with renewed attention. "And whom, exactly, are you doing?"

"What?" I narrow my eyes.

"You said you were free to do anyone you want."

"No," I shake my head. "You did."

"And you didn't correct me," he barks. "So, answer the question. Who are you doing?"

"No," I push back, my anger returning. "You can't guilt me into answering anything."

"I don't do guilt. And, if you join me, you will never have to worry about guilt again."

"Is that why you sided with Luke?" I smirk. "His empty promises do it for you?"

"A guiltless existence is one of many reasons," he nods. "And trust me, that promise of unlimited pleasure has been fulfilled and then some."

"Well, we each made our beds, and now we have to lie in them." I don't need a reminder of how Dante spends his time when he's not here. It's burned in my mind.

"The last thing I'm doing when I'm in my bed is lying in it," he grins.

"Who you sleep with is none of my concern, Dante," I say with disdain.

"I think we both know sleeping is not involved, Diablo," he shoots back, a sardonic smile pulling at his lips.

I stare at him, wondering where the being I once knew has gone and how this dance between us hasn't destroyed me yet.

"You know I won't stop," his eyes lock onto mine. "None of us will until all of you are back on our side."

"I know," I take a deep breath, my desire to fight

beginning to wane. "But do you have to make it so difficult? It doesn't always have to be this painful."

"It isn't. My time here is full of —"

"Pleasure," I cut him off. "At the expense of my pain."

"It wouldn't be painful if you joined me."

"You're impossible," I take a deep breath, this argument getting us nowhere.

Dante reaches into a bowl of fruit on the counter next to him and grabs an apple. "Angel, I'm a sure thing," he winks, then takes a bite.

"I'll...take your word for it," I lick my lips, looking from his mouth to the apple.

"Tell me, Diablo, have you ever taken a bite?" The innuendo in his question is obvious.

I step back, eyes glued on the teeth marks in its soft, milky pulp. "What do you mean?"

"Ever taken a bite of the forbidden fruit?"

"Stop," I hold my hand up. "I'm not playing this game with you."

"You should try it," he continues, taking a step towards me, closing the space between us again. "Go on. One bite won't hurt."

Despite the amount of skin I'm showing, I feel flush and sweat beads at the nape of my neck. "I'm...fine."

"Well, this," he waves the apple back and forth in front of my face, "you can have. The bartender, you cannot."

"I don't want it," I nod to the apple. "That, or him."

Dante tilts his head, looking at me in silent contemplation. "Are you sure?"

"I don't even know him," I roll my eyes.

"Well, he wants to know you. But poor soul, or soulless rather," Dante laughs at his joke. "He will never have what belongs to me."

This push-pull between Dante and me is tiring, and I feel my resolve fading by the second. "It doesn't matter what he wants," I rub my temples, "or anyone because they can't have it."

"Not even if they asked nicely?" he raises an eyebrow.

I drop my hands in exasperation. "Not even if they got down on their knees."

"Well," he sets the apple down on the counter next to us, and a server that appears out of nowhere picks it up and hands him a napkin. "It shouldn't have happened that way."

I watch as she undresses Dante with her eyes. She's exactly the type he would use to satisfy his hunger. Easy and interested in him.

"You're right," I nod, ignoring her ample breasts spilling out of the tight leather vest she's wearing. "You shouldn't have said anything."

"No," he holds out the napkin after wiping his hands. The server grabs it, and their fingers brush. But while the server's eyes flicker with the contact, Dante's eyes remain focused on me. "The bartender deserved what was coming to him. And he will get what comes next if he looks at you again."

"But you said—"

"Our kiss," he cuts me off. The server looks from Dante to me, then walks away, lips pursed. "That's what I was referring to, not that insipid pourer of drinks."

"You mean your kiss."

"It may have started as mine," he leans in, breath fanning my face. "But you were more than willing."

"Oh, is that what you felt?"

"I'm not talking about my arm," he grins. "I've had nails dug into my skin before."

23

"You're disgusting."

"Irresistible? Yes. Disgusting? No."

"Whatever," I shake my head.

He laughs, clearly enjoying this nauseating repartee. "All I was trying to say is our first kiss shouldn't have been like that."

"By calling it our first, you're implying there will be more."

"All in time," he says with infuriating confidence.

"Even if it's an eternity?"

"Good things come to those who wait," he winks.

I let out a weary breath. "Don't be so sure of yourself. I've resisted every temptation thrown my way so far."

He looks at me with a strange expression on his face. "Every...one?"

At first, I didn't understand why he looked at me like he was. But then I realize what I've just alluded to, and I want to kick myself.

"Diablo," he runs a finger along my shoulder. "Are you telling me you've never been kissed?"

"Did you...forget my virtue?" I stammer, his touch making me tremble.

"Oh," he licks his lips. "I remember. I just figured —"

"Just figured, what?" I cut him off, ignoring the flutter in my chest.

"There must be some reason you fell."

"And you think it was so I could have my share of quickies?" I cringe when I hear the word come out of my mouth. Sometimes, Dante brings out the worst in me.

"Do not underestimate the benefit of a good quickie," he laughs.

I close my eyes, wanting to get as far away from this topic

as possible. "What I meant to say," I take a deep breath, then open them again, "is we each had our reasons."

"Fair enough," he concedes. "But aren't you the tiniest bit curious to try that free will we fought so hard for?"

"With an obsessive bodyguard ready to pounce on anyone that looks at me, why bother?"

"First, I do not obsess," he smiles. "And second, I am not your bodyguard. We both know I'm much more than that."

"Your understanding of our connection is grossly inflated."

"You fell with the rest of us," he ignores my response. "Why honor that virtue if it no longer bestows in you light?"

"Well, you almost destroyed the bartender for looking at me. I can't imagine what would happen if someone were to touch me."

"No one will ever touch you," he says firmly.

"Exactly!" I throw my hands up in exasperation. "So, why even ask if you already know the answer?"

"Because there are ways to experience pleasure which do not involve another," he leans in. "To scratch that itch, if it were."

"I find no pleasure in hearing about your sexual adventures, Dante."

"I'm not talking about that," his voice drips in suggestion.

I shake my head, trying to make out the riddle of his words. It takes a moment, but my cheeks start to burn once I do.

When it's clear that I know what he's inferring, a slow, suggestive smile pulls at his lips. "Satisfying oneself can be ever so enjoyable, Diablo."

I shake my head, disbelieving he would approve of anyone touching me, including myself. "You'd be okay with

25

that?"

"Hell yes," he lets out a wicked laugh. "I'd encourage it. I might even watch."

"You'd like that, wouldn't you?" I roll my eyes.

"Oh angel," his eyes burn into me. "You have no idea."

The air between us thickens, and I turn my head. "I'm done talking about this."

"Come now," he tsks. "Don't be embarrassed."

"I'm not."

"Then why do you look away?"

"I was bored with this conversation. "But…" I turn back around. "I'm looking at you now. Satisfied?"

"Not yet," he smirks. "But soon, I hope."

The way he's looking at me makes my heart race. We need to talk about something, anything else. "Tell me something, Dante."

"Yes?" he tips his head.

"Why can you do whatever you want, with whomever you want, but a bartender can't even look at me?"

"It's simple," his response is even and confident. "I am your salvation."

I let out a bitter laugh. "You…my salvation?"

"Since The Fall, your existence has been an endless cycle of regret."

"You mean an endless cycle of this," I cross my arms and let out an exhaustive sigh.

"We all know what it feels like being cast aside," he continues. "But with us, you will never feel alone again. You will only feel acceptance."

"It's not that simple," I shake my head, wishing it were.

"It is," he brushes my cheek, his touch drawing fire. "You just have to let it. The sooner you do, the sooner it ends."

Those very words are the first thing Dante's said in centuries that I agree with–the end. Although what it looks like to him is far different than what it looks like to me.

"Now," he smiles. "What do you say we get on with our night, hmm?"

I shift nervously, already anxious about whatever he's planning. "Where are we going?"

"Meet me here at five," he drops his hand, the heat from his touch fading. "And I was going to suggest you wear something nice, but maybe just…wear something."

"Can you at least tell me what you have planned?" I ask, needing some kind of idea of how I should dress.

He holds my gaze, considering the question, then shoves a hand in his pocket and turns to leave. "Be here at five, Diablo," he calls over his shoulder. "And don't be late."

I watch him walk away, wondering what just happened and also how I can be both infuriated and intrigued at the same time.

5
DANTE

I shake my head, shocked by what I've just learned. Diablo's never kissed anyone, never touched herself. I can't believe it. But it's a relief if I'm being honest. The idea she and the bartender had something going on drove me red with rage. Had she said anything to indicate they were together or had been well, hell hath no fury.

Of course, I know she's right. Technically, Diablo can do what she wants when I'm not here. But the idea drives me crazy. Now that I know I'm the only one who has ever tasted her sweet lips, I plan to keep it that way.

"What's that shit-eating grin for?" Vinny shoots me a curious look as I slide back into the booth.

However, the best part about what just happened was realizing how I could finally win Diablo's fealty. It wasn't about showing her what she could have. It was about honoring what she'd been–an angel of the highest order. Her light was among the brightest.

"No reason," I reach for my drink. "Where's Lila?"

"She went home to get ready for tonight. And, Diablo?"

I look over my shoulder and, seeing she too has left, turn back around. "Same."

"Was seeing her again everything you thought it would be?" he takes a sip of his beer.

I tighten the grip on my glass, thinking about the moment Diablo first walked into *Saints*. How the room shifted, and everything faded away but her. "It was," I lift my drink and take a sip. "Looks like you and Lila are off to a good start."

"She's a wildcat," Vinny laughs. "It's going to be fun having her around."

"Well," I hold up my glass. "Congrats, brother."

"We're not there yet," he taps his bottle to it. "But after tonight, I sure as shit hope we'll be. You might have your work cut out for you, though."

"Always," I shake my head. "Diablo can fight all she wants, but I'm playing to win this time."

"Oh yeah?" he raises his forehead. "Got something up your sleeve?"

Until I have a plan, I'm keeping quiet. One thing is for sure, though, I need to play my cards right and be on my best behavior, which means I need to keep my anger and hunger in check. None of the usual games this time.

I need to show Diablo a different side of me. One I've kept hidden for so long, I'm not sure I can even find it. But for her, I will try. I'll do anything if it means she's with me when I leave.

"Everything okay, buddy?" Vinny asks when I grow quiet.

"Sure," I shrug. "Why?"

He nods at my hand, and when I look down, I see that I've dug my fingernails into the tabletop. I take a breath and stretch it out. "Just…anxious."

"Now that I understand." Vinny polishes off his beer and slams the bottle down on the table.

Anxious is an understatement. A better word would be fixated. I'm more determined than ever to win Diablo's loyalty, and no one better get in my way. Like that bartender. If he looks at her again, I'll burn this place to the ground, with him inside.

As I turn back to Vinny, I see the fruit bowl and get an

idea. "Hey, Vin...how about we go get our ink?"

We've both gotten a new tattoo whenever we're back in Eden. It commemorates the passing of another hundred years. Every tattoo I have is part of my story, just as every bit of ink on Vinny is his.

"Been saving this just for today," he pulls up the sleeve of his shirt and points to a spot of fresh skin on an otherwise fully tattooed arm.

I finish the rest of my drink and then push up from the booth. "Well then, let's go."

I'm optimistic as we leave *Saints* and navigate Eden's familiar streets at full throttle. By the time we arrive at our destination, unbridled confidence fills me.

"Anybody here?" I call out as we push through the door of *Scorched*, Eden's oldest tattoo shop.

A tall man steps out from the back and looks around. His eyes narrow when he doesn't see anyone, but once they see us, his face brightens. "Is it already that time?" he strides towards Vinny and me, arms open.

He embraces us, and Vinny pats him on the back. "Good to see you, JJ. Looking good."

"Well, one thing about that statement is true," he laughs and steps back. "The other is horseshit."

"How are you, old friend?" I laugh and shake my head. JJ's mahogany-colored hair is thinner since the last time we were here and slightly gray at the temples.

"Old...I'm old," JJ grumbles. "But things are good–just another day in paradise. But you two," he clasps my shoulder with one hand and Vinny's with the other. "Man, you haven't aged a day."

As old as Eden itself, JJ was the first soulless here and knew our history. He's the only one of them worth a damn and has been a friend to both Vinny and me.

"I could have sworn you two were just here," JJ looks at the calendar.

"Time flies when you're up to no good," Vinny's eyes shine with a hint of mischief.

"That it does," JJ turns back to us. "How are things out there?"

"Same," I shrug.

"So, they're good," he laughs, knowing well who we are and what we do.

"That they are," I grin.

"Well," he rubs his hands together. "It's time for new ink, yeah?"

"You know it," Vinny pushes his sleeves up.

"So," JJ looks from me to Vinny. "What are we doing this time?"

I walk over to the sketchbook JJ keeps at the front and flip through the pages. After finding what I want, I point down at the image. "How about…this?"

"Well, that's twisted," JJ rubs his goatee.

Vinny looks down at the book and shakes his head. "I think it takes the cake as the most twisted, alright."

"You have no idea," I flash them both a sinister grin. The design is the perfect way to honor what I hope will be my last trip to Eden.

"Okay, so you're set, Dante," JJ looks at Vinny. "What about you?"

Vinny turns the book to him and looks down. After flipping through a few pages, he points to an image. "You got it," JJ nods. "Who wants to go first?"

"I'll go," I clap my hands together. I want my new ink as soon as possible. The sooner it is, the sooner it's part of my story.

"Alright," JJ waves. "Let's go."

I look around as we make our way to JJ's workstation. "Place has changed a bit."

"Well, I have indoor plumbing and power now," he snickers.

I shake my head at his dry humor. "You had both the last time I was here."

"True, but they weren't the best. What was new wasn't always dependable in the 1920s."

I think back to the era. It was a time of big parties fueled by industrial and economic growth and even bigger scandals. Eden grew tenfold that decade. The value of one's soul plummeted in contrast to luxury and lavish lifestyles.

"But this," JJ picks up a tattoo gun lying on a table. "I'd say it's the best invention of the twentieth century. That work of art on your back would've taken a tenth of the time.

I settle into the tattoo chair and close my eyes, a phantom pain shooting down my back with the memory. After The Fall, I wanted to mark my new body with a reminder of what I'd given up. When we met JJ and learned of his talent for carving, he made it possible.

Using only a needle and thread dipped in soot, it took a couple of weeks to etch the design into my skin, but when he finished, JJ had given me back my wings...with a twist. Each started at the scars where mine once began, and instead of feathers, flames fanned across my shoulders.

That day he turned something heinous into a work of art, and whenever I looked at my back now, I saw power, not disgrace. I would forever be in JJ's debt for giving that back to me.

"So, how are you really, Dante?" JJ slips on a pair of latex gloves and readies his workstation.

"Oh, you know," I take a deep breath. "Focused and anxious."

"And Diablo…how is she?"

I think about my raven-haired angel with eyes the color of emeralds and a rebellious spirit that matches my own. "She's good."

"Yeah?" JJ looks up.

"Yeah," I nod. "Going to be a handful this time, though."

"Well, that's good. Someone has to keep you in line," JJ laughs. "Alright, buddy, let's get to work."

As JJ begins, I think back to the day that Diablo and I were bound. I wanted to protect her, even then. Her eyes were so full of fear, so unsure of what her existence would be.

The undecided fought with us and should have been free to exist as they wished. To rebel for your freedom and then be stripped of both it and your reason for existence was a cruel punishment on Luke's part.

That's why I stayed the course to win her over. I didn't want her to bear our punishment forever. I wanted her to embrace what she could be. Yet, no matter what I said or did, she seemed to carry a great weight, and I'd always wondered what she fell for and how it could be worth her pain.

My eyes shoot open, and I sit up as a new realization hits me.

"Hey," JJ puts a hand on my shoulder and pushes me back down in the chair. "No moving."

"Sorry," I ease back into the chair.

As important as what Diablo had once been was why she fell. I needed to find out what she wanted so I could make her believe she could not only have it but that I was the one that could give it to her.

This could work, I think excitedly. Honoring who Diablo had been while trying to help her get what she fell for was a foolproof way to win her loyalty.

"Alright," JJ drops the gun and slides back in his chair when he finishes. "What do you think?"

I look down at my forearm, and the tattoo's perfect. It's an apple, shaded in a way, so it seems like it is reflecting light, and there is a snake wound around it.

"You're a genius, JJ," I clench my fist, and the snake's tail moves with the flex of my muscle.

He rubs petroleum jelly on my arm, covers the fresh ink with a bandage, and removes his gloves. "I know you won't keep this on, but humor me until you leave?"

"You got it," I get up from the chair and reach for my wallet. "What do I owe you?"

"Aw, come on," he waves my hand away. "We both know your money's no good here."

I shove my wallet back into my pocket. "Thanks, my friend. I owe you a drink."

"You got it," he nods, then breaks into a coughing fit.

"Hey," I place a hand on his shoulder and take note of his pallid cheeks. "You, okay?"

"Yeah," he presses a hand on his thigh and takes a deep breath. "Go ahead and tell Vin he's up."

"You sure?"

"Yeah, yeah," he waves me off.

"Alright," I study him for another moment, then turn to get Vinny.

"Hey, Dante," JJ calls as I reach the walk-through that connects the front and back of the shop.

I stop and turn. "Yeah?"

"Your time in Eden this round...do you think it will be the

34

one?"

I know what he's asking. Will this be the century Diablo leaves Eden with me? "Yes," I say with conviction. Something tells me that this time things will change forever.

"A word of advice," he says while preparing his workstation for Vinny. "Be good to her. Keep her safe. No matter what."

Despite the nature of our relationship over the millennia, I've always felt a fierce need to protect Diablo. The idea of anything or anyone hurting her filled me with a fiery rage. "I plan to."

JJ doesn't say anything else. He simply nods and watches as I make my way to the front of the shop.

"You're up," I clap at Vinny when I come through the door.

"Well," he gets up. "Let's see it."

I stick out my arm and lift the bandage. "Aw man, that's sick."

"He's a master," I agree.

"Alright," Vinny moves his neck from side to side and makes his way to the back of the shop. "See you in a bit."

Vinny's swagger makes me laugh. He's the best, and this existence wouldn't be the same without him, that's for sure. But as JJ lowers his gun and gets to work, his words slam into me and pull my focus back to Diablo–*Protect her, she's not like the others*. They repeat the entire time I wait as if they are the most important words I need to know.

6
DIABLO

When I walk through my front door half an hour later, I'm surprised to find Lila standing in the kitchen waiting for me. I jump and put a hand on my chest. "You scared me!"

"Why...did you think I was a burglar?" she taps her nails on the counter.

I ignore her obvious sarcasm, set the wings down on the floor, and slip off my heels. "I don't know, maybe."

"First, no one in Eden would dare do anything to you because of Dante. And second, what happened with you two?" she asks impatiently.

I let out an exhausted sigh. "You were right."

"What did I tell you?" she gloats, a triumphant smile pulling at her lips. "Eating out of the palm of your hand, right?"

"Not exactly," I call over my shoulder as I make my way down the hall to my bedroom.

"What do you mean, not exactly?"

I reach for the robe hanging on the back of the door and slip into it, tying the sash around my waist, then heading back to the kitchen. "I mean, at first he was, and then, wasn't."

Lila lifts a brow and shoots me a curious look. "Did something happen after I left?"

I open the fridge and grab two bottles of water, handing one to her. "Depends on when you left."

"Well," she reaches for the one I extend to her. "I was there long enough to see Dante lay that kiss on you."

Heat creeps up my neck, remembering the feel of his lips on mine. It was unexpected and caught me by surprise. "So, you saw that?"

"Sure did," she smirks. "Was it as hot as it looked?"

Hotter, I think, as I unscrew the top of the bottle and take a sip. I didn't hate it, as I said. I hated how it happened. Still, I couldn't stop thinking about it. The feel of Dante's lips haunted mine all the way home and even now.

But I don't say any of this. Lila may be my oldest friend, but there are some secrets no one should ever know. "How about we talk about what was going on with you and Vinny?" I shift the focus back to her.

"Oh, you know," she waves her hand airily. "Just making up for lost time."

"Oh, is that all it was?" I take a sip of water.

"Sure," she unscrews the cap of her bottle and does the same. "Can't give him everything in the first five minutes. But I'm not here to talk about Vinny and me."

"Speaking of," I shake my head. "Why are you here? Shouldn't you be at your place, getting ready for tonight?"

"Diablo," she presses her perfectly glossed lips together. "That hurts."

"Oh," I pinch her, "you know you're always welcome here."

My home is like hers, and at one point, it was. We were roommates for a long time, but when I walked in on her and Vinny making out a couple of hundred years ago, she got her own place.

"I know," she brightens. "I was just practicing. How'd I do?"

"The pout? It was flawless. Whatever you want from Vinny, you will, without a doubt, get."

Lila is impossible, but I adore her. It's hard not to. It is who she was and always will be. Kindness was her virtue, and when the world was dark, it was she who filled me with hope.

It's why I can't bear to see her siding with Luke. Being on his side is contrary to all she is. But the adoration she feels for Vinny is as apparent as his for her, and being with him is the one thing that can make her swear fealty.

"Excellent," she flashes me a megawatt smile. "I plan to use it on Vin tonight. Now, the reason I'm here. I wanted to make sure you were okay."

"Of course," I look at her, puzzled. "Why wouldn't I be?"

"Diablo," she exhales. "I know the whole sex-on-a-stick vibe isn't your thing. But man," she shakes her head with admiration, "did you work it like it was."

"Yeah?" I chew my cheek.

"Oh yeah," she nods with approval. "Every eye in the room was on you, and nobody's burned hotter than Dante's."

My cheeks grow warm, and I look down, the idea I'd gotten to him sending a fiery thrill through me. "Yeah?"

"Girl, yes. You made me proud. And, by the way, you've got the body; you need to use it to your advantage."

Lila coached me for weeks, sharing tips on assuming control while making Dante feel like he had it, and her advice worked. Things felt different in those first moments together, and there wasn't anger in his eyes but intrigue.

"I'm not sure if it worked, though." My smile fades, remembering how fast things shifted, and his usual domineering self assumed control.

"Oh, it worked," Lila insists. "Everything about him hardened the minute he saw you."

"Lila!" my eyes widen like saucers.

"What?" she laughs. "You know it's true. Dante has major

BDE."

"Stop!" I spit out a mouthful of water.

"Why…is it warranted? Tell me it is."

I'd felt every inch of Dante pressed against me earlier at *Saints*, and it was warranted. "I wouldn't know," I brush my hair over one shoulder and fan myself, the room suddenly feeling hot.

"Oh, come on, Diablo," she grins. "Dante is the hottest. You know it. I know it. Even Vinny knows it. And the two of you together, I'm surprised you don't combust when you look at each other."

"Well, he made me hot, that's for sure."

She lifts an eyebrow and grins. "Yeah?"

"Yeah," I nod. "With anger."

"Didn't look like that to me," she smirks at me and shakes her head.

"You left too soon."

"Oh?" she leans against the counter. "There's more?"

My forehead scrunches, remembering Dante's insult and the admission he pulled from me. I could only imagine what he was planning to do with that information. Then again, he couldn't do much since his notion wasn't totally accurate.

No, I hadn't been with anyone, and yes, his lips were the first I'd kissed, but I knew my body–both where I liked to be touched and how.

"He thinks I'm his possession," I clear my throat, needing to keep that subject, and Dante, as far apart as possible.

"Well," she considers my comment. "I don't think they can help it."

"Wait, did I hear you correctly, Miss Tell Him Who's Boss? I just said he thinks he owns me."

"I know," she holds out her hand. "But hear me out. It's

been what...five millennia, and their only goal in all of that time has been to get us to swear our fealty?"

"It's not their only goal. In case you didn't know, daemons have done quite well for themselves in the outside world."

"I know," Lila admits. "But when it comes to us, that intense focus on our fealty is all they know. They can't help but be possessive. And, in a way, they're all we know, too."

"Dante is not all I know," I respond a little too defensively because, in a way, she's right. His pull on me transcended body and spirit.

"I'm just saying," she considers a different response. "The bond we have with them, we'll never find with another."

"Well, one thing you said is right. The power they have on us, we too have on them."

"I said that?" she laughs.

"I read between the lines," I smile. "And...that's what I told Dante. I have power, and he shouldn't forget it."

"You didn't," she sets her bottle down on the counter.

"I did," I straighten. "Well...in a manner of speaking."

"Man," she looks at me, shaking her head. "You really are fighting fire with fire."

"Wasn't that the whole point of today? To let Dante know I have power, too."

"Oh, he's aware," she grins.

"Why do you say that?" I ask, curious about her comment.

She stares at me as if the answer is obvious. "You can tell by the way he looks at you."

"Like a wolf would its prey?"

"No," she rolls her eyes. "Like he's ready to burn down the world, and you hold the match."

"He doesn't look at me like that," I push back. But I can't deny that the idea of the heat in his eyes not being fueled by anger but something else entirely stirs a flutter in my chest.

"Yes, he does," Lila insists. "And if Vinny looked at me like that, we'd never leave the bedroom."

"Oh, he does," I smile. "And when he's here, you don't."

Lila blushes. "Vinny looks at me like he wants me, yes. But there's that, and then there's the way Dante looks at you."

I shift the attention away from Dante and me for a second time. "You're going to swear your fealty, aren't you?"

"I…haven't decided," she looks down.

Lila may say she hasn't decided, but I know she has. I can hear it in her voice and see it in her eyes. She wants to be with Vinny. He worships the ground she walks on, and they are great together. Who could begrudge her for wanting to be with him?

"I won't be mad if you do," I say when she grows quiet. "Sad, definitely, but never upset for doing what makes you happy."

She looks up. "You…won't?"

"No," I reach across the counter and squeeze her hand. "It will just take some time for me to get used to you not being here. It's been us for so long."

"What if there was another way?" she holds my hand in hers. "One where we can all be together, like before?"

"There isn't," I say with brutal honesty. There was no point in talking about things that weren't possible, no matter how badly I wanted them to be true.

"But what if there was?" she asks again.

I know Lila wants to believe everything will magically work out, but the truth is, it won't. There isn't a way out of this endless cycle between Dante and me that doesn't involve my fealty, and I'm never going to do that.

That's how I came up with my plan to fight fire with fire. I

41

thought if I could get him to feel even a fraction of what he'd made me all these centuries, he'd understand, and we could come to some kind of truce.

"We both know the only way we can all be together is under Luke's thumb," I sigh. "And that's never going to happen. But I think it will take more than strutting around half-naked to get Dante to listen to me."

"I bet he would if you were totally naked," she cracks a smile, lifting the weight that settled over us.

I think of the image that flashed in my mind when Dante and I kissed. It stirs longing and hope, which scares me because I'd buried them centuries ago.

"I'll leave that to his soulless groupies," I push the image from my mind, knowing it will never be us. "In fact, there's one back at *Saints* right now, anxious to give him what he wants."

"He doesn't like them, you know." Lila is aware of Dante's appetite for indulgence, and she also knows how much I hate hearing about it.

"Oh, he likes it," I roll my eyes. The idea of Dante not liking anyone ready and willing is almost laughable.

"Sure, he likes it," she says with air quotes. "But he doesn't like them the way you think."

"I don't think anything."

She looks at me, skeptical. "Are you sure about that?"

"What are you hinting at, Lila?"

"I'm not hinting," she sighs. "I'm saying maybe, deep down, you don't hate Dante at all."

Of course, I don't hate Dante. I could never hate him. And when I said it earlier, I didn't mean it. But the way I feel is complicated.

"Remember, the opposite of hate is love. Without one, the

other cannot exist."

"True," I consider the two emotions. "But there is a lot in between that can fuel one and destroy the other."

"Yeah, but which one?" her chocolate eyes shine.

I set my bottle down on the counter and grip the edge with both hands. If we were playing chess, Lila would have just stolen my queen. "Thank you for your help today."

"For you, anything," she smiles. "Besides, that outfit looked a thousand times better on you than me. On a separate note, do you know why that bartender would challenge Dante the way he did?"

"Not sure," I shrug. "Never seen him before."

"Well, whatever the reason, do me a favor…stay away from him?"

"You think Dante would hurt him?" I hated the idea of anyone getting hurt defending me, even if it was someone I didn't know.

"I'm not worried about the bartender."

"You think Dante would hurt me?"

"Never," she says with absolute confidence. "He would sooner go to war again than hurt you. But that mortal instrument you're so fond of, I can't be so sure won't be hurt in the crossfire."

I wince at Lila's words. They are more accurate than she knows. The human heart breaks and mends, each fracture deeper and harder to heal than the one before. And every century, my heart breaks and heals like clockwork.

"Okay," she taps her hand on the counter. "I need to run, and you need to get ready for tonight. Where are you two going to kick things off?"

"I have no clue," I shrug. For all I know, we're spending the night at *Saints*.

She looks at me, clearly surprised. "Dante didn't tell you?"

"Nope," I cross my arms. "What about you and Vinny?"

"Oh, you know," she winks.

"Right," I laugh and walk her to the door, pulling it open. "Do you want to grab a coffee in a couple of days?"

"Totally," she kisses me on the cheek. "I'll need the caffeine after all the late nights I'll be having."

I shake my head and watch as she bounces down the stairs and into the afternoon sun. "Hey, Lila?" I call out as she reaches the end of the drive.

She stops and slips on a pair of sunglasses. "Yeah?"

"Thank you."

"Anytime, babe," she blows me a kiss and pushes through the gate.

I watch until she fades from view, and then I turn back around to head inside. When I do, I see something strange on the other side of the street. It looks like a shadow but is distorted, almost like a cloud.

I do a double-take, and seeing nothing when I look again, head back inside and close the door–the only shadow hanging over me is that of my impending night with Dante.

7
DANTE

I look at the tattoo on Vinny's arm and shake my head. "Man, I never thought I'd see the day."

"What day?" he asks, looking around. We're at *Saints*, and he's waiting for Lila, and me, Diablo.

"The day you, my friend, were wrapped around Lila's finger."

"I am not wrapped around her finger," he scoffs.

"That fresh ink on your arm says otherwise."

Vinny looks down at his newest tattoo. It's an elaborate, cursive letter L, with a sword running through it and vines twisting around the hilt. "Well, what can I say," he looks back up and grins. "When you know, you know."

"So, you're admitting it."

"Sure," he shrugs. "Why not. You should try it sometime."

"Never gonna happen, brother." No one will ever wrap me around their finger. Caring is a detriment, which makes you weak, and my station is about strength. "I don't need that kind of complication."

"You may not want it," he crosses his massive arms and laughs, "but you already got it, so why not just go with it."

"What are you talking about?" I'm not sure when this conversation flipped to me, but it needs to go back to Vinny.

"Come on, man…I saw you and Diablo earlier."

"And?"

"And…I could feel the sparks on the other side of the room. That's a complication you most definitely need."

Vinny can read me better than anyone. Still, it makes me a little uncomfortable that he can see how Diablo affects me.

"Right now, my focus is on her fealty."

"That's it?"

"That's always it."

"Come on," he claps a hand on my shoulder. "It's Diablo. She's a total doll. There isn't one daemon that didn't wish he were bound to her."

Even Vinny, who only has eyes for Lila, knows Diablo is special. And he's right. She's perfect. But if she doesn't get here soon, I'm going to change my mind on doing things differently and take her to the private lounge in the back and bend her over my knee.

"All I'm saying," he continues, "is don't fight it. Maybe, give in and go with it."

"I'm not fighting anything."

"Okay," he rolls his eyes. "If you say so."

"Vin," I take a deep breath. "If you don't stop, I will hurt you."

"Hurt me all you want, brother. I have the cutest nurse to kiss my boo-boos and make them better. In fact, can you punch me below the belt?"

The memory of kissing Diablo slams into me. Damn, if she isn't the best thing I've ever tasted. If her lips taste that sweet, I can only imagine what the rest of her tastes like or what it would feel like for her luscious lips to go below my belt.

"Finally," Vinny lets out an eager breath and gets up from the booth. I turn and see Lila walking toward us. When she reaches our table, she greets me coolly, wraps her arms around Vinny's neck, and draws him into a kiss.

He rubs his hands up and down her sides, then steps back as she twirls around in front of him. She's wearing leather pants, knee-high boots, and a pink off-the-shoulder sweater.

"You look like a piece of cotton candy, and I want a taste," he runs a hand across his chin, eyes shining.

She smiles and reaches for his hand, eyes drifting down to his arm. "Is that for me?"

"Perhaps," he grins. "Do you like it?"

Looking back at him, she says two words that render Vinny speechless. "I, love."

He's a lucky bastard to have finally won her over. If only Diablo were that easy. "So, when are you making it official?" I look from Lila to Vinny, seeing her fealty all but certain.

"We haven't talked about it yet," Vinny shoots me a look that says a thousand words. Four coming at me the loudest– shut the fuck up.

I hold up my hand in apology. Fealty is a big decision. I know this and don't want to rock the boat. But honestly, it looks like it will be smooth sailing for Vinny and Lila from here on out.

Lila ignores the question and turns her attention to me. "Where's your new tattoo, Dante?"

"Same place," Vinny responds.

The apple on my forearm peeks out from under the rolled-up sleeve of my black button-up shirt. I can tell she is trying to get a better look, so I push it up further so that she can see all of it.

"Well," she looks back up. "That's…interesting. How'd you come up with it?"

"You know, the whole apple thing earlier," Vinny smiles, then stops when he sees the confusion on Lila's face. "Oh, wait, you left by then, that's right. Well, after you left—"

The look I shoot at Vinny stops him cold. Coincidentally, it comes with the same message he sent me with his own cool look seconds earlier.

"What apple thing?" Lila narrows her eyes, looking from him to me.

I yank my sleeve back down and adjust the rolled cuff so that it doesn't wrinkle. "Diablo will know."

She crosses her arms and sticks a hip out. "Oh?"

By the look on her face, I can tell there's more she wants to say. "Yes, Lila?"

"Don't hurt her, Dante. She's not as tough as you think."

"Is that why you put that outfit together?" I snort.

"How did —"

"Come on," I cut her off. "Give me some credit. I know Diablo better than anyone, and that outfit wasn't her."

"Maybe it was, and you don't know her as well as you think?"

"She would never have cooked that up on her own, and you know it."

I know my angel better than anyone, and she wouldn't use lingerie to prove a point. It's not her style. Not to mention, Lila knows how much Diablo misses her wings, and giving her a pair to wear, black, nonetheless, seemed crueler than anything I'd ever done.

"For your information, she loved it," Lila holds her hand out to inspect her nails. "And judging from your reaction, so did you."

I can't help every part of me is drawn to Diablo. She could be wearing nothing but a T-shirt and jeans, and I'd like it.

I try to shake off the memory of her walking towards me, all body and skin. "Why do I doubt it was her idea?"

"Doubt me," she shrugs. "I don't care. What I do care about is Diablo. Don't hurt her."

"I would never —"

Lila is now the one to cut me off. "You would, and you have. Maybe, give it a rest this time."

The muscle in my jaw tics, and Vinny slips his hand into Lila's and squeezes it. "Why don't we focus on us and let those two figure things out."

She looks up at him and then over at me, apologetic. "I'm sorry. I just…"

"You're going to leave, and you don't want her to be hurt any more than she will be," I finished her thought.

The look in her eyes tells me I'm right. I know Lila will be with us when we leave Eden this time. But I can't say the same about Diablo, and the thought of leaving her behind, yet again, makes me ache.

"I'm not the monster that you think I am, Lila. I know losing you will be hard for Diablo."

"I don't think you're a monster, Dante," Lila takes a breath. "Quite the contrary. You and Vinny are my family. But so is Diablo. And I just wish there were a way we could all be together."

"I want her with us, too," I say with conviction. "And I'm going to do everything to make sure that happens. But…" I continue when I see Lila open her mouth to interject. "I give you my word that I will not hurt her."

"That's the thing, Dante. You can't make that promise. Diablo feels things deeply, and sometimes it hurts her more than she lets on."

I knew Diablo's ability to feel was strong. It's why I'd tried to arouse both fire and desire in her in the past. If she could feel regret and anger, she could also feel pleasure. And if she knew how good it felt, she'd side with us and have an existence filled with every emotion possible.

"This time will be different," I cross my arms.

Vinny lifts his chin in acknowledgment. My answer is good enough for him. But Lila continues to look at me, not backing down. She's determined when it comes to those who matter to her and reminds me of Vinny. They are a lot alike in that regard.

"I would sooner burn the world to the ground than hurt her. You have my word. Okay?"

Lila smiles for the first time since this conversation began. "Okay.

The tension between us lifts, and she returns her focus to Vinny. But as I wait for Diablo, I can't shake the feeling that things aren't okay. They'll only be okay when she is next to me as Lila is with Vinny.

8
DIABLO

I'm on my way to meet Dante when my cell phone rings. I reach into my bag to see who it is, and an unknown number flashes on the screen.

I consider not answering but decide to when curiosity gets the better of me. "Hello?"

The reply is computer-generated and stops me in my tracks. "What can speak without a mouth?"

I look around, wondering if someone is playing games with me. "I'm sorry?"

"What can speak without a mouth?" the question repeats.

Assuming it's a wrong number, I'm about to hang up. But then a conversation comes to mind, stopping me.

Establishing a truce with Dante was not the first idea I had to change things between us. Initially, I wanted to see if there was something that could unbind us somewhere in the contract that bound the Fallen. There was one problem with that idea, however. It had been missing for thousands of years, and no one knew its whereabouts.

I'd always thought it odd Luke lost the very thing he used to impose his rule over the Fallen. At the same time, I knew there were many treasure hunters over time, desperate to find proof of our existence. It could be anywhere.

My desire to find the contract led me to enlist the help of Eden's notorious computer hacker, Minerva. She was known for her ability to do the impossible. I figured if anyone could find it, it was her.

We spoke only once, and she was cool throughout our conversation–giving me no indication if she would look for it or when I might hear from her again. I'd given up on hearing from her again, given how much time had passed. But thinking about her cryptic response before we hung up–*When I've found something, you'll have the answer*–it hits me. This call is from Minerva. She's found something, and I need to answer the question to know what.

I close my eyes and repeat it in my mind, and when I realize it's a riddle, the answer comes to me. "An echo," I reply quickly, holding the phone tight.

The line is quiet for a moment, and then I hear her voice. "Hello, Diablo."

My hands start to shake, and I take a deep breath to steady my nerves. "It's good to hear from you, Minerva. I wasn't sure I would."

"I said I'd call when I had news," she quips.

I imagine a young woman with blue hair and gray eyes rimmed with eyeliner. I do not know what she looks like, of course. No one does. Her face is unknown, but the rumors of her abilities are not, and her reputation underscores her attitude.

"So, you found something?" I can hear the hope in my voice, and I'm sure she can, too.

"Take a look at what I just sent you," she says casually.

"I didn't get—" I start, then stop when a chime on my phone cuts me off.

"Click on the file," she instructs, "and when prompted, enter 060607."

I hold the phone out and click on the message. When the prompt pops up, I enter the code as instructed and wait for the document to load. When it finally opens, I'm speechless.

Fragments of a language that was once as familiar as my wings fill the screen. Enochian, the tongue of the angels.

The ability to read and speak Enochian was stripped from us when we fell, and the symbols staring back at me are as foreign to me now as my mortal body once was. I don't know what I'm looking at or if it's even the contract.

I bring the phone back to my ear, fighting the tears that threaten. "How did you get this?"

"There's a reason I'm the only hacker in Eden, Diablo." Her response is curt, but Minerva's earned the right to be arrogant. Stories of her abilities carry like an electrical current. It's why I sought her help.

"Where was it?" I swallow, trying to steady my voice, which shakes more than my hands.

"The Vatican."

"The Vatican?" I narrow my eyes. "What are they doing with it?"

I'd never cared for the church's rhetoric or caustic representation of Heaven's messengers, nor its manipulation of history to fit their narrative. To know they had a document that belonged to my kind was infuriating.

"A couple of years ago, they began a digital Noah's Ark," she explains, the sound of fingers moving swiftly over a keyboard, clicking in the background. "A lifeboat for artifacts that span the history of humankind. Only, it's not the artifacts themselves, but 3D renderings that will make it possible to recreate them, should the originals ever be destroyed."

Minerva pauses for a moment, and I tap my foot impatiently, anxious for her to continue. "After we spoke originally," she begins again, "I started running queries across the web, and they hadn't returned anything for the past year until today."

I want to know everything, but I don't want to appear too eager. "Is there more?" I manage to ask, as cool as I'm able.

"More isn't the word; try everything. Nearly every important artifact back to the beginning of man is in that vault. Well, and woman," she adds with sarcasm.

"No. I mean like this."

"Ah," she laughs. "Gotcha. Yes, that is one of four in the lot. They look like they're from some kind of scroll."

My heart starts to pound deep in my chest. "Do you have all of the pieces?"

"Not yet," she says casually. "I could only grab this one before the back door that I used to access their system closed."

I was desperate for her to get all the pieces so I could find someone to translate them and see if it was the contract. "Can you get the rest?"

"The security is top grade. Every day the password changes, and only one person receives it. I'm sure you can guess who that may be."

Minerva is right. I did know. The head of the church would be the only person trusted with such information, but you had to go through The Swiss Guard to get to him, and their security was legendary. "So, it will be hard to get the rest," I say, soberly.

"Sure, for an everyday hacker. But I am not your everyday hacker."

"So, you can get them?" I brighten.

"I can," she confirms. "But it's going to cost you."

I knew it would. I'd been around long enough to know nothing was free, in our world or the mortal one. Still, I can't help but feel irritated by the response.

Once upon a time, I sat among the highest of the angels, and Minerva was soulless, which meant I outranked her in

Eden. Her nerve to ask me for anything fills me with righteous indignation. "Do you know who I am?"

"I wouldn't have taken the job if I didn't," she responds evenly. "How is Dante, by the way?"

My back stiffens. "How do you know him?" I ask crisply. Dante is both feared and respected among the soulless. Minerva could have easily told him what I was looking for or already told him what she'd found.

"I did a job for him years ago," she says casually.

A flicker of jealousy sparks, making my fingers twitch. "And just what kind of job was that?" One where she gives, and he takes, no doubt. It's precisely the kind of transaction he'd make.

"Calm down," she laughs. "He's cool but not my type."

"No?" Wasn't Dante the type of every soulless—brooding, dark, and handsome?

"No,"' she says candidly. "He's not on my team."

"Your team?" I repeat, not sure what she means.

"He's got a dick."

I draw in a sharp breath with her response. "Oh," my cheeks burn. "I'm…sorry."

"Hey," she lets out an airy laugh. "All good. No harm, no foul."

I nod to myself, not sure what to say next. Thankfully, Minerva continues. "You're a lot like him."

I bark out a laugh, the idea ridiculous. "Not even close."

"Totally," she insists. "Dante's straightforward, and you're honest. Two sides of the same coin."

Dante and I couldn't be more different. Yet the comparison makes my skin tingle. I clear my throat and push him from my mind. "Well, as I said, whatever you want, I can pay."

While most daemons amassed wealth and power, given

their greed and access to the world, the undecided were left to make a living in Eden.

Eden was like any city, with stores and commerce, and for centuries I'd run its only bookstore. But when the internet came along, sales suffered, and it closed a few years back.

I still make a living with books, but the internet has helped me do more than just sell them. I now specialize in finding rare and unique works for customers in our world and the mortal one. I do well financially, and it's the guise under which I enlisted Minerva's help.

"Well, be that as it may," she continues. "I don't take money. I require another type of payment."

"And that would be?"

"Information."

"What kind of information?" I laugh awkwardly.

Her response is direct and to the point. "You'll know when the time comes."

I can't imagine what information Minerva could want but would agree to anything at this point. "Just let me know when you have the others," I reply confidently.

"Will do," she confirms. "When I have them, I'll be in touch."

I'm about to ask when that might be, but she's already hung up.

I pull my phone from my ear and stare at it, stunned. Could I finally have the answer I've been looking for after all this time? The idea of fighting fire with fire means getting close to Dante, and I'd prefer not to go there, if possible. It would make things easier if it were the contract. Unbinding seems easier.

I shove my phone back into my bag and continue making my way down the street when the smooth timbre of his voice cuts into my thoughts. "I wondered how long you were going to keep me waiting."

I look up, surprised to see I'm already at *Saints*. Standing there, with the light of the setting sun casting an ethereal glow, a moment from long ago comes to mind. It's faint, but through the haze of time, I see one thing clearly–Dante. He steals every thought. Every step. Even the beat of my wings.

9
DIABLO

Dante is wearing a black shirt, gray slacks, leather loafers, and a steel watch. He looks like a model, and I can't help but feel a pang of attraction.

Wow, I say under my breath. But the way his lip tugs up at the corner tells me I said it loud enough for him to hear.

"I could say the same," he grins. "This century certainly agrees with you."

"Oh," I look down, forgetting what I'm wearing for a moment. "Thank you."

After trying on a dozen outfits, I settled on a cream wool sleeveless jumpsuit with an asymmetric neckline. Paired with the camel-colored kitten heels and clutch that I chose, it is appropriate for anywhere we may be going.

Between the two of us, however, Dante is the breathtaking one. The tattoos on his forearms, visible thanks to the rolled-up sleeves on his shirt, combined with his clothing, exude edge and power, and I can't stop staring.

"So," I clear my throat, ignoring the butterflies in my stomach. "What are we doing tonight?"

Dante shoves a hand in his pocket and smiles warmly. "I thought we'd go somewhere and catch up."

"Ah," I pull my clutch to my chest, knowing well what that means. The first few hours together were usually bearable. Dante was less arrogant in the beginning, cool even. But eventually, the niceties ended, and by the end of the night, the games would begin.

"Is that okay, or would you like to do something else?" he asks.

"Sure," I finger my neck nervously. "Where are we going?"

"You'll see," he pulls a set of keys from his pocket and crosses the street, stopping next to some kind of sports car.

"We're getting into that?" I point at the sleek, gunmetal gray sportscar with rims that look like spiderwebs.

He clicks the key fob in his hand, and the horn beeps, and headlights flash. "Answer your question?" he grins.

I hurry across the street, ponytail hitting my back, and when I reach the passenger side, he's holding the door open.

I look at him, both surprised and impressed. "All this, and manners, too…I had no idea."

"There are many things about me you don't know," he taps the hood while I slide into the seat.

I pull my leg inside, adjust the way I'm sitting, and then set my clutch down next to me. "Such as?"

"I have patience when the situation calls for it." He closes the door, then walks around to the driver's side. In the last century, he's found patience, and I feel like I'm going to jump out of my skin? I can't help but laugh at the irony.

As he slides into the driver's seat, his smell fills my lungs. It's a mix of orange and sandalwood and evokes a feeling of nostalgia. Ignoring the memory, I run a hand on the seat's smooth leather. "When did you get this?"

"I bought it last year and had it shipped here. Thought it would be fun to drive around the island."

The contract barred daemons from Eden outside the required ten days, and they relied on the soulless to help manage their affairs on the island during the years away. Many daemons had homes in Eden, and they had to rely on the soulless to help manage those properties, as well shipments before their arrival–like cars, the last two centuries, and horses and carriages in those which came before.

The undecided may outrank the soulless in Eden, but as Luke's servants, they were Eden's gatekeepers and came and went as he or the legion needed. I'd always envied them for this. They sold their souls, yet we were the ones confined to Eden. It seemed unfair.

Dante lifts the cover for the ignition switch on the center console and flips it up. The engine roars, loud and strong like a lion. "Beats a Touring, right?"

"You remember?" The last time I saw Dante behind the wheel of a car was in 1921, and the Nash Touring he drove to Eden was the height of machinery for its time.

"I remember everything about our time together," he looks at me and revs the engine. I reach for the seat belt and fasten it with a click. "Does it scare you?" he arches a brow.

"The car or your memory?"

"The car," he smirks.

"I don't scare easily, Dante."

He locks his eyes on mine and grins. "Good."

I press my legs together and ignore the tingling sensation the engine's rumble sends up and down my thighs.

"I meant what I said earlier," he releases the brake and pulls away from the curb. "You look terrific."

"Thank you," my cheeks flush. "I didn't know what to wear. You didn't give me much to go on."

"It's perfect. Certainly, better than your last outfit. Well, some of it," he winks.

He's baiting me, but I don't fall for it. "You don't look bad, yourself."

"Well, thank you," he says with confidence.

We race down Eden's streets, past the city limits. "So, where are we going?"

"A town I know up the coast."

"We're…what?" I look over at him.

He meets my eyes and smiles, then turns his attention back to the road in time to veer right at a fork in the road. "You look surprised?"

"Probably because I am."

He darts his eyes at me a second time. Almost as if he thinks I might open the door and jump out. "Why?"

"Because we never leave Eden."

"Sure, we do," he scoffs.

"No," I look at him pointedly, "we don't."

"Well," he considers my response. "We are. Is that okay?"

Honestly, yes. It was more than okay. I'd wanted to get out of Eden for thousands of years. Although, as exciting as leaving will be, I can only imagine what he's planning.

"So, what will it be? A brothel in Barcelona or a strip club in Seville?"

He laughs and tosses his head back. "What makes you think that's what we're doing tonight?"

"Because you like the flesh, Dante."

"I do," he confirms without apology. "But, no…I thought we'd try something different this time. Like, dinner."

"Dinner?" I repeat, caught off guard for the second time in minutes.

"Yeah," he nods. "You know, food, wine, conversation." I look at him, speechless. "What?" he laughs.

"Just as we never leave, we certainly don't eat."

"Oh, I eat," he laughs wickedly, and my cheeks burn with the inference. "Are you sure we haven't gone out to dinner before?"

"I'm positive. I would remember if—"

"If what?" he asks, curiosity in his voice.

"If you treated me normal." I look down at my lap, the admission stinging. I crave normalcy with Dante.

"We're not normal, Diablo," he rests his elbow on the door. "Our entire existence defies normal."

"I know that, obviously," I exhale. "I mean, I can't even leave Eden but once a century, and only then, with you. But I just meant that we never go out because you're always focused on my fealty."

"We can go out, and I can still want your fealty. The two are not mutually exclusive."

"Really?" I look at him, skeptical. Who is this Dante, and what has he done with the one back at *Saints*?

"Would you rather we not and get right down to business?" he says, voice tight. "Because I can turn this car around and go back and get started if you prefer."

"No," I bite my lip and look down. I didn't think the Dante I'd come to know had disappeared entirely.

Dante pushes back in his seat and grips the wheel tight, taking a deep breath. On his exhale, he straightens and continues, his voice again at ease. "Do you know the definition of insanity?"

"Rebelling?" I respond dryly.

"Doing the same thing, over and over, and expecting different results," he says candidly, ignoring my sarcasm. "For five thousand years, we've done this, and nothing's changed. I thought, maybe it was time to do things differently."

"So, you're not going to subject me to your usual antics?" I turn to him, looking for some kind of sign that will tell me what he just said is a lie. But I don't see one.

"Not unless you want me to."

62

I don't know what to say. Here I am, ready to dig my heels in and fight, and just like that, Dante's changed the game? No, I don't think so. He was a daemon, his very existence rooted in tricks and cons. What better way was there to get one to play into your hands than by making them think you were doing exactly as they wanted.

I wait for him to say something else, but surprisingly, he doesn't say anything. He simply keeps his eyes on the road and navigates us through the tunnel that connects to the mainland with a smile.

Twenty minutes later, we arrived at a small seaside town. Perched on a cliff, it appears lost in time. A stone rail runs along the water's edge on one side of the road, and a row of white stone buildings overlook the Mediterranean from the other.

After parking the car, Dante turns off the engine and reaches for the door. "You ready?"

Lights dangle from café patios that line the street as the bell over the door of a shop nearby chimes. "This is where we're having dinner?"

He sits back and stares out the window, his expression softening. "So much has changed over the millennia but not this place. That's why I like it."

I drink in the blue-green waves of the water, changing color with the setting sun. "It's beautiful but isn't exactly what I thought you'd be into."

"And that is?" he raises an eyebrow in question.

"Small towns…simple pleasures."

"I enjoy places and pleasure of all kinds," his eyes flicker.

"Didn't think you'd appreciate what small towns have to offer," I clarify.

"And just what do small towns offer, Diablo?" The way he

says my name makes my chest tighten.

I ignore the feeling and search for the right word. "I don't know. Sentimentality, or perhaps, beauty."

The feel of his touch startles me, and I turn slowly to find his knuckle grazing my cheek. "I appreciate sentimentality and beauty."

"And this place," I push down the lump in my throat, "has those qualities?"

"It does," he nods. "And the company." He looks at me for a moment, then drops his hand and turns to the window.

I follow his gaze to a large fountain across the street. In the center, a young girl holds a bucket and has a fish on her head. The expression on her face is melancholic, and the fish is nearly as large as the girl herself; its tail cracked.

It's crumbling but still working. The water that circulates is murky. And the design is both unique and quirky. But it's also familiar. I don't know why, as I'm sure I haven't been here before. But when I look away, a memory slams into me.

It's long ago, and Dante and I sit at that same fountain. The sun is high overhead, and fluffy white clouds paint the sky, but there's an ache in my chest and despair deep within me, despite the day's beauty.

"We've been here," I swallow, a phantom pain from that day making me wince.

"We have," he nods softly.

I close my eyes, the memory squeezing the air from my lungs. It was one of our most miserable times together. Dante arrived in Eden that century with a chip on his shoulder, and we spent every one of the ten days fighting. When he left, I was so desperate to be rid of him that I never said goodbye.

"I guess I...forgot," I say quietly, my voice barely a whisper.

"You forgot?" he asks, an edge of disbelief in his own.

I nod, unable to repeat the lie because I didn't forget. I chose to bury the memory because it hurt too much.

That was the last time I saw the Dante I once knew. When he returned the next century, he was different. He changed during the time apart, returning with an insatiable desire that he enjoyed satisfying, then filling me in on the details.

I never wanted to remember that day, but I could feel others trying to claw their way back into my mind now that I had. They were memories of the times that came before when being with Dante wasn't painful.

I close my eyes to push them away, but they crash into me, a storm of memories and emotions.

He grabs my chin with his thumb and forefinger and gently turns my face to him. "I'd like to take you to dinner, Diablo. Will you allow me to do that?"

When I look in his eyes, I don't see derision or motivation. I see a hint of who he once was. It pierces through that day's awful memory and reminds me of when I longed for his return.

"I haven't been the most…. tolerable," he lets go of my chin. "I'd like to change that. Would you let me?"

I stare back at him, remembering the first rule of manipulation. Feign friendship. "Are we really being honest here, or will you threaten to spank me if I say something you don't like?"

"I will only spank you if you want." I inhale and straighten, and he sits back, putting his hand on the wheel. "I'm kidding."

I ease slightly but don't know what to say. "What's your endgame, Dante?"

"Oh angel, you know the answer to that question."

"No," I shake my head. "Not my fealty. This one. Here, now."

"Look," he says with utter honesty. "I want your fealty. I won't lie. But..." he adds when I start to respond. "It's just dinner. Making up for the past. Hell, rewriting some of it."

I wanted to believe Dante, but a part of me screams not to. Not because I don't think he can change, but because if he had, it would mean I would have to as well, and I'm not prepared to do that. Winning my freedom from Dante was my focus. It had to be. And if agreeing to dinner got me one step closer to that goal, then so be it.

"Okay, Dante," I take a deep breath and reach for the door. "We can have dinner."

He is already there before I can open it, holding the door open with one hand and extending the other towards me.

I place my hand in his, and he helps me out of the car, flashing a beautiful, enigmatic smile. But when I return it with one of my own, I can't help but feel as if we're both hiding something.

10
DANTE

"Well, you certainly know how to make an entrance," I whisper in Diablo's ear as we wind through the restaurant.

At first, it stirred pride, knowing she was with me, a boost to my already rousing confidence. But then, it became irritating. From the car to the restaurant, every guy we passed stared at her. The look in their eyes made me want to smash every one of their faces, but I resisted. The side of me I need her to see, want her to see, one of charm and poise.

"They're not looking at me," she counters as we take our seats.

"Well, I beg to differ," I smile and hand her a menu. Usually, I find humility feigned and pretentious, but not with Diablo. With her, it's natural and charming.

Her fingers brush mine as she reaches for the menu, and she clears her throat and looks down. "So, what do you recommend?"

Diablo is beguiling. I wasn't lying when I said this century suited her. She didn't just give every mortal a run for their money. There simply was no contest.

"The gazpacho is wonderful," I say with confidence. "The paella, perfection."

"Good to know," she browses the menu and sets it down, and looks around when done. "This place is lovely," she removes an errant strand of hair from her eyes with a delicate finger. "How did you find it?"

It's a beautiful evening. The sky is clear, and the

temperature mild. From where we sit, we have an unobstructed view of the water, and the Spanish sweet peas that twist along the wall fill the air with their rich perfume.

I wonder if I should tell her that I come here every year to mark the passage of time. Days apart, then years. Measurements of equal significance. "I've been here a few times on my way to Marbella," I say instead.

"Ah," she nods, a smirk pulling at her lips. "Makes sense."

"What makes sense?" I sit back, admiring the glow of the setting sun on her skin.

"Marbella, the car, clearly you're enjoying the luxuries of this century."

"Is that a bad thing?"

"No," she shakes her head. "Not when the business you do, which allows such luxuries, is conducted with integrity."

I've known Diablo far too long not to be able to read her as well as I can. That's how I know she's trying to provoke me. "Would you like some wine?" I ask politely.

"That's it," she arches her brow. "You're not going to say anything?"

By not responding the way she assumed I would, I've piqued Diablo's curiosity, and that's good. When one is curious, they are open. And that's what I need her to be. I need her to see me with an open mind and let her guard down.

"Am I going to respond to your barbed comment?" I grin. "No, I'm not. What you and I do when we are not together is, as you said earlier, not the other's concern. Which means how I go about my business is, well, my business."

The words taste sour, but I say them anyway. To sell the idea that I am not who Diablo believes me to be, I need to say and do differently than she expects.

Diablo studies me. "Really?"

"I don't like it, but it's what it is." That wasn't so hard, was it? To fight my very instinct to show her who's boss. The glint of surprise in her eyes was worth it. "Now, back to the wine. Would you like to get a bottle?"

She rests her hands gently in her lap and sits back. "Sure. What do you suggest?"

When the server arrives, I request one of the best wines on the menu, and then he turns his attention to Diablo to take her order. He goes over today's specialties, eyes never leaving her face, and when she asks about a specific item, he leans in a little too close while explaining it to her. It takes every ounce of restraint in me not to lunge across the table and knock his teeth out. There's a line between impulsive and protecting what's mine, and when it came to Diablo, the latter drew the fiercest reaction.

When it's my turn to order, I feign ignorance on how to pronounce a dish and motion for the server to lean in, speaking low enough so only he can hear. "If you and every other asshole in this restaurant don't stop looking at my dinner companion like she's on the menu, I will filet you. Do you understand me?"

The server's eyes widen as he straightens, scribbles on his notepad, and hurries away.

"What was that about?" Diablo asks once he's gone.

"Hmm?"

"The server…he left in a hurry."

"Did he?" I glance over my shoulder, pretending not to notice. "Given the wine I chose, he probably assumes there's a good tip for him if he doesn't keep us waiting."

She places her elbows on the table and leans in, peering at me with her hypnotizing green eyes. "Tell me, Dante, are you used to everyone cowering in your presence?"

The question makes me laugh. "I can't help it if power frightens."

"It doesn't scare me."

I stare back at her, and she neither squirms nor shifts uncomfortably. "Is that so?"

"No," she lifts her chin, meeting my gaze head-on. My beautiful angel is fire and willpower. A combination that both fascinates and arouses me.

A new server returns, holding a bottle of wine out for my inspection, careful to keep his eyes on me and not Diablo. That means the other server delivered my message. Good.

I look at the label and nod in approval, then the server pours a small amount into the glass in front of me and waits. "Go ahead," I push it towards Diablo. "Tell me what you think."

She reaches for it, and my eyes zero in on her mouth as she places her lips delicately on the rim and takes a sip. "It's good," she smiles, swiping a finger gently along her lower lip. "It tastes like cherries...and violet."

My body's response to her is visceral, every muscle in me responding as she licks her lips. I motion for the server to pour us each a glass, then shift in my seat to ease the growing tightness in my pants.

Ten days, I remind myself. Ten days and then I can, what? Satisfy the hunger I've put off fulfilling with whomever I find first? Surprisingly, the question doesn't ease the tension in my body; it makes it worse. I want Diablo to myself so badly I can taste it, and the idea of that not happening makes me want to break something.

I push the thought to the back of my mind, reminding myself to focus on the here and now. A lot can change in ten days, and who was to say we won't be indulging in one another by the end?

Once the server fills both glasses, he places the bottle on the table and heads back inside. "To new beginnings," I hold up my glass.

After a moment of hesitation, she reaches for her wine and taps it to mine. "So, business appears to be going well for you this century," she says after taking a sip.

"Better than any before," I nod, lift my glass, and sip.

Diablo knows I buy and sell companies. I've done it successfully for hundreds of years. But she doesn't know it's the business of secrets that fuels my enterprise. They're easy to acquire when you move in the circles I do, and from world leaders and CEOs to the social elite, I know things that could make heads spin.

Secrets make it possible to buy companies cheap and sell for top dollar. Money is no object to those with skeletons in their closet–both what one is willing to pay and lose. And nothing has shaped the last century more than secrets and lies.

"And you?" I take a sip of wine. "How is the bookstore?"

"Oh," she looks down into her glass. "It closed a few years ago. I'm a book dealer now."

"There's a market for that?" I ask with genuine curiosity.

Her eyes light up. "Oh yes. You wouldn't believe how much one would pay for a first edition Shakespeare."

I grin, knowing exactly how much one would pay for that which they desire. "I can probably imagine."

Diablo tells me more about her work, and I'm mesmerized just listening to her. She possesses an intellect that matches her beauty and a passion for literature that's infectious.

"The internet is the only reason I can do what I do," she sits up and sets her glass down. "I can search anywhere."

"Ah," I take a sip of wine, trying to shake off the spell she cast over me. "Now that I understand. The internet has been good for your business and so, too, has it been for mine."

"Oh?" she leans her elbows on the table and runs a finger around the rim of her glass. "How so?"

I set my glass down and clear my throat, pushing aside how beautiful she is. "Internet companies tend to be started by narcissists. They will do anything to have the world in the palm of their hand, and when their companies are failing, it is precisely this which is their undoing. They will take whatever you offer to preserve what they've amassed."

"When it was first available, I didn't know what to think," she places her hand on the table and pauses, considering her words. "It felt like a blessing and a curse. All that information and access to the world outside Eden."

"And has it been...a blessing or a curse?" I tilt my head with curiosity.

"It's been a little of both," she admits. "In a way, I get to experience the world while being reminded that I'll never be a part of it."

My chest pangs at the hint of melancholy in her voice, and for the first time in this existence, I feel something I haven't before–empathy.

Diablo has more appreciation for the world than any Fallen, yet she is forbidden from being a part of it, aside from the time we are together, and she can leave with me. If anyone should experience it up close, it's her.

"To be honest, I'm surprised he allowed it in Eden," she continues, turning her attention to the water. "Then again, letting us see what we cannot have, is something he would do."

By he, I know she means Luke. He's the only one of us

Diablo refuses to call by name, and conversations about him never end well. But she's right. Luke did let the undecided have access to the internet for ulterior motives. He believed if they saw the world, they'd want to be a part of it and swear allegiance.

However, I didn't want to say this and get into an argument about his Machiavellian ways and have dinner go to shit. Instead, I reach for my wine and take a sip, responding in the most impartial way possible. "The internet was inevitable. As times change, so too must Eden."

Diablo sits back, appearing to ease with my response. "The world changed so much this past century. It makes me wonder how it will change in the next."

I had the same thought before coming to Eden. In fact, it's the same thought I've had for centuries. Each new one is rooted in the subject of us–will this be the one where things change between Diablo and me?

I look down at her empty wine glass, then back up, noticing her cheeks are pink. "Diablo, how often do you drink?"

"Not that much," she confesses.

I knew the wine would help loosen her up. It's why I suggested getting a bottle. But the flush of her cheeks and sudden candor tells me she should probably eat something before drinking any more. "How about we hold on having more wine until our food arrives?"

"Why?" she laughs. "Are you afraid I'm going to get sick in that fancy car of yours?"

"No," I smile, both amused and aroused by her boldness.

"Right," she smirks. "You probably have dozens just like it. Perhaps, you're worried I'll become too loose-tongued."

"Oh, on the contrary," my body hardens. "I think I'd quite

enjoy your loose tongue."

I've never seen her like this–no feigned bravado. No hesitation. Just raw, honest authenticity, and it's sexy as fuck.

Her cheeks turn from pink to red with my comment, and I reach for her glass and pull it towards me. "For your information, I know wine hangovers are the worst. You'll thank me."

"Is that so," she hiccups, which makes her giggle.

"Yes," I smile wider, unable to help myself. The sound of her laughter pierces my chest and stirs my desire for her. "That's so."

She eyes me curiously. "Are you always this concerned about your dates?"

"I don't date," I shake my head.

"No?" her brows shoot up.

Surprisingly, her questions don't frustrate me. I find her inquisitiveness alluring. "Dating isn't for me," I reply simply.

"Not one mortal, in five thousand years, has ever caught your eye?"

There has never been anyone that's captured my interest. Mortals are the means to an end. Bed them, then forget them. "Does that surprise you?"

"Well," she holds her hand out. "Have you seen you?" The moment the words come out of her mouth, I know she regrets them. "You know what I mean," she clears her throat. "Young...and successful."

I reach for my glass, enjoying the hole she's digging for herself. "Young?"

"I meant..." she stammers.

"I know what you meant," I lock my eyes on hers and grin. My angel just revealed a card she hadn't planned on showing.

74

"I was just saying," she takes a deep breath. "This existence can be lonely, and I would understand if you found someone who made it less so."

"Well, I haven't," I say before she expects me to say something similar because I won't. The very idea of someone else getting to be with her in the years that I am unable irritates me. Nope. No way. Diablo belongs to me. And the sooner she realizes it, the better she will be.

"You know, Diablo, I could make sure you never have to worry about your business, or anything else, for that matter."

Her forehead pinches in confusion. "What do you mean?"

"I mean, I could make sure you are taken care of and never have to worry about money again."

She grabs the arms of her chair and leans forward. "Why would you do that?"

Man, I've really fucked up over the millennia. She's suspicious of even my desire to give her. I have my work cut out for me. "You should have the best, and I can give that to you."

"No matter what I decide?" she asks with brutal honesty.

I know what she's asking. She wants to know if my desire to give to her relates to whether she swears her fealty.

The subject is always tenuous, so I consider my response carefully. "Your happiness and your fealty are not related."

"But they are," she sits back. "Intrinsically."

I hold up a hand and clarify. "I simply meant that I can want one without it being contingent on the other."

"You've never cared about either before. Why now?"

"Of course, I have." I know the things I've done to get Diablo on our side. But I did it for her. If only she could see that. "I won't make excuses for what I've done in the past. All I can do is move forward."

"That's just it," she looks at me with sadness. "Sometimes, we can't move forward. Sometimes, we're stuck, forever looking back."

I press the tips of my fingers together and think about the word forever. It's as much a part of my existence as she is. "Here's the thing about the past, Diablo. It isn't infinite. Once you let it go, the future is there, waiting."

II
DIABLO

"Are you sure you had them?" Dante asks, lips twitching in amusement. We've been standing at my front door for the past five minutes while I search for my keys.

He's surprisingly calm, but he has been all night, much to my surprise. It was disarming, and why I had so much to drink. I kept waiting for the other shoe to drop and drinking helped soothe my nerves.

"Yes," I sigh with frustration. Despite my bag being impossibly small, my fingers tingle, and everything I touch feels unfamiliar. "I locked my door when I left."

I hate to admit it, but Dante was right. I should have eaten something before having more wine. But when he pulled the whole 'I can take care of you' card, the fighter in me reached for my glass and pulled it right back. I was incensed that suddenly now, after all this time and all he'd done, he cared.

By the time our food arrived, I'd polished off a second glass, and when the server came to clear our plates away, I'd made it through my third, and my cheeks were warm, and a low hum vibrated through my body.

If Dante noticed, he pretended not to. But judging by the way he looked at me now, something told me he was well aware and enjoying every minute of watching me fumble.

"Would you like some help?" he asks cheekily.

"I just don't understand. It's like Mary Poppins' bag."

"Mary, who?" he looks at me, confused.

"Poppins," I look up. "You know, the nanny."

"Oh, I've known a few nannies," he flashes me a devilish grin. "But never Mary, whomever."

The thought of Dante with someone makes me lose focus for a moment. "She's a character in a story," I shake my head to clear my mind. "And she has this bag," I dig through my own and finally pull the contents out. "It holds all kinds of stuff. Like a plant and a coat rack, and —"

"What's that?" Dante asks, cutting me off.

I look up, startled by the tone of his voice. "What's what?"

"That," he points to my hand.

I look down at my compact, cell phone and lip gloss. "A mirror?"

"No, the other."

"Lipstick?" I hold my bag upside down, giving it a shake. "Ah-ha!" I smile excitedly when my keys fall out.

I bend down to pick them up, but he's beat me to it. "The cell phone," he says accusingly, gripping my keys. "Is it yours?"

I shoot him a wry smile. "Good guess, Sherlock."

"Why didn't you tell me you had a cell phone?"

"I don't know," I laugh, and Dante grabs it out of my hand and taps the screen. "Hey!"

"No passcode?" he shakes his head. "Really?"

"I don't need one," I watch in disbelief as he opens the keypad and dials a number. A second later, his pocket rings, and he hangs up. "Did you just call yourself?"

He hands me back my phone, reaches into his pocket, and pulls out a phone. After a few taps on the screen, he shoves it back in. "Now I have your number. And seriously, you need to put a passcode on your phone."

"Why? No one in Eden would touch my phone."

"No," he says with certainty. "No one in Eden would dare

mess with you. But out there," he nods in the direction of the mainland, "they would in a heartbeat."

"What does it matter? I doubt you plan on us leaving Eden again in the next ten days?"

"Maybe we will," he shrugs.

"Well, I'm not changing my ways for a maybe."

Dante presses his lips into a discerning line and stares at me. "Regardless, now you have my number."

"Money and a phone number," I roll my eyes. "What will you offer next?"

He leans in, eyes drifting from my eyes to my mouth. "Do not underestimate what I would give to you, angel."

His words still me as heat shoots down my spine. "You could have just asked for my number."

"Would you have given it to me?"

"If you'd asked nicely. Now," I shove my things back into my bag and hold out my hand. "May I have my keys?"

Dante drops them into my hand and waits for me to open the door. Once we're inside, I flip on the lights and drop my bag and keys onto the entryway table.

"I'm sure it's different from wherever you live now," I close the door behind us. "I'm thinking…penthouse with a view?"

He swings his head in my direction, and the grin on his face confirms I'm right. "It's changed since the last time I was here."

What began as a simple cottage had grown over the years into a spacious home filled with natural light and an open floor plan. "It has," I nod.

Dante looks around the kitchen, taking note of the white marble countertop, stainless steel appliances, and bowl of oranges in the center, then makes his way to the living room.

I follow him and stand next to an oversize chair with a cream pillow and cashmere throw.

"Is this new?" he looks out my large bay window.

"No," I shake my head. "The view is, though."

Since he was here last, I'd purchased the property on either side of me and added a rock wall around the perimeter and a garden.

He looks down at me, and his nearness makes my chest flutter. "You always wanted a yard full of peonies."

"I did," I smile, surprised he remembered. "So, I planted them."

He holds my gaze for a moment, then turns from the window and studies my corner bookshelf. It's sparse, with only a few books and a few items. "For a book lover, I expected a bigger collection."

"Oh, that's not all of them," I look at it awkwardly. "That's just decoration."

"So, where are all your beloved books?" he asks, curious.

"Well...that's the other thing that's changed since you were here last. My study. It's expanded a bit."

"Well, let's see it," he shoves a hand in his pocket.

"Oh, I don't know. It's personal."

"Personal?" his eyes light up. "You just spent an hour at dinner talking to me about books. So, show me where you keep this passion of yours."

If fighting fire with fire will work, I have to let Dante see all of me. Including the place that I love most. "Fine," I exhale. "Come with me."

We make our way down the hall, past my bedroom, stopping at the end in front of a wood door with a top arch, black iron hinges, and round hammered clavos.

"And here I was, thinking you were showing me your

bedroom on the first date," he looks down at me, eyes smoldering.

"But you don't date," I ignore the heat passing between us. "So, it doesn't count."

"For you, I'd break all my rules. And for the record, every moment between us counts."

"Dante," I hesitate, wrapping my hand around the ornate door handle. The world on the other side is like stepping into my heart, and if he is trying to get in there as a way to get to me, I didn't think I would be able to take the betrayal.

"Diablo," he wraps his hand around mine. "Let me in."

My heart thumps deep in my chest as he pushes the door open, and we step inside–the smell of wood and parchment greeting us. In this space, time does not exist, only words and worlds of the past and those still to come.

Without me having to say anything, I want him to understand why it's my favorite place in the house, and when I look over and see his mouth open as he looks up, something tells me he does. "This is incredible," he marvels at the curved ceiling.

My heart lurches with his approval. "Yeah?"

"Yeah," he makes his way further into the room, eyeing the bookshelves that line the walls.

"It was a lot of work," I look around, remembering how long it took to plan and build out.

"Oh, I bet," he looks down to the polished wood floors that run from wall to wall, then over at the leather tufted couch in the center of the room, with an ottoman in front. "It's amazing."

"Amazing as in, wow? Or as in, whoa?"

"As in wow,"' he looks at me. "How did you do all this?"

I look around, drinking in my beloved space. "I guess,

with time, anything is possible."

"Where did you get the idea?" he asks. When I look over, I can see that he's impressed by the look on his face.

"I was online one day and saw a picture of Trinity College, and well...it became a passion project."

"It looks a lot like it," he looks up. "The ceiling and the color of the stacks."

"You've been?" I ask, surprised. The library at Trinity College was on the list of places I wanted to see someday, along with The National Gallery, The Louvre, and countless other places.

"Yeah," he laughs. "I do read."

"I know you read," I cross my arms and lean back against a shelf. "Just didn't take you for someone who visits libraries for fun."

"I was in Ireland and needed to look into a few things," he says casually.

"What's it like?" I ask dreamily.

"For a book lover such as yourself, the best way to describe it is probably, well... Heaven."

The comparison makes me smile. "I'd love to see it."

"We should go," he suggests. "I have a plane. It would be easy to take a trip there."

"You do not," I shake my head in disbelief.

"Of course, I do," he smiles. "It makes my work easier."

I wonder what it's like to be Dante. To travel wherever and whenever he wants. "Well, maybe someday we can go there." The word hangs in the space between us. Someday-part dream, part promise.

"What's over there?" Dante nods towards a glass case on the far side of the room.

"Ah," I push up from the shelf and make my way over to

it. "It's every one of Shakespeare's plays ever published."

"Don't most lovers of Shakespeare have copies?" Dante does the same.

"Yes," I draw out my response as we meet at the case. "But more special." I wonder if I should tell him what they are. No one knows. He'd be the first.

He lifts a curious brow. "How so?"

"Do you promise not to say anything?"

"Of course," he says with raw honesty. "You can trust me." I hesitate, my eyes searching his. "Look," he holds out a hand. "You have my word. No matter what I've done in the past, you can trust at least that."

Dante is right. He was forthright and candid, and when he said he was going to do something, he did. He'd never lied or broken my trust, per se.

"Okay," I take a deep breath. "I'll tell you. But if word ever gets out, I will know it was you. Lila doesn't even know."

"Duly noted," he nods. "And by the way, I'm honored you'll tell me something you've never told your best friend."

"There are things you've kept from Vinny, right?"

Dante looks at me for a moment and replies simply. "Only one."

The way he's looking at me makes my palms sweat. "So then, you know that some secrets are best to remain hidden."

"I do," he confesses. "But sometimes, it's not about keeping it quiet, but waiting for the right time to reveal it."

My head swims, and my heart races as I prepare to tell him the truth. "These are first editions," I say as if hypnotized.

He looks down into the case. "But those are in the British Library."

With the break in his focus, air rushes into my lungs, and I shake my head, clearing the haze from my mind. "How…do you know that?"

He looks back up and smiles. "I know a great many things, Diablo. One does not get ahead in the mortal world without being a learned individual. So, tell me, how are these first editions?"

I can see why Dante does well in business. His intelligence is attractive.

"What's in the British Library," I swallow and push aside his dangerous combination of smarts and sex appeal, "is what historians believe to be the first collected edition of Shakespeare's plays. But these are the first published individual copies. They are the true, first editions."

Dante's eyes widen at my confession. "How did you get them?"

"Well," I pause, wondering how much I should say. "As I said at dinner, you can find anything online. And underground communities and networks have been around for thousands of years, and Eden is no exception."

He shakes his head and grins.

"What?" my stomach tumbles nervously.

"Remember the 'do it with integrity' line you fed me at dinner?"

A flash of righteousness hits me. "It's not—"

"Wait," he holds up a hand. "If you let me finish...I was going to say I'm not judging you. That's not what I was saying."

"Then what are you saying?" I cross my arms, wondering if trusting him had been a bad idea.

"I was merely going to say that just as I have done things for my passions, so have you."

Dante was right. I couldn't condemn his actions if I didn't mine. At the same time, I can't help but think protecting a few books paled to whatever he'd done over the years.

"You're right," I sigh.

"I'm what?" he holds a hand to his ear.

"You're right," I say again. "Okay?"

A look of satisfaction fills his handsome face. "Can I tell you something?"

"Depends," I take a deep breath. "Will I regret it?"

"Some of the businesses I've bought, their leaders have been the worst. The world is better off without them. You protect words, and I protect the world from those who should not have power. When you think about it, we're not so different."

I bite my lip and look down, thinking about that simple statement. Was there a bit of angel still left in Dante?

"Don't worry," he says when I grow quiet. "I won't say anything about what's in the case. And this is amazing," he looks around. "Thank you for showing me."

I'm stunned by the compliment. I trusted Dante and didn't regret it. In fact, sharing this with him unlocked something I hadn't felt in a long time–understood.

"Well," I look at the door. "It's getting late. Shall we?"

"Yeah," he exhales. "I guess so."

We're both quiet as we make our way back down the hall. "Thank you for tonight," I say once we reach the door.

"It was a good night," he smiles. "I should be thanking you."

Dante is right. It was a good night. Surprisingly so. "Dinner was nice. Your recommendations were spot on."

"The food and the company were perfect," he flashes me a smile. "You should come with me to a few of my business dinners. You'd charm a CEO out of their company without even knowing you'd done so."

I laugh and tuck my hair behind my ear as I open the door. "Goodnight, Dante."

"Goodnight," he stares at me for a second longer, then makes his way down the steps. "Oh, and Diablo," he stops and turns when he reaches the end of the drive. I froze, wondering if I'd been too quick to let my guard down, and it was time for the other shoe to drop. "I meant what I said earlier. If you need anything, just call."

I nod stiffly but promise nothing, waiting until he's driven off before going inside. Once I do, I lean back against the door and exhale in relief. I'd tried to fight fire with fire tonight, but I can't help but feel that the only walls that chipped away were mine.

At the same time, I'm not afraid of what our second day together might bring. For the first time in forever, I'm curious. And curiosity is a lot better than fear.

12
DANTE

Diablo wasn't wrong when she guessed I lived in a penthouse. I do. It's in the building I own along the river in London, which serves as headquarters for my corporation. It's spacious and has the best view, with museum-worthy artwork hanging throughout. But when I'm back in Eden, the comfortable flat I'm at now is home. It, too, is a space I enjoy.

Vinny and I bought the building centuries ago, and it has everything we need. One floor is a garage for our bikes and cars. Another is a full-sized gym with a pool. Then one floor is his, and the other, mine.

I've decked out my place with a bar and pool table, a flat-screen TV covering nearly one wall, and a large table made of a slab of oak and high-backed antique chairs with purple velvet seat cushions. It's rustic and comfortable, and I wish we could come to Eden more often because it's a great space.

The flat and penthouse couldn't be more different, but both feel like me. Whereas the ultra-modern space in London is flawless and austere, this building with its aging brick and faded windows has charm and character. Like my homes, I was a blend of many things, and I realized this applied to Diablo, too.

Being with her tonight wasn't at all what I expected. I enjoyed myself and found it easy to be who I thought she wanted me to be because I was being who I also was.

In the mortal world, I was poised and intellectual. One had to be to move in the circles I did. And Diablo matched me in charm and wit and also made me laugh. I couldn't have imagined a better first night together.

But seeing the way the world responded to her reminded me of my other side–the one that wanted to claim her.

I reach into my pocket and toss my phone down onto the bed, unbuttoning my shirt hastily and ripping it off. Being with Diablo in that beautiful library, I couldn't stop thinking about how I wanted to make her mine. Against the stacks. On the polished wood floor. Spread out on one of those leather couches. Fuck, I'd devour her whole on one of those.

The blood in my veins turns to fire just thinking about it, and I realize it's not the soulless or even the outside world I need to worry about–it's me. Every time Diablo is near me, I want to touch her. I am the only one that can ruin my plans and need to get it together.

Deciding to blow off some pent-up energy, I change into my workout gear and head to the gym. I'm surprised when I push through the door and see Vinny on the bench press. I didn't expect to see him tonight. I figured he and Lila wouldn't come up for air for days.

I make my way over to him and stand behind the bench. I know he won't need a spot since he's stronger than me. But still, it's a habit.

He's lifting three hundred pounds, and I don't have to ask what's got him pumping so much iron. The look on his face says it all. At the same time, I can't help myself. "Trouble in paradise, already?" I smirk and look down.

He does a couple more reps, then pushes the weight to the bar and sits up. "Lila and I got into it tonight."

I reach down for his water bottle and hand it to him. "About?"

"Where to live," he grabs it and takes a drink. "She wants

Paris, but I'm not into all that crap. London is home. Your work is there, which means mine is, too."

"Your work can be anywhere," I shrug. I'm used to calling Vinny any time of day, and he's used to going anywhere, for anything. He's the only person I trust as my right hand, and he shares my success. My wins are his wins.

"All I'm saying is don't let it be something she changes her fealty over."

"Oh, that's not happening," he gives me a sly grin. "The fights are epic, but the make-up sex," he blows a chef's kiss. "I'd fight with her for eternity if I get to fuck her as I did earlier."

I shake my head, envious for a second time today. "If things are good, then why are you here?"

"She had to take care of something. I figured, why not get in a workout before getting in another one with her later." He laughs, and I do, too. "How was your night?"

"Honestly, it was good. Diablo's different this time."

"Well yeah," Vinny moves his neck from side to side. "We all saw that."

I narrow my eyes, and he holds up his hand. "Chill, brother. I was going to say she doesn't seem afraid of you, that's all."

"She isn't," my shoulders ease. I know Vinny wasn't inferring anything, but I can't help my possessiveness over her. It's instinctual. "Can't hold her alcohol worth a damn, though."

"No?" he takes another sip of water.

"No," I shake my head and laugh. The memory of her wine flushed cheeks pulls at my chest. My angel is bright, with a keen mind for business. While I want to take care of her, knowing she can take care of herself is a major turn-on.

"And man does she love books."

"So…when does the real work begin?" Vinny waggles his brows. "I'm sure you're anxious to get started."

"You know, I've been thinking about it, and I'm doing things differently this time." I'd already made progress with Diablo. More so than in any other century. And I'm confident my approach will work.

"So, not the usual fun and games?" he looks at me, dubious.

"Nope," I shake my head.

"You?" his brows shoot up.

"Sure," I shrug. "Why not?"

"Dante," he shakes his head. "You're my brother. I know you better than anyone. And you need sex, my man. How are you going to manage without it for ten days?"

Honestly, it wasn't about managing because the truth was, I didn't want anyone else. All night I could feel my desire for Diablo. It wasn't a matter of ten days, and then I could satisfy my hunger with whomever. I only wanted it to be her.

My longing for her. I'd felt it in the past, but her stubbornness had always pushed me to satisfy that hunger elsewhere. But now that she was letting me in, I didn't want anyone else, and this was the secret I'd never told Vinny.

"I'll deal with it," I say simply. I could go without sex. I didn't always have such a voracious appetite. And seeing that fountain tonight reminded me of this.

The argument Diablo and I got into the last time we were there together had been vicious. I was hell-bent on her fealty, and she was just as focused on refusing me. I was angrier with her than I'd ever been when I left.

When the next century rolled around, that anger joined forces with my need to make Luke proud and twisted into

90

darkness fueled by selfishness and greed. To sate it, I found whatever soulless I could find, and this hunger, this cycle of wrath and pleasure, only grew in the centuries that followed. It was my need for Diablo that lit that match.

Regret cuts into me thinking about it, and I can't help but wonder–had I changed my approach with her back then, would things be different now?

Vinny takes a sip of water and looks at me from over his water bottle. "Dealing with it is not an answer, brother."

It's not. I know. But the truth is, I'll never want another the way I do her, and I don't want to use others as a substitute anymore. My focus was on winning her, and that's all I was thinking about right now.

"It's the only one I've got," I shrug. "So, take it or leave it."

"Well," Vinny gets up and claps me on the shoulder. "If it works for you, then it works for me."

"It does," I confirm, more for me than him. "Now, do you want to grab a drink when I'm done?"

"Sure. How long will you be?"

"I'm going to run and then lift a bit. An hour?"

"Okay," he reaches for a towel slung over a rack of weights next to the bench. "I'll spot you when I'm out of the shower."

"Sounds like a plan."

Vinny leaves, and I head over to the treadmill. Peeling off my shirt, I toss it to the ground and reach into my pocket for my phone and wireless headphones. After finding my playlist, I slip in my earbuds and press start.

After twenty minutes, my heart rate is steady, so I increase the speed and incline. "Hey," Vinny comes over after thirty minutes. My body is warm and glistening with sweat. I remove an earbud and lift my chin in acknowledgment.

"Drinks have to wait. Lila needs me."

"Everything okay?" I ask, keeping my pace.

"Yeah, she's at Diablo's."

"What's she doing there?" I ask, my curiosity piqued.

"I don't know. Didn't ask." His phone vibrates, and he looks down, reading a message that's just come in. "I think you'd better look at this."

I decrease the speed on the treadmill and hop off, coming over to where he stands. I remove my other earbud as he holds up his phone, and I read a text from Lila.

Hey, could you come over? Something's off.

My back straightens, and I look up. "Is she still at Diablo's?"

Vinny writes back to ask and presses send. A few seconds later, another text comes in.

Yes. Are you coming now?

The idea that something is happening at Diablo's makes my heart pound and fingers twitch. "I'm coming with you."

"Let's roll," he shoves the phone into his pocket.

We take the stairs to the garage, passing the row of cars until we reach our bikes, and with the keys already in the ignition, slip on our helmets, start the engines, and race off.

We fly down Eden's streets and arrive at Diablo's house minutes later. I storm up the walk, pound on the door, and after what feels like forever, it opens. "Dante?" Lila looks at me, confused. "What are you doing here?"

"Vinny got your message," I say as I come through the door and call out Diablo's name.

She comes down the hall seconds later with a shocked expression. "What are you doing here?"

She's wearing a T-shirt that reveals a hint of her stomach and pajama bottoms and looks irresistible. But it's the flush in her cheeks that arouses me.

She rolls her bottom lip under her teeth as her eyes flit from my face to my chest, and when I look down, I realize I'd raced out of the gym so fast that I forgot to grab my shirt. I'm standing in her living room in nothing but gym shorts and shoes.

She's speechless as she stares at me, lips slightly parted, and I know what's causing her cheeks to turn such a beautiful shade of pink because I recognize the look. She likes what she sees. If I knew it would take me being shirtless to get this kind of reaction out of her, I'd have walked around without one years ago.

"Why are you both here?" Lila asks Vinny as he walks through the door.

"Top dog had to go all alpha," he reaches for her and nips at her neck.

I keep my attention on Diablo. "Lila's text said something was up. Are you okay?"

Diablo clears her throat and shifts her attention to my face. "After you left, I saw something."

"What did you see?"

"Some creepy looking dude in the shadows across the street," Lila responds, smiling in Vinny's embrace.

"What?" I turn around and storm outside.

"He's not there now," she calls out as I push through the gates and look down the street.

"What's up?" Vinny asks, coming up behind me.

I speak low enough so only he can hear. "Has anyone been followed from the mainland lately?"

"Not that I know," he shakes his head. "Why? Is that where you were tonight?"

I look up and down the street again. "Yeah."

"Do you think someone followed you?"

I blow out an angry breath. "Wouldn't surprise me. Every asshole in the restaurant was staring at her."

"Do you see anything?" Lila calls out. I look to the door and notice Diablo standing behind her.

"Do you want me to check it out?" Vinny asks.

"No," I run a hand through my hair and shake my head. "Not tonight. Go be with Lila."

"Are you sure?"

"Yeah," I take a deep breath. "I'll stay here tonight and keep an eye on things."

"Alright," he claps my shoulder, then turns around and heads back into the house. "Hey, sweetness. Let's go!"

Lila jumps into Vinny's arms as he makes it to the door, and envy hits me again.

When I make it back inside, Lila is saying goodbye to Diablo. "Vinny and I are going to go, but Dante's here. See you in a couple of days for coffee, as promised."

Diablo offers Lila a grateful smile and reaches out to hug her. "Thanks for coming. I'm sorry to bother you."

"Girl, of course. Call me anytime."

Once the two pull apart, Vinny throws Lila over his shoulder. "Okay, we're out. See you tomorrow, brother."

"Have a good night," I lift my chin as they head out the door but keep my eyes on Diablo.

"We will!" They laugh in unison.

I wait until I hear them speed off before speaking. "Now, do you want to tell me what happened?"

Diablo makes her way into the living room and curls up in the oversized chair, pulling a pillow to her. I follow and stand in front of her, arms crossed. "I was getting out of the shower, and I heard a knock."

I try to ignore the fact she was in the shower and the thoughts it brings to mind. "A knock?"

"Yes," she continues. "But when I went to see who it was, no one was there."

"And the creepy-ass dude?"

"After I called Lila, I watched from the window to wait for her, and that's when I saw someone standing across the street. I thought it was the shadow I saw earlier, but it was someone, not something."

"Wait." I hold up my hand. "Back up. You saw what earlier?"

"Before I left to meet you at *Saints,* I saw a weird shadow across the street."

"So, twice in one day, you saw something strange?" She looks at me and nods stiffly. I bend down so that we are at eye level. "Why didn't you call me?"

"I don't know," she shrugs. "I'm used to calling Lila, I guess."

"Well, not anymore. Now you call me."

"Dante," she exhales and closes her eyes. "It's not that easy."

I grip the arms of the chair and lean in. "What's not that easy?"

"Calling you," she opens her eyes and stares at me. They bore into me and made me ache.

"Why not?" I smile softly, trying to ease the situation. "All you have to do is tap on my number."

She pushes up from the chair, and I drop my arms and turn, watching as she walks over to the fireplace. "It's not easy, Dante," she takes a deep breath, "because, for a long time, you've been the last person I would call if I needed something. I'm sorry, but it's the truth."

Her words sting, but I've been a real jerk to her the last few centuries. She didn't owe me any apologies.

I stand up and turn to face her. "I meant it when I said you could call me if you needed anything."

"I know," she looks at me, face filled with a mix of apology and apprehension. "It's just...going to take some time to let my guard down."

"I understand." The words taste like rusty nails. I may understand, but that didn't mean I liked it. "But I want things to be different between us."

She studies me, apprehensive. "Do you really, or are they just words?"

"I meant it," I say with sincerity, and I do. Earlier, I had only been saying it. But everything shifted sometime between dinner and the moment I thought Diablo was in danger. Her safety is more important to me than anything–even my plan to win her fealty.

She looks at me as if she will find the truth the longer she stares. "Okay," she says finally, as if she found it, or at least enough to let more of her guard down. My mouth curves upwards. "But you need to be patient."

"I told you," my smile grows. "I have patience when the situation calls for it. But for the record, I'll be staying here tonight."

"Is that necessary?" she exhales.

"It would make me feel better." We are always careful when we come to Eden, and I'd never had anyone follow me. Still, I'm angry with myself for potentially bringing a whack job to her door. "It's just a precaution," I add to ease her fear and reluctance.

Seeing I'm not going to take no for an answer, she nods. "Fine. You can take the spare room at the end of the hall."

"The couch is fine," I hold up my hand.

"You won't sleep well out here. You can use the—"

"Who says I'll be sleeping?" I cut her off. "I'm staying to keep an eye on things and make sure you're safe."

"Are you sure?" she looks at the couch, dubious.

"Yes," I insist. "Now, why don't you go back to bed? I'm going to take a look around outside."

"And then you'll be in?"

"I'll be in as soon as I've finished outside." She's worried but doesn't want to say so. Her need to know I won't be gone long pleases me and confirms I made the right decision to stay.

"Alright," she says after a beat of silence, then turns on the balls of her feet.

I watch as she makes her way out of the living room, her cute little ass tempting me. "Goodnight, Diablo."

"Goodnight," she calls back.

"Oh, one favor?" I ask as she starts down the hall. She stops and looks over her shoulder. "Could I use your shower? I was in the middle of a workout when we came over."

"So, I noticed," her eyes flit from my chest to my face. "There's a bathroom in the spare room. It should have plenty of towels and whatever else you might need."

"Great, thanks. I'll take another look around outside and then be in."

"My pleasure," she smiles softly, then turns around and continues to her room. "Goodnight, again."

Once her door is closed, I head outside, keeping my eyes open for anything that raises a flag. The idea someone may have followed us makes me furious–unless it's someone here like, that nosey bartender. He seems like the kind of indignant prick that would do something like this.

After taking several laps around the property, I head back inside and text Vinny and ask him to look into the bartender tomorrow. When done, I make my way to the shower. As I pass Diablo's room, I notice a light under her door. She's still awake, which means she probably can't sleep, and it only annoys me further.

I'm fuming by the time I step under the water and have to turn it up hot to stop the burn of anger on my skin. No one fucks with my angel and gets away with it. No one. There will be blood on my hands when I find out who's doing this.

13
DIABLO

I set my book aside and close my eyes, trying to push Dante from my mind. At one time, the idea of him in the next room would have shredded my nerves. But when I agreed to let my guard down, something in me shifted, and instead of anxiety, a different kind of energy coursed through me.

It'd been a surprise to find him standing in my kitchen, fists clenched, ready to fight whatever meant me harm. But an even bigger surprise was seeing that body. Vinny was strong, but that kind of brawn was intimidating. On the other hand, Dante was fiercely hot, with cut muscles I wanted to touch.

Every inch of him was perfection–strong shoulders, chiseled abs, and toned arms that could hold and break anything that got in his way. And those tattoos, I knew he had them, obviously, but didn't know the extent.

Seeing them cover his chest kicked my pulse into overdrive. I wanted to trace the ink with my fingertips and hear the stories behind each. Although I had a feeling, I knew the one for the apple and snake on his forearm. I saw it earlier when we were at dinner but ignored it. Something telling me commenting on it was just what he wanted.

The shower in the spare room turns off, and I open my eyes and turn my head. I'm anxious to know if he found anything while looking around outside.

Ignoring the idea of his naked body under the water, I push up from the bed and make my way across the hall, hesitating for a moment before knocking.

"Come in," he answers.

I open the door and find him next to the bed, phone in hand. He's wearing a tight black shirt and boxer briefs that fit like a layer of skin, and his hair is wet.

"Everything okay?" he looks up and sets his phone down on the nightstand as I enter.

"You're...dressed," I swallow, pushing down the heat creeping up my neck. Hot was an understatement. Just looking at Dante set me on fire.

"Would you rather I not be?" his lip quirks up.

Honestly, I wouldn't mind if he never wore a shirt again. "No...I mean, yes. I mean..." I fumble for the right words. "I wasn't sure if you had anything to wear."

"I keep a change under the seat of my bike. Never know when I may need something."

"Ah," I reply crisply. I could only imagine how often Dante needed a change of clothes when he wasn't here. He'd probably used showers in more bedrooms than I could count.

"When daemons get together, all hell can break loose," he laughs. "It's proven to be a good idea over the years to have a change of clothes nearby."

His explanation puts my mind at ease. Though, I'm not sure why. He is who he is. A couple of hours of good behavior wouldn't change centuries of bad.

I clear my throat and focus on why I came in. "I wanted to make sure you got what you needed."

"I did," he crosses his arms. "Shower was great, thanks."

"My pleasure," I tuck a strand of hair behind my ear. "And outside? Did you find anything?"

"Not really," he turns his attention to the window. "But can I ask you a question?"

"Sure," I look down and scrunch my toes into the floor.

He turns back around and sits down on the bed, pulling a leg up. "How have things been here lately? Have you seen anything out of the ordinary?"

"It's Eden. A city of fallen angels and lost souls. Define what you mean by ordinary?"

"Good point," he rubs his forehead. "How about, have you noticed any changes?"

Eden was a far cry from what it'd once been. It was beautiful when we first arrived, with beaches that stretched for miles. But then the soulless came and turned the peaceful isle into a superficial metropolis.

"Everything about Eden has changed." I walk over to the bed and sit down gingerly on the opposite side. "This side is quieter than before, and there are more soulless than ever, which has changed the energy."

I'd often wondered if that was Luke's plan all along. Give the undecided paradise, then take it away so we'd side with him out of misery. I wouldn't put it past him. He was, after all, a schemer, and it was something he'd do.

"Okay," Dante runs a hand through his wet hair. "Another question. Earlier, you mentioned an underground network. How does it work?"

I turn to him, brows raised. "Do you not know?"

"Not really," he confesses.

"I thought daemons knew everything that happened in Eden?" I ask, unable to hide my smugness.

"We know what we care to know," he shrugs.

"And you didn't care to know about the network before?"

"No," he shakes his head. "But now that I know you're communicating with it, I do."

The honesty of his response, combined with the way he's looking at me, makes my skin tingle. "I don't know much about it, to be honest. I have a contact, and she's the one who gets me what I need."

"Hmm," he presses his lips together. "Maybe I should talk with Luke. See if—"

"No," I cut him off. He looks at me, curious, and I think about my response.

I want to tell Dante that being on Luke's radar doesn't exactly thrill me, but I need to tread that line carefully. Since the beginning, he's been on Luke's side, and his loyalty runs deep.

"What if it was nothing?" I suggest. The less we talked about Luke, the better. "I don't need someone overhearing you, then spreading rumors about me seeing things."

"No one will spread rumors about you," Dante shakes his head.

"You don't know Eden as I do." Rumor mills were a dime a dozen here; gossip a kind of currency for those with no souls.

"Well," he takes a deep breath. "I do know that no one wants to piss me off. And spreading rumors about you would do just that."

His response is absolute and does something unexpected. It doesn't just weaken more of the wall I'd built but knocks a hole, and through it, I see Dante more clearly than I have in centuries. He doesn't just think I'm his possession. He cares about me. Maybe we could come to some kind of truce. Perhaps, we could be friends.

I place my hand on the bed and weigh my response. "Maybe, just keep this between us for now?"

He looks down at it, then back up. "I'll look into it and keep it on the down-low. Okay?"

I let out a sigh of relief. "Thank you."

"Was there…something else?" he asks when I grow quiet.

"I can't sleep," I look around the room. If Lila still lived here, we'd watch a movie or talk. But she doesn't, and it reminds me how lonely I am.

"I would have thought all that wine you had tonight would have made you pass out a while ago."

"Hey," I look over at Dante, ready to let him have it. But when I see him grinning, I ease. "I did drink a lot, didn't I?"'

"Yeah," he smiles softly. "You did." He leans back against the headboard, puts one arm behind his head, and stretches his legs out. "Are you feeling okay?"

"I'm fine," I push myself up on the bed and do the same. "I had a lot of water after you left earlier."

"That's good," he looks at our stretched-out legs. "You know, when I can't sleep, I listen to music."

"What kind of music do you like?"

"All kinds. I have a great collection at my place."

"Oh yeah?" I look up. "Tell me about it."

"The collection?" he turns and meets my eyes.

"Your place. I assume you still live in London?" Even though daemons moved to a different place every century to protect the secret of their immortality, Dante always considered London home.

"You are correct," he nods. "You were also correct when you guessed it was a penthouse."

"Of course, it is," I roll my eyes.

"I'd love to show it to you sometime," he looks at me. "I think you'd love it."

Going somewhere, anywhere with Dante, sends an unexpected thrill through me. "I'd like that."

We grow quiet, and I look down and play with an invisible thread. "What's the world like?"

He rubs his chest and considers the question. "Big."

"Well, I know that. I mean, what's it like, really? All I've experienced is when we've left Eden, and that's been limited."

He takes a deep breath, considering my question. "It's busy, complicated, and strange."

"What?" I look at him in disbelief. "What about wondrous, exciting, and alive?"

"When you know and see the kinds of things that I do, it taints your view. Man can be ugly and ruthless."

"That's an interesting observation, coming from a daemon."

"It's one thing if that's who you are. It's another when your altruism is feigned. We never hide our true selves. But man spends his whole life on a stage, under a mask."

"Okay," I considered his comment. "But what about the beauty of Earth? You have to admit, the oceans and mountains, not to mention the creatures that call it home, can be pretty breathtaking."

"Sure, there's beauty to it," he shrugs and turns to me. "But honestly, sometimes the most beautiful things in existence are right in front of you."

He's right. No matter the time that's passed, Dante has always been the most beautiful thing in front of me. Even before this existence.

"Heaven was beautiful," I say softly. "Do you miss it?"

He exhales. "You know I can't answer that, angel."

I lay down on my side and lay my head on the pillow. "I'm sorry."

"Don't be," he does the same and locks his eyes onto mine. "Can I ask you something, though?" I hesitate for a moment before nodding. "Why did you do it?"

I know what he's asking. He wants to know why I fell.

He's asked me before, and I answer the only way I'm able each time. "I had my reasons."

Like always, he nods and accepts my answer. "Why don't you get some sleep?" he suggests when my eyes start to close.

"I already told you…I can't sleep."

"Well, those droopy lids of yours say otherwise. But I have something that might help if you can't keep them closed." He reaches for his phone and scrolls through the music library, "It helps me when I'm restless."

"Before you do that," I look up when he sets the phone down on the bed between us. "I need to say something."

"Okay," he looks at me. "Shoot."

"I'm…sorry. For what I said earlier at *Saints*. I don't hate you."

His lips curve up. "I know. You were angry, and you had every right to be. I'm the one that should be apologizing."

"No," I place my hand on his arm. "It's fine."

I don't want Dante to apologize for kissing me. I may not have liked how it happened, but I don't regret it. It awakened something in me, and these last few hours with him have felt good.

"It's not," he looks at me, the tenderness in his eyes matching that of his voice. "You don't deserve my anger. You never have. I'm sorry for how hard I've pushed. The things I've said and done…I never meant to hurt you. I promise I'll do better."

His confession takes my breath away, and I'm stunned into silence.

"Now," he taps his phone. "Close your eyes and get some sleep, angel. Tomorrow is another day."

Tomorrow, I think, and close my eyes as a guitar's gentle picking fills the air, followed by a soft voice that sounds like it's singing a lullaby. The song is haunting and tranquil, and I can see why it helps Dante when he's restless. The melody alone calms me, and when it ends, I feel something I haven't felt since I fell–peace.

I linger in its perfect stillness, my spirit at ease, and for the first time since we began, I wish these ten days didn't have to end. Instead, I wish I could stay in this moment indefinitely.

14
DANTE

I was mesmerized watching Diablo sleep. The way she folded one hand under the pillow, her mouth drawn into a delicate bow, and her hand on the bed beside me, stilled my heart. I wanted to stay where I was and bask in her nearness. But reminding myself why I'd stayed, I got up and pulled the blanket at the end of the bed over her, closed the door, and made my way to the living room.

I lied when I said I didn't find anything outside. I did–a broken branch near her bedroom window and matted grass along the wall. It could be nothing more than an animal, so I didn't feel the need to say anything and alarm her. But, combined with what she said about Eden feeling different, it was enough to raise a flag.

I alternated between looking out the living room window and walking the grounds all night, noting every detail from one lap to the next. I had a funny feeling that someone was watching me at one point. The skin on the back of my neck prickled, and the air seemed to turn still. But when I turned around, nothing was there.

When morning arrived, I called Vinny and asked him to meet me at the coffee shop next to our place. I could tell by the murmur in the background he was with Lila, but when I heard a belt buckling and keys jingling, he was on his way.

"Hey, brother," he greets me with a shit-eating grin an hour later. "How was your night?"

I reach for my coffee and push the one I got for him across

the table. "Long."

"Oh yeah?" he pulls out the chair across from me, flips it around, then sits down, folding his arms over the back.

"Mine too," he takes a sip. "Thanks, I needed this."

"No problem," I lift my finger in response. "But I'm sure our long nights were for different reasons."

I was more tired this morning than I'd been in a while. The idea of wanting to keep Diablo safe and watch her was draining. I wasn't used to the combined weight of care and concern.

"You're probably right," he tips his coffee at me. "Speaking of, last night was for the record books."

I look at him and shake my head. Listening to him lately, I'm beginning to think he's the insatiable one.

"Should I just get a tattoo on my arm that says Lucky Bastard and flash it whenever we see each other?"

"You may want to, brother," he laughs.

I take a sip of coffee and continue. "So, Diablo and I got to talking last night."

"Damn," he shakes his head. "I'm sorry. That talking shit gets on my nerves at times. Sex first, talk second. Why is that so hard?"

"It wasn't so bad, actually," I shrug.

"Is that part of your plan…talk her into submission?"

The idea of Diablo in submission to me for anything lights a fire in my chest. "Say what you want, but we had a bit of a breakthrough last night. We're actually in a good place, and I want to keep it that way."

"Careful, Romeo," Vinny laughs. "You just might find yourself falling for Juliet."

Vinny's comment makes me smile inside. He has no clue just how accurate it is, given her love of Shakespeare. "Talking aside," I smirk at him, then turn serious. "I'm glad I stayed because I think someone may be watching her."

"What?" he straightens. I can tell by his reaction that he's as annoyed by the possibility as I am. Fealty or not, you don't mess with our angels.

I tell him what I found, and he agrees–the matted grass by the window could be an animal. But when I told him it felt at one point like someone was watching me, Vinny agreed; it was suspicious. Our senses are unparalleled, and for me to feel that meant someone likely was.

"She also told me about the underground network. Do you know much about it?"

"Not much," he admits. "Been around forever, though."

"When did you first learn about it?"

"Oh man, I don't know, let's see…a couple of centuries ago?"

"I never paid it much attention," I admit. "Didn't have a reason to. Bootlegged goods and all that."

"But now that Diablo mentioned it, you're paying attention."

"I didn't say that."

"Didn't have to," he grins.

"Whatever," I look away, more than a little irritated at the moment with how well Vinny can read me. "Do you think the network is being careless and bringing the wrong eyes back to Eden?"

"Well," he considers the question. "The soulless have been coming and going from Eden forever. I don't know why they would mess up now. Maybe Luke knows?"

I pick at the coffee sleeve on my cup, thinking about how Diablo responded when I brought him up last night. I was earning her trust and didn't want to risk it by involving him when I said I wouldn't. "Let's keep this between us for now. Cool?"

"Sure," he takes a sip of coffee. "You got it, brother."

"And keep an eye on Lila." Not that I have to say anything. Vinny will keep her close.

"She's already at my place. I'll just tie her down if I have to. A little restraint in the bedroom is hot," he flashes me a roguish grin.

"Whatever you need to do to keep her safe," I laugh. "Speaking of, I'm planning to take Diablo out of town for a few days. Just as a precaution. I want to be where I'm one step ahead of things and want to show her London. I didn't realize how cooped up she was here."

"Hey," he laughs. "You don't have to explain it to me. I think it's a good idea, and about fucking time you two get off this island for longer than a few hours and go somewhere together. Plus, the penthouse is the safest place there is."

"Agree," I look around, ignoring his other comment. "Hey, can I ask you something? Does it feel different around here?"

"Define different," Vinny asks.

"When we got here, it looked the same, and it felt the same. But now, I don't know. Diablo said something last night that didn't resonate at the time, but it does now. She says it's different, and she's right. We're in a coffee shop in a city of sin."

"Well, it's a good thing. I needed the caffeine after the night I had."

"Vin, I mean it," I say with seriousness. "I can't put my finger on it, but something's off. There's an energy in the air that wasn't there before. It's peculiar. If I didn't know any better, I'd say we were in Los Angeles on a Saturday morning."

"Well, *Saints* is still there," he counters.

"Yeah, but how long until it turns into a Gap? The soulless next to us are talking about fucking yoga!"

I grow quiet as Vinny looks at me. "What do you want me to do?"

"While we're gone, will you dig around a bit?"

His eyes light up. "Shake some bones, rattle the cages?"

"Exactly. And look into that bartender. Something about him doesn't sit right with me."

"Say no more," Vinny sticks his fist out, and I bump mine to it. "I'm on it."

We finish our coffees and head back to our place. "Now it's my turn to ask you something." Vinny pulls the door open, and we begin climbing the stairs. "Are you really concerned that someone is watching Diablo, or is this about something else?"

"Of course," I stop and look at him. "Why would you ask me that?"

He stops and turns to me. "I'm just wondering if you're focusing on this, so you won't have to focus on something else–like the fact you have feelings for her?"

"Come on, man, that's ridic—"

"Dante," he cuts me off. "It's me. I see the way you look at her. Eden's not only different, but you are, too."

"I'm trying a different approach," I say defensively.

"Yeah, yeah," he nods. "You told me. But it's more than that. I saw it last night when you thought she was in danger. You nearly broke her damn door down."

"I did not," I laugh dryly. But Vinny's not wrong. I did almost break Diablo's door, and she is changing me. I can feel it.

"Yes, you did," he laughs back. "You didn't even put your shirt on. You thought she was in danger, and you bolted."

"Wouldn't you do the same for Lila?"

"Damn straight, I would," he crosses his massive arms. "But Lila and I are together. She knows how I feel about her, just as I know how she feels about me."

"And?" I match his stance, waiting for him to elaborate.

"Do you know how Diablo feels about you?"

I stare back at him, not wanting to answer. There's a connection between Diablo and me that neither of us can deny. But how she feels about me, I don't know.

"But that's not even the biggest question," Vinny continues when I don't say anything. "That question, my friend, is can you admit how you feel about her?"

"That's what I thought," Vinny claps me on the back.

"It's…complicated," I shrug, not knowing what else to say.

I've always known how I feel about Diablo, but it's different this time. It may have started as part of a plan to win her fealty, but it was always about wanting her. I was drawn to her like a moth to the flame and liked who I was with her.

"Well, it doesn't need to be. And you better know what you want," Vinny points at me. "Or Lila is coming for your balls and then mine."

The idea that my friend built out of bricks could be scared of the petite angel that owns his heart makes me laugh. "I promised Lila I wouldn't hurt Diablo, so your balls are safe."

"But have you thought about what happens if she doesn't swear her fealty? I sure as hell don't want to be around your moody ass if she's not with you when we leave."

I try to ignore the question. The idea of her not being with me makes me bristle. "I'm not moody."

"Hell, yes, you are!" he rumbles. "Every century, it's like

112

clockwork. Diablo doesn't swear her allegiance, and you are hell on wheels for a good decade. Don't get me wrong. I love the ride. But I don't know," he stops and takes a breath. "Maybe it wouldn't be so bad making more love and less war."

"I've got it under control, Vin."

"Are you sure about that?"

"Yes." I blow out a heated breath. This conversation was frustrating me more by the second.

"Oh yeah?" he crosses his arms, studying me. "You have nine days, and if you fail, it's another one hundred years until you see her again. How does that make you feel?"

I clench my fist, the idea of being separated from Diablo one I didn't want to consider. "Don't," I shake my head, needing him to stop before I punched something.

"But what if that happens, Dante? I'm serious. You need to think about it."

"I said, don't!" I clench my jaw so tight my teeth gnash. The anger coursing through me is explosive, but it's not at Vinny. It's in response to the very real possibility he's posed.

Vinny looks at me and waits for me to calm down. When I do, he puts a hand on my shoulder and looks me in the eye. "Now that I got your attention, I need you to listen to me, brother. You are my best friend, and if you want to burn the world down, I'll give you the gas and the match. But you need to stop and think about what you want. If it's Diablo, then go for it. Give her everything you've got. Because let me tell you something, this endless cycle of pursuing their loyalty, it's bullshit. You deserve to be at peace, just as I do."

I open my mouth to respond, but he continues. "That's why I gave in with Lila. She makes me happy, and I'm not ashamed to admit it. So, we're daemons. So, what. We can still want ruin. But it doesn't have to be us that we destroy. Don't deny what you want because of some idea of how you think we should be."

Vinny's right. I can't deny it. There's no doubt I not only want Diablo but need her. And I've never needed anyone.

Vinny watches me, waiting for me to say something. "Maybe you should be the brains of the business, and I'll be the muscle."

"Shit, man," he laughs and grips my shoulder. "I thought you were going to lay me out."

My brows shoot up. "Me, lay you out?"

"I've trained you," he smirks. "You're capable."

"I'd never do it, man."

"Never say never, my friend," he pats my shoulder again. "You never know what you would do for the one you are bound to."

He's right. I'd burn the world for Diablo.

"So, when are you leaving?' he asks as we continue making our way up the stairs.

"In a couple of hours. I still need to pack and ask her if she wants to go."

"Ask, not tell?" Vinny looks up at me, surprised.

"I know, right?" I shake my head. "I'm assuming she'll say yes, though, so we'll be gone for a few days."

Vinny reaches for his keys as we hit his floor. "Any special plans?"

"Maybe," I say as casually as I can. But the truth is, I've been working on a surprise for Diablo all morning and can't wait to see her face when she finds out.

"Well, enjoy yourself," Vinny shoves his keys into the door. "And who knows, this may be the trip that finally does it," he wags his brows.

"Maybe," I shrug as casually as I can. But secretly, I'm hoping it is the trip that changes everything. "So, earlier, you said it was a night for the record books. Does that mean Lila swore her fealty?"

"Brother," he grins. "She screamed it."

When he pushes the door open, I see Lila waiting for him. "Hey Dante," she giggles as he wraps an arm around her waist and kisses her neck. "Everything, okay last night?"

"Everything was fine." I look at Vinny, a silent exchange passing between us. We agree–keep all possibilities between us for now since all we have to go on is suspicion and questions.

"Good," she smiles, noticeably relieved. "So," she looks at me as Vinny pulls her closer to his side. "I'm sure he told you about my fealty?" I don't say anything. I'd hate for her to be mad at him for telling me if he wasn't supposed to. "Do me a favor," she continues when I neither confirm nor deny that I know. "Don't tell Diablo."

"Lila," I shake my head and run a hand through my hair. If Diablo is going to trust me, I can't keep secrets from her.

"Please," she pulls away from Vinny and steps toward me. "I know you care about her, Dante. And don't try to deny it. It's beyond obvious at this point. But please," she says again. "Don't tell her. She has to hear it from me."

I don't want anything to ruin the trust I'm building with Diablo, but I want to do right by Vinny, too. "I won't lie to her."

"I don't want you to. Just don't tell her proactively."

I know Lila is conflicted with sadness over leaving her best friend and the joy of being with Vinny. It has to be hard for her.

"Look, I'm taking her out of town for a few days," I look

from her to Vinny. "You two enjoy this time and celebrate, and when we're back, you can tell her."

Lila steps back to Vinny's side and exhales. "Thank you, Dante."

The three of us stand there, looking at one another in silence for a moment. "So, you're taking Diablo out of town?" she asks with unmasked interest.

"I am, but I haven't said anything yet, so don't tell her before I get there."

"I won't," she grins, the irony I'm now asking her not to tell Diablo something not lost on either of us. "But you need to spoil her, Dante. I mean it. Treat her like a queen. Spare no expense. You can afford it, and she deserves it."

Man, between the two of them, they were really giving it to me today. "I got it covered, Lila. But on a separate note, has anyone ever told you two that you're perfect for each other?"

Vinny tightens his hold and kisses the top of her head. "Maybe a time or two," she smiles.

"Look," I reach for my keys. "Now that you're with us, Lila, you have to know…you have not only the legion behind you but also me. If you ever need anything, I'm here. Vinny has my back, and I, his, always."

"Thank you," Lila shoots me a genuine smile. "That means a lot."

"Of course," I nod. "Now, I have to go and get packed. You kids have fun," I shoot them a naughty look and then head to my place. "See you in a couple of days."

Once I've packed my bag, I make a few calls and then lock up. I've come after Diablo in the past, but those times were in vain. I wanted her fealty. Now, I'm coming after her with everything I've got because I want her. I just hope I don't burn both of us in the process.

15
DIABLO

When I wake up, I'm in the spare bedroom with a blanket draped over me. For a moment, I'm confused about why I'm here and not in my room, then I remember and sit up.

I can't help but feel a bit of whiplash with all that had happened between Dante and me. From our dinner together to his determination to keep me safe, he'd managed to reverse centuries of resentment in one night.

My plan to fight fire with fire had frayed at the seams, and the wall I'd built, was crumbling. But I didn't care. The thought of Dante was no longer painful. I couldn't wait to see him again and wondered what the day would bring.

After getting out of bed, I make my way to the kitchen to make some coffee. I'm reaching into the cabinet for a cup when there's a knock at my door. I look through the peephole and, seeing Dante on my doorstep, pull it open.

"How did you know it was me?" he frowns. "It could have been anyone."

I point to the hole in the door and shake my head. "Good morning to you, too."

"Sorry," his expression softens. "Good morning."

My stomach flips at the sight of him. He looks effortlessly handsome in jeans, a white T-shirt that stretches across his chest, and a leather riding jacket.

"What time did you leave this morning?" I grip the door handle.

"Early. I met up with Vinny for coffee." He looks down at

my pajamas. "Did you just get up?"

"Maybe," I tuck a strand of hair behind my ear and look down the path, seeing neither his bike nor car. "How did you get here?"

"I walked," he motions to the tray in one hand and a bag in the other. "Can I come in?"

"Oh, of course," I step aside. "Did you say you walked?" I close the door once he's in the kitchen.

"I did," he sets a bag and tray down on the counter and hands me a coffee.

"Thank you." I reach for it appreciatively and inhale its rich aroma. It smells like almonds and honey and makes my mouth water. "Why did you walk over?"

"I wanted to get a feel for things. Figured, what better way to do that than on foot. It's not that far."

"It's not," I agree, taking a sip. The coffee tastes as divine as it smells. "I walk it all the time. But you're you."

He looks at me, amused. "And that means?"

"I didn't take you for the casual stroll type."

"You sure have quite a few preconceived notions about me, don't you?" he places a hand on the counter. "For the record, I appreciate a good stroll now and then. But this wasn't for leisure. I was checking out your neighborhood."

"Ah," I nod. "See anything interesting?"

"Not really. It's quiet on this side of town like you said last night."

I take another sip of coffee and nod at the bag. "What's that?"

"Muffins. I figured you'd need something to nurse your hangover. And I thought it would be good for you to eat something before we go."

"I don't have a hangover," I look from the bag to him.

"And what do you mean, before we go?"

"No hangover?" he crosses his arms. "Wow, now that's impressive. And in response to your question, we're heading out of town for a couple of days. That is if you want to go?"

"We're...what?" I shake my head, not sure I heard him correctly.

"You asked about the world, and I think it's time you saw it. And," he exhales, "I want to be the one to show it to you."

I set my coffee down, put my hand on the counter, and looked at him. "That's it?"

"Yes," he smiles. "That's it."

"There's no other reason we're leaving?"

"You shared your home with me, and now I want to share mine with you."

"We're going to London?" I straighten.

"We are if you —"

I don't let him finish. I throw my arms around his neck, and he tenses for a moment, then wraps an arm around my waist and pulls me close.

"Are you serious?" I whisper excitedly as the heady smell of leather fills my lungs.

"Yes," his lips ghost my cheek.

I pull back when I realize I've been hugging him longer than necessary. "Sorry."

"You don't have to apologize," he grins.

"I'm just...still getting used to this. You and me, getting along."

"And...do you think we're getting along well enough to come with me?" he asks, tapping his fingers on the counter.

I consider not going, and every fiber in my body revolts. I want to go to London with Dante. More than anything. "Well," I reach for my coffee. "My calendar is pretty booked,

119

but I think I could manage to fit it in."

"Good," he exhales with obvious relief. "I'm glad you agree. It's a good time to get away." My face falls, and with it, his as well. "What's wrong?" he asks, concerned.

"You found something last night, didn't you?" Dante looks away, and I grab his arm. "Didn't you?"

His eyes search mine, and he takes a deep breath. "It's probably nothing."

I look down, not sure how this news makes me feel. Worried there was something to be found or disheartened, it was the only reason we were going away.

"Yes, I found something," he tips my chin up. "A broken branch and some matted grass by the fence. And before you ask, yes, it does cause me concern because of something you said last night. You said Eden felt different, and you're right. I feel it, too."

His blue eyes lock me in place, and I swallow. "And that's why we're going to London?"

He takes a deep breath and drops his hand. "I want to get away for a few days to give Vinny time to look into it. And —"

"So, it's business," I cut him off,

"If you let me finish," he shakes his head, lips curving up. "I also want to get you out of here and show you the world. When you told me you wanted to see my place, I thought, why not now? You deserve to see the places you've dreamed about."

I inhale, the softness of his voice and sincerity in his words stealing the air out of my lungs. "Oh."

"This is for you. If someone is watching you, I want you somewhere I can keep you safe. And, selfishly, I want to be the first."

The intensity in his eyes makes it hard to look away. "My

first, what?"

"The first one to show you the world…and everything else you will allow me to be."

Fire shoots down my spine at the suggestion in his words. "Okay," I drop my questions. "When do we leave?" It didn't matter why we were going. We were leaving Eden together, and that's all that mattered.

"A car will be here in twenty minutes," he smiles.

"Wow," I shake my head. "You were certainly optimistic."

"Maybe a little," he grins. "Can you be packed by then?"

"I can be ready in fifteen. But I need to know what we'll be doing so I can bring the right clothes."

"Whatever you bring will be fine," he insists. "And if you forget anything, my staff can get it."

Dante's phone buzzes, and he reaches into his pocket and looks at it, forehead scrunching.

"Go ahead and take care of that." But he's not listening. His focus is on whatever message has just come in.

I make my way down the hall, and my mind is spinning by the time I get to my room. Clothes, I need clothes. For a couple of days. How many…two, three? And what will the weather be, raining or warm?

I use my phone to check the forecast, and when I have an idea of what the weather will be while we're there, I grab my overnight bag from the closet and start throwing clothes into it.

I can't believe I'm going to London. Going to London with Dante. Going to London with Dante and staying with him at his house. With each layer of the thought, my excitement grows.

By the time I've packed, dressed, and ready to go, I'm so jittery with excitement that I nearly miss my phone ringing. I reach for it, and I freeze when I see an unknown number.

It's only been a day since I talked to Minerva, but my feelings have started to change in that time. To be honest, my feelings about Dante have always been complicated. But do I want to separate from him forever? That, I'm not so sure of anymore.

I let the call go to voicemail and shove my phone in my pocket, deciding to call her later. When I get to the kitchen, Dante is thrumming his fingers on the counter while looking out the window. He appears confident and in control even from behind, and I feel his pull over me.

"Fifteen minutes," he turns and looks at me approvingly. "And one bag? I'm impressed."

"I probably brought too much, but I wasn't sure what I'd need. Plus, I only ever use this bag for sleepovers at Lila's, and I wanted to be able to pack it full of stuff at least once."

"As I said," he smiles and grabs it out of my hand. "Anything that you need or forget to bring, my staff can get for you."

"Well then," I look around. "I guess I'm ready."

"Alright," he reaches for the door with his free hand and opens it. "And right on time, because the car's here."

A black SUV pulls up next to my gate, and I watch as a driver in a suit gets out and opens the trunk.

As we make our way to the door, it dawns on me that this is the first time I've left Eden in five thousand years, and the realization sends a wave of panic crashing into me. My home has been my safety net. My haven away from a world I've never really known. What if the world is too much?

Sensing my apprehension, Dante reaches for my hand and squeezes it. "Vinny will come by and keep an eye on things when you're gone. It will be fine."

Heat surges between our palms and comforts me. "It's not that. I'm not worried about my house. It's me. What if the world doesn't like me?"

"And what if it loves you?" he gives my hand another squeeze. "Only one way to find out."

Nodding, I take a deep breath and look around one last time, then look up at Dante and smile. "Alright, let's go."

While I should be concerned someone could be following me, I'm not. I feel safe with Dante and know he will protect me. I hadn't planned on trusting him so quickly, but now that I do, my belief in him has eclipsed everything.

16
DIABLO

When we pull up to the building that serves as the headquarters of Dante's corporation, my mouth falls open. He's not only built a business but an empire; the throne on which he sits at the top of a glittering tower of steel and glass, more magnificent than any in Eden.

The building is tall, sleek, and angular on one side and extends higher than others in the skyline. It casts a shadow down to the street below, and as we exit the car that picked us up from the airport, I can't help but feel tiny in its presence.

As we make our way through the lobby and to the elevator, Dante takes great pride in telling me about the architectural feat that the building is and the awards it won. Every detail is perfect, from the glossy floors to the sleek furniture. But it's the space at the top he calls home which leaves me speechless.

When the elevator doors open, we step into an entryway with a large mirror and table underneath and five staff members. They're all men, stand with their hands behind their backs, and wear black suits and ties with an earpiece.

Dante slides his leather duffel bag off his shoulder, and the first of the five men reach for it. Then, he grabs mine and hands it to the second in line. Seeing there are no other bags to tend to, the other three men turn and disappear through a door that opens on the right.

The entryway matches the aesthetics of the building, but when Dante grabs my hand and pulls me left, we step into another world entirely. In front of me is a grand foyer with floor-to-ceiling windows that offer an unobstructed view of the city. It's the kind of space you would see in a magazine, not an item out of place.

To the right is a massive fireplace, with an abstract painting hanging above, three gray leather couches arranged in a u-shape in front, and a solid marble table situated in the center. While to the left is a spiral staircase with a curved glass balustrade, capped with a steel handrail and a cluster pendant light fixture that hangs down the center.

Dante looks at me, and I know he's waiting for me to say something, but I'm too stunned to speak. His lips pull into a sly grin, and he squeezes my hand and nods for me to look to our left.

Waiting at attention is another group of men wearing suits and earpieces. The first is older than the others and has salt and pepper-colored hair. He stands with his chin up, a red silk handkerchief in his front pocket, and leather folio tucked under his arm.

Next to him are three more staff, standing with their hands behind their backs, eyes trained ahead. Judging by the walkie-talkies on their hips and gun holsters peeking out from beneath their jackets, they're some kind of security.

"Wills," Dante nods to the older man as we make our way over. "Didn't expect me back so soon, right?"

"It's good to see you," the man tilts his head and smiles.

"I'd like to introduce you to my friend, Diablo."

The older man looks at me and nods in acknowledgment. "It is a pleasure to meet you."

"Diablo, this is Wills," Dante looks from the older man to me. "He runs the house, my personal affairs, and a few other things, but I won't bore you with the details."

"It's lovely to meet you," I smile politely.

"Diablo is more than a guest here," Dante looks back at Wills. "Whatever she needs, please make sure that she gets it."

"Absolutely," Wills nods again and turns to me. "If there is anything special you would like to have in the kitchen, please let me know. And of course, after Lillian helps you unpack, she can tend to any personal items you may need."

I turn to Dante and raise an eyebrow. "Lillian?"

"Wills, excuse us for a moment," Dante holds up his hand and pulls me aside, speaking low enough so only I hear.

"Who's Lillian?" I ask, eyes narrow.

"Lillian is my stylist and helps manage the house, but she's agreed to be your assistant while you are here."

"Your what?" I look at him, confused. "My what?"

"I go to many events and have to look the part, and Lillian knows style better than anyone. And I thought she would be the best at helping you with anything you might need while here."

I chew my cheek, wondering with envy how close he is to this, Lillian.

Dante leans in as if reading my mind and whispers in my ear. "I don't fuck the staff if that's what you're thinking."

I inhale sharply and pull back, shocked by his directness. "I wasn't—"

"I saw the look in your eyes just now when you heard her name," he cuts me off. "That flicker of jealousy sent a heat surge between our palms."

"I wasn't...I'm not...." I stammer, frustrated that my body's natural reaction is betraying me.

"You are," his eyes light up. "And it's hot as hell. But you have no reason to be jealous of anyone, ever."

"Well, who is she?" I can't help but ask. "If I'm to trust

her…it would be nice to know who she is."

"See," he runs his thumb along my chin. "Hot…as fuck."

I let go of his hand and cross my arms–the mix of insecurity and possessiveness that I feel, both strange and unfamiliar. "How long have you known her?"

"First, I would not entrust you to anyone I did not trust myself. Second, Lillian is two hundred years old and an attendant, like Wills."

"What?" I shoot the older man a furtive glance. I didn't know Dante had attendants.

Luke had his minions, and so too did daemons. But, unlike the soulless, attendants gave up their lives to serve daemons, not their souls, as Luke required from those who served him.

Luke didn't like attendants. He considered them a waste. But he begrudgingly accepted their existence and only allowed them in Eden when the daemon that sired them was permitted.

I look at Wills, wondering how old he was and what brought him to Dante. "Why did he give up his life?"

"You will have to ask him and Lillian their reasons. It is their story to tell, not mine."

I look up at Dante, his cobalt eyes swallowing me. Knowing Dante had chosen not to steal souls but grant eternal life to those he deemed worthy, proved the angel he'd once been, was still a part of who he was.

"I can answer whatever questions you have later," he reaches for my hand again and squeezes it. "For now, can we get back to Wills? I want to make sure everything is ready for our stay."

I exhale and nod, and we step back over to where the staff waits. "Sorry," Dante addresses Wills. "Please continue."

Wills clears his throat and hands the leather folio tucked

under his arm to Dante. "You will find everything you need for tonight in here. I am working on your other request and should have an update soon."

Dante scans the contents and nods. "Everything looks in order. Thank you for doing all of this on such short notice."

"It was my pleasure. Will you be needing anything else right now?"

"No," Dante shakes his head. "We're good for now. I'll find you later to talk through a few things."

"Very well," Wills nods to Dante, then turns to me and smiles. "If there is anything I can do while you are here, please don't hesitate to let me or Lillian know."

"I will," I smile warmly. "Thank you, Wills."

After saying goodbye, he makes his way down the hall and disappears around the corner.

Once he's out of sight, Dante turns to me. "I need to brief these guys on a few things. Why don't you go look around, and when I've finished here, I'll come and find you?"

"Are you sure?" I look down the hall to our left. It seems daunting and endless. "I can go to my room if it's easier."

"No," he laughs. "I meant what I said. You are more than a guest here. Please, go wherever you'd like, and when I catch up with you, I'll give you the official tour."

I look at the security staff, who are anxiously waiting for Dante. "Alright," I sigh. "If you don't find me, send out a search party."

"I will always find you," he winks before turning his attention to the men waiting.

I make my way down the hall, and it feels endless. More than a dozen rooms of varying size and appearance line each side, and I take note of the consistencies that carry through each.

The first is the white marble floor that extends throughout the penthouse. It's shiny and flawless, with crisp black lines that run through thick gray veins, and the only place I don't see the pristine stone is where rugs cover the floor for aesthetic purposes.

The second thing I notice is the lighting. Each room has canned lights recessed into the elevated ceilings and modern lamps on tables, with bases made of gold iron in abstract shapes.

There is also exquisite museum-worthy artwork in every room; each hung perfectly, with a ceiling-mounted accent light above to illuminate each piece. As well as collectibles all around, some of which looked ancient.

Everything is perfect, down to the pillows on the chairs, and I can't help but notice that Dante has built a palace in the sky, similar to the kingdom we once called home. The marble floor resembles the clouds of Heaven, and the artwork is as unique and extraordinary as the angels.

I'm lost in the irony, wondering if he can see it too, when I find myself standing in front of double doors with privacy glass at the end of the hall. I'm curious to see what is on the other side, so I push through and freeze when I see the space around me.

The room extends the entire width of the building–ceiling and walls, except the side from which I entered, made of glass–and it's filled with all kinds of plants and flowers, including peonies, my favorite. Their heady scent fills the air as sunlight streams in from above, and the blue sky surrounds us.

"Do you like it?" Dante's voice startles me. I spin around and find him leaning against the doorway.

I'm not sure what to say. Words don't seem to do the

space around me justice. "It's...breathtaking."

Dante pushes up from where he's leaning and comes over to where I am. "It's been a labor of love for the gardener."

I drink in the lush vegetation all around me as Dante reaches out to touch a large, heart-shaped leaf that is dark green and leathery.

"It's incredible," I marvel. "I've never seen anything like it."

He turns to me, stirring a familiar flutter in my chest. "It is," he agrees, eyes never leaving my face.

Last night Dante showed me a side of him that he'd buried under centuries of anger-fueled purpose. A side that relied on music when he couldn't sleep and stayed with me because he thought I was in danger. If those parts of light still existed in him, perhaps those of dark weren't to be feared but accepted.

"So," he shoves a hand in his pocket. "How much of the house have you seen?"

"I've only been down this hall so far," I admit.

"Come then," he nods towards the door. "Let me show you the rest. Although, something tells me this may be your favorite space."

"I think you're right." I drink in the space around me as I follow Dante through the glass doors and back down the hall.

We pass the foyer and continue down another hall, Dante pointing out a gym, game room, and kitchen. There is also an enormous dining room with a window overlooking the city on one side and a hand-painted mural that runs the length of the wall on the other.

When we reach the end of the hall and stop at a set of double doors, Dante freezes. Unlike those leading to the garden, these are wood and painted black.

"What's in there?" I point.

"It's...private," he holds out his hand for me to turn around. "Why don't we —"

"Is it your bedroom?" I cut him off.

"No. It's...just a room," he peers down at me.

"What?" I laugh. He'd been so open, and now suddenly, this is 'just a room?' "Come on, Dante, show me."

"No," he says more sternly. "You don't need to worry about what happens in there."

I look at him, confused. Was there more to Dante's business than I knew? I wonder why he's being so elusive, and then another thought hits me–it's not business that goes on in that room. It's something else entirely.

My stomach plummets, and my heart starts to pound. It's a room for pleasure–where he satisfies his hunger with those who are willing to submit.

I should let it go. Just turn around and go back the way we came. But a force stronger than curiosity pulls me forward. "What are you doing?" he looks at me in shock as I reach for the door.

"Show me," I say again, trying to move around him, but he steps in front of me, and I slam into his chest.

The air between us crackles, and his eyes flash. "Why do you want to see what's in there so badly?"

"I want to see every part of your home...of you."

He runs a finger along my jaw and holds my gaze, locking me in place. "There is nothing in that room that will tell you what you don't already know."

I place a hand on his chest, and his muscles flex. "I'm not afraid."

He stares at me for a moment, and then his expression softens, and his mouth curves up. "How about I show you to your suite? It's getting late, and we need to get ready."

"Ready?" I ask, confused. The surge of adrenaline that coursed through me seconds ago wanes, and the intensity of the moment we were just in fades.

"We are going out, and before you ask where, it's a surprise. But we need to get a move on because we have a schedule. So, shall we?" he holds out a hand.

I look from him to the door. Deciding to pick this battle another day, I nod and follow him back the way we came. But I can't help but look over my shoulder as we walk back down the hall–more curious than ever to see what is on the other side of those doors.

17
DANTE

As we make our way back down the hall, I look at Diablo out the corner of my eye, wondering what just happened. She couldn't possibly know what was in that room. And even if she did, why would she want to see it?

At one time, I wanted nothing more than to introduce her to the pleasures of pain. Now, I want to drown in the desire of only her and never step foot in that room again. The being I am with her and who I've been in the past are not inextricably linked. In fact, they're growing further and further apart.

Once we reach the second floor, I guide us down the hall and stop at a set of white double doors. "This is your suite. And mine is there," I point to the double doors at the opposite end.

The tension that pinched her brows minutes ago is gone, and her lovely features are again at ease. "Are there other rooms?"

"Midway down this hall, you will find a walk-through that connects to the other side of this floor. That's where the rest of the guest rooms are."

"How many are there?"

"I don't know," I laugh with honesty. "Would you be more comfortable on that side?"

"No," she turns back to the door. "This is fine. You're just a ten-minute walk down the hall if anyone comes for me."

I hear the sarcasm in her response, but the idea makes my jaw tic. "That won't happen. You're safe here."

"I know," she says with certainty. "I'm locked away in a tower with the world below."

"As it should be."

"Locked away?" she cocks an eyebrow.

"Looking down on the world," he grins. "Now...are you ready to see your suite?"

She motions for me to open the doors, and when I do, we step inside, and her mouth falls open.

A wall of windows flanked by gold satin drapes that fall to the floor line one side of the room, and a giant bed with a cream tufted headboard, oversized pillows, and marble nightstands are on the other. While across from the bed is a fireplace, with double doors on either side–one for the closet and the other for the bathroom–and a writing desk under a picture window in the corner.

Seeing Diablo in this room that I designed for her takes my breath away. It is a space fit for a queen, down to the detail, and I'm anxious to know if she likes it.

I watch as she makes her way to the window, trying to read her response. Does she like it? Hate it? "This is too much," she says, turning from the window. "My entire house would fit in here."

"It would not," I let out a relieved breath and laughed softly. "And it's the least of what you deserve."

We stare at one another, silence filling the space between us, then the sound of a throat clearing pulls both of our attention. I turn and find Lillian standing there, watching us. "Ah," I smile and hold out a hand. "Diablo, this is Lillian."

Diablo looks at the older woman with dark hair pulled into a bun and sky blue eyes, and her face lights up. If she didn't want to admit she was jealous before, her response now is every indication that she was.

Lillian makes her way toward Diablo and looks her up and down with a hand on her chin. "You were right," she looks over at me. "Your measurements were spot on."

Diablo shifts uncomfortably under Lillian's gaze, and her modesty makes every inch of me ache with affection. She's a charming combination of confidence and innocence, and the feeling of wanting to show her the world and protect her from it floods me.

"Oh," she reaches for Diablo's hand and pats it. "I'm sorry. The designer in me always looks at the canvas first. It's lovely to meet you. You are every bit as Dante described."

Diablo eases and smiles back at Lillian. "It's nice to meet you."

"Lillian knows fashion better than anyone," I shove a hand in my pocket. "She's the only one I would trust to help you get ready for tonight."

Lillian glows at the compliment. "He is being kind, but also right."

Diablo laughs, and it fills me with warmth. "Do you know where we're going tonight?"

"Ah yes," Lillian holds up a finger. "But I have been sworn to secrecy. However, every gown I have pulled is worthy of your evening, so do not worry."

Diablo looks over at me, curious. "Gowns?"

I shrug my shoulders mysteriously, offering nothing more than a sly smile.

"Oh, my dear," Lillian clasps her hands together. "There are dresses, and then there are gowns. The latter, worthy of entrance and event."

"But how will I know which to pick if I don't know where we're going?" Diablo counters.

"My dear," she smiles. "There is not one option of those I

have pulled for you that will not be acceptable."

Her response is kind yet authoritative. And she's right. Lillian was head designer for a Paris couture house during the time of Empress Josephine, and her eye is impeccable. There was likely not a gown Josephine wore that Lillian did not have a hand in making, and had I given her more time, she would have made a dress for Diablo for tonight.

"So," Lillian smiles. "Shall we look at the gowns I've pulled and see what interests you?"

Seeing that as my cue to leave, I dip my shoulder towards the door. "This is where I say goodbye, for now."

"I have put a rack of tuxes in your room," Lillian says as I reach the door. "Let me know what you select, and I can make adjustments if needed."

"Noted," I nod, then look at Diablo. "I'll see you in a couple of hours."

She looks at me and doesn't say anything, but she doesn't have to. The look on her face says it all. She's excited, and I am, too.

Lillian's voice begins to fade away as I leave the suite and make my way down the hall to my room. I'm pent-up sexually, and the thought of Diablo trying on gowns doesn't help. The idea of her naked makes my fingers itch with need.

Instead of heading to the gym downstairs, I hop on the treadmill in my suite to ease my tension. Opting for the surround sound instead of my earbuds, I load an up-tempo playlist and push play.

After running for an hour, I feel in control again, and when done, I head to the shower and let the steam fill my lungs and hot water relieve my muscles, thinking about the night ahead.

I'm excited to introduce Diablo to a world she's never

seen. Mine, outside Eden. And can't wait to see her dressed up.

After drying off, I wrap a towel around my waist and grab my phone to check in on things and see a text from Vinny.

How are you two? Getting along?

I shoot off a quick response.

Of course.

As it tends to, our exchange turns into a conversation, which makes me laugh, thanks to his caustic humor.

Vinny: What are you doing tonight?
Me: It's a surprise.
Vinny: Come on, it's me.
Me: Exactly.
Vinny: Planning to make her scream fealty?
Me: No comment.
Vinny: Satisfy your appetite yet?
Me: Why don't you worry about your own.
Vinny: No need. It's satisfied 24/7.
Me: Stop.
Vinny: Never. Don't be jealous.
Me: I'm not.
Vinny: You sound it. Go get some.
Me: I'm good, thx.
Vinny: Are you sure about that, brother?
Me: Yes. New topic. Find anything?
Vinny: Not yet.
Me: Bartender?
Vinny: Can't find him.
Me: What does that mean?
Vinny: It means Vinny look, no find.
Me: Get on it and let me know.
Vinny: Yup, already doing.
Me: I know you're doing something else.
Vinny: I can do both. One, preferably.

Me: Yeah, yeah. Talk later.

I toss my phone down on the bed, put both hands behind my head, and take a deep breath. That bartender pisses me off. I'm still irritated he was looking at Diablo that first day at *Saints*. If I find out he's been lurking around her house, I'm going to tear him apart, limb for limb.

A knock at the door pulls me out of my building irritation. "It's me," Lillian calls from the other side.

"Come in," I adjust my towel.

The door swings open, and she steps into the room. "Well, which did you choose?"

"Honestly, I didn't look." I run a hand through my wet hair. "I'm assuming the Brioni is there?"

"It is," she makes a beeline for the rack in the corner. "When did you wear it last?"

"Fall, last year."

"Okay," she removes one of the hangers and inspects the tux hanging from it. "It should be fine, then."

"Fine?" I scoff. "I sure as hell hope so. It costs enough." Made of Vicuna fur and stitched with white gold, it's one of the most expensive tuxedos money can buy.

"Never underestimate the price of society," she says with a knowing smirk. "I once made a dress for Josephine that would have been five hundred thousand dollars today. And that was simply a dress for tea."

"Ah," I watch as she brings the tux to my closet and places it on the suit valet. "But look where that got her."

"Married for love...and divorced for politics," Lillian says dryly. "You remember the time, well."

"Paris, 1804," I grin. "No better time to be a daemon."

We both laugh, and she comes back into the room. "By the way, you should use the emerald and onyx cufflinks."

I look at Lillian in surprise. "She chose green?" I would have thought Diablo would choose a gown in a softer color.

"I suggested them because they will match her eyes."

Diablo's eyes twisted me and soothed me and everything in between. It's one of the reasons I had the garden built. I wanted a room filled with their rich, lush color.

"She means a great deal to you, doesn't she?" Lillian asks.

I make my way over to the window and stare out across the city, silent. There wasn't a cloud in the sky. It was going to be a beautiful night.

"You do not need to say anything," she continues. "I once lived amongst liars and thieves. I know the smile of benevolence and that of malice. And since she has been here, yours has been neither but another entirely."

Lillian, like Wills, knows everything about my existence. She knows who Diablo is and why we are bound. She also knows where I go once a century and why I am in such a mood when I return.

"I just want tonight to be perfect," I hold my thumb to my chin, thinking through my plans for tonight. "She deserves that."

"And I suspect you have done everything to ensure that happens?" she tips her head.

I exhale and turn from the window. "I hope so."

"Well, good luck," she smiles at me warmly. "I hope this night is all you want it to be."

"Thank you," I nod at her appreciatively. "For helping her and everything else you've done for tonight."

"It is my pleasure. Selfishly, I want everything to go your way. It would be nice to see this side of you more," she smiles, then rolls the rack out of the room and closes the door softly behind her.

139

I take my time getting dressed, and once I'm ready, I head downstairs. I'm pacing in the foyer, wondering how the night will go. But when I see Diablo at the top of the stairs, everything stops, and all I see is her.

She's wearing a black strapless ball gown, with a full layered skirt and a green sash around the bodice, emphasizing her tiny waist. And her hair is pulled up and held in place with a large metal hair comb embellished with green crystals that catch the light and shimmer against her porcelain skin.

"Wow," she smiles when she sees me. "You look incredible."

The tux I'm wearing is everything it should be, and I've slicked my hair back to show off my chiseled features, but it pales compared to her. She is breathtaking.

I take in every inch of her, eyes lingering on her smooth shoulders and perfect breasts pushed together by the gown's corset top, and a fierce pang pulls at my chest. "You're stunning."

Diablo blushes and places a hand on her stomach, and looks down. "Is it too much?"

"No," I shake my head. "You're perfect." My pent-up energy from earlier returns, and the urge to trail kisses down Diablo's neck slams into me. "Well," I clear my throat and push them both aside, holding out my arm. "Shall we?"

She descends the stairs and takes my arm, and when we touch, electricity shoots through me. "Now, will you tell me where we're going?" She looks up at me. Her eyes are lined in charcoal pencil, making the green pop, and her lashes appear endless. She could ask me for anything right now, and I'd give it to her.

I point up, and we make our way to the roof, where a helicopter awaits. After helping Diablo into her seat and

140

ensuring her gown is tucked in safely, I slide in next to her, and the pilot starts the engine. Once the rotator blades are moving at full force, we lift off and make our way to the private runway outside the city, where my plane awaits.

An hour later, we land on another private runway, then climb into a waiting car, which takes us to our final destination. "Dante," she presses her hand to the window. "Where are we?"

One of the benefits of flying by private jet is that customs will come directly to the plane to clear passengers. It's what made it possible for my crew to take care of the necessary paperwork when we landed and keep our location a secret until this very moment.

"Milan," I smile.

She turns to me, eyes wide. "Are you serious?"

The excitement on her face makes me melt, and I point to the window. "Take a look."

She looks back at the window as new and old buildings blend into one another as we make our way into the city. But when we finally stop outside a neoclassical building on a small city square, her face lights up with recognition.

"La Scala," she whispers.

"You wanted to see the world, and what better way to start, than a night at the opera. And not just any opera, but the most famous one in the world."

I became a corporate patron decades ago but hadn't been for a while. When I learned what was playing tonight, I knew we had to come.

"I can't believe I'm here," she turns to me, eyes glistening. The look on her face reaches into my chest and fills me with something I've never felt before. Joy. Giving her this moment has made me happy, and it's a strange, welcome sensation.

The driver hops out, comes around to the back of the car, and opens my door. Once I step out and adjust myself, I hold a hand up to let him know I'll be taking it from here.

After making my way to Diablo's side, I open the door and hold out my hand. She reaches for it and steps out of the car, adjusts her gown, and then weaves her arm through mine.

We make our way to the entrance, and she tugs on me to stop. When we do, she looks up, drinking in the rusticated entrance, balustrade parapet, and three arched entryways with wonder.

"What do you think?" I ask, taking note of the expression on her face. I want to remember every moment of this night.

"I can't believe I'm here," she looks at me.

"Believe it," I smile. "Good surprise?"

She shoots me a dazzling smile, and my heart lurches again. "The best."

I can't help but smile back. "Shall we?" I nod towards the entrance.

She nods, and we head inside, taking note of everything as we make our way through the lobby and up the stairs to my private box. When we arrive, an usher dressed in traditional robes greets us and hands me two programs, then holds the privacy curtain open for us to step inside.

Diablo takes a seat in one of the red velvet-covered chairs, and I sit down next to her. "What are we seeing?" she peers over the balcony's edge.

I hand her a program, and she stares at it for a moment, then pulls it to her chest and looks at me. "Romeo and Juliet."

The fact it's playing isn't just serendipitous. It's fate. "Good surprise?"

"The best," she smiles.

The lights dim, and the audience grows quiet and takes

their seats. But when the curtain rises and the music begins, I am the one that's still.

She looks down at the stage, eyes glistening, and I know it's not just a good surprise but the best one she's ever had. Her smile lights up the space around us, and it fills me with unexpected emotion and tugs at my heart. It's joy, pure and simple, and I don't think I've had a better moment in all of my existence.

18
DANTE

Watching Diablo is better than any performance I've ever seen. She looks so lovely sitting there, moved by everything from the costumes to the music, that I don't even realize I've spent the entire first act mesmerized by her until the curtain falls and lights come up for intermission.

I get up from my seat, wait for her to adjust her gown, then offer my arm and guide us to the bar.

"Are you enjoying yourself?" I ask, noting the sparkle in her eyes. It's her first opera, her first real night out, and the world doesn't just welcome her but bows at her feet. Patrons gush as we pass, and they're not wrong to respond that way. Diablo is the epitome of ethereal beauty.

"I am," she places a hand over her chest, enthralled. "It's so beautiful. But I wouldn't have taken you for a fan."

"Well, there is something wonderfully tragic about the opera," I flash her a wily grin. "And...it comes with the territory."

"And what territory would that be?" she asks, curious.

I order two glasses of champagne and hand one to her. While she's taking a sip, I grab a program from a side table. The best way to answer is to show her. "This may clarify things."

She looks down at the program in my outstretched hand. "I already have one back in the box."

"I know," I shake my head and smile. I once found her tenacity frustrating but now find it endearing. "Just take a look at the back."

She reaches for the program and turns it over. "It's a list of sponsors."

"It is," I nod. "Check out the top. Founders Circle."

"Primordial Holdings," she reads aloud, then looks at me. "Is that your company?" When I respond with a wink, she smirks. "Clever name."

"Does that answer your question?" I lift the glass and take a sip of champagne.

"It does," she does the same. "Although, I already assumed. What about Vinny? Does he do this well for himself?"

"Vinny has been instrumental in my business and plays an important role. My success is his success."

"Does he, too, come to the opera as part of the territory?"

"Vinny, no," I shake my head. "This isn't his kind of thing. He hates glitz and glamour."

Diablo looks up at a painting on the wall while sipping her champagne. "Doesn't that get lonely...going to events by yourself?"

"Not really," I drink in the curve of her shoulder and the back of her neck. "As I said at dinner, no one has ever captured my interest."

"I still find that hard to believe," she turns her attention back to me, expression dubious. "Given your...history."

"Interest and sex are different, Diablo. You do not need one for the other."

Surprisingly, she doesn't shy away or avert her eyes. Instead, she challenges me. "You could have anyone you want. Surely, someone could satisfy both."

"Yes," I lock my eyes on hers. "Someone could. But I'm not looking for someone. There is only one."

The air between us charges, and I can see she's about to respond, but the lights overhead dim once and then again, stopping her.

"Ah," I set my glass down on a table nearby, then take hers and do the same. "That means intermission is over, and we need to head back to our seats. So, how about we continue this conversation later. Shall we?" I hold out my arm.

We make our way back to the box, and as the second act unfolds, I can't help but think about what she said. She's right. I could have anyone I wanted. Yet, I don't have the one I want, and all the money in the world can't buy her because she's priceless.

A fierce longing pulls at me as the music builds towards the finale. It's potent and sits like a rock on my chest as we make our way out of the theater and back home. Only once we are in the car on the way back to the penthouse, and she lays her head on my shoulder and closes her eyes does the weight lift.

"We're here," I whisper in Diablo's ear when we arrive. She moans softly and snuggles deeper into my shoulder.

It was a wonderful evening, and I didn't want it to end. But it was a long day, and I am sure she's exhausted.

I lift Diablo out of the back seat and pull her to me, then carry her into the building and up the elevator, careful not to step on the yards of satin falling to the ground. Once we make it to the penthouse, I lay her down gently on the couch in my study. I'll bring her upstairs and put her to bed shortly. But right now, I need a drink.

I take off my jacket, remove my tie, unbutton my shirt, and roll up the sleeves. After knocking back a bourbon, I pour another, head over to the window, and look out across the city.

It was a good night, and everything went according to plan. There was no doubt that Diablo was growing more comfortable with me, and I was becoming more addicted to her presence. But I had no clue where we stood, and it was unnerving for someone like me who craved control.

The sound of someone knocking pulls my attention from the window, and I turn to find Wills in the doorway. I hold up my finger and point to where Diablo lies sleeping. He nods and steps into the hall, and I go out to meet him.

"What is it?" I ask, pulling the door closed softly behind me.

"I thought you might be hungry," he says in a hushed voice.

"Oh," I shove a hand in my pocket. "Right." I'd planned to cook dinner when we got back, but those plans changed when she fell asleep. She had to be hungry. Between the muffin this morning and a snack on the plane earlier, she hadn't had a real meal all day.

"I could have the kitchen put something together and bring it here if you'd like," Wills suggests.

Diablo stirs, and I look over at her. As much as I hated to wake her, she really should eat something. "That's probably a good idea," I turn back to Wills. "Feel free to bring it in whenever it's ready."

"Very good," he nods and leaves.

I make my way over to her and set my drink on the table, then bend down, brushing away a strand of hair from her forehead. "Angel, do you want something to eat?" I whisper, lips ghosting her cheek.

Her eyes flutter for a moment, then open, and when she sees my face inches from hers, she pushes herself up from the couch and looks around. "Where are we?"

147

"At the penthouse," I smile. "You fell asleep in the car."

"I did?" She lifts a hand to her head and blushes. "How did I get here?"

"I carried you. And with that gown of yours, trust me when I say, it was quite the feat."

"Oh," she sighs. "I'm...sorry."

"Don't be," I laugh. "I'm not."

"Well, thank you," she flashes me a tired smile that makes my chest twinge.

"Wills is going to bring in something to eat. He thought we might be hungry. That's why I woke you."

"Food," she licks her lips, and I see the sleep beginning to lift from her eyes.

"Let me get you some water," I straighten and go over to the bar and pour her a glass. As I make my way back over, Wills appears with two staff members carrying trays.

She reaches for the glass appreciatively and takes a sip, watching as they set the trays on the table in front of us. There are fruits and cheeses and all kinds of meat. It's enough food to feed an army.

She admires the spread and looks up at Wills. "This is incredible. Thank you so much."

I sit down next to her and reach for my drink. "I was going to cook for you but guess I should have thought about when we'd be getting back."

She takes another sip of water. "You can cook?"

"I am a man of many talents," I wink. "You haven't seen anything yet."

Once the staff has finished arranging the trays, Wills bids us goodnight and closes the doors behind him. "I'm sorry about dinner."

"Don't worry about it," I reach for a plate. "I'll cook for

you tomorrow."

"What will it be," she asks as I put meat, cheese, and fruit on it, then had it to her. "Takeout or pizza?"

"For your information, I am an excellent cook," I say with confidence as she pulls the plate to her lap. "It will be homecooked and wonderful."

"I'll be the judge of that," she smiles, reaches for a slice of cheese, and takes a bite. "Oh, this is good."

"Well, eat up," I fix a plate for myself. "There's plenty."

We power through the food, both of us hungrier than we thought, and when done, sit back. I'm at ease with one hand behind my head and my knees spread apart.

"Thank you for tonight," she says dreamily, legs tucked under the skirt of her gown–one arm draped along the back of the couch, the other resting gently in her lap.

"It was my pleasure," I turn to look at her. "Did you enjoy yourself?"

"It was an unforgettable first," she sighs. "The music, the costumes, the company…all of it was perfect."

"Good," I exhale with relief, and we both grow quiet.

"Remind me which room is this again," she looks around. "I saw it earlier, but I can't remember, honestly. There are so many rooms."

"This is my study. I have an office downstairs on the executive floor but wind up here a lot."

"It's nice," she drinks in the room. It's spacious, with several leather couches, a fireplace, and a large black lacquer desk near the window. "Why are we here again?"

"Honestly," I smile. "I needed a drink after carrying you through the streets of London."

"Stop," she laughs softly.

"I'm kidding. I needed a drink after the long day we had. I

planned to put you to bed when done, then Wills popped in, and well," I hold out a hand to the trays in front of us. "The rest is food history."

"I'm glad he did," she smiles happily. "I would have hated for the night to end that way. It was a long day but an amazing one. I can't believe we went to Milan."

"Believe it," I smile. "And not just Milan, the greatest opera house in the world."

"I know," she pats the couch excitedly, and I can't help but smile at her unbridled joy. "So, tell me, what do you like to do when you stay in?"

"Well," I take a deep breath. "Remember that music collection I was telling you about?"

She arches a brow in question. "Yeah?"

I turn my attention to the far side of the room, and her eyes follow. "Why don't you go take a look?"

She pushes up from the couch and crosses the room, stopping in front of a set of sliding doors. She pauses to look at me and, when I nod for her to continue, pushes one aside, revealing a state-of-the-art entertainment center and music collection bigger than any.

She drinks in the endless rows of records and CDs, shaking her head. "Why didn't you ever tell me?"

I get up and make my way over to her. "About liking music?"

"No," she shakes her head. "That music is to you, what books are to me."

"Honestly," I shove a hand in my pocket. "It's just easier to be what people expect you to be. Then they're not disappointed when they learn who you really are."

"And just who are you really, Dante?" she asks, eyes luminous.

My heart thumps deep in my chest, desperate for this connection with her. "Why don't you tell me?"

She locks her eyes on mine, lips slightly parted as if she's about to say something, then shifts her attention to the shelf and reaches for an album. "Is this…any good?"

"Ah," I reach for it and look at the jacket. "This is a classic."

"Isn't everything a classic when you're as old as we are?" she asks wryly.

"Good point," I smile. "I meant classic as in classic rock. This album is by one of the greatest bands of all time, Led Zeppelin." I look up and find her staring at me with a blank expression on her face. "Stairway to Heaven? Whole Lotta Love?"

She holds a hand to my head and furrows her brows with feigned concern. "Are you feeling okay?"

"They're songs," I pull my head away, and she laughs. "Here, let me play one for you. You'll see."

I move to the audio equipment and lift the lid on my turntable. Some artists sound best on vinyl–others digital. The album I hold is best when played as initially recorded. It's why I have a record player when they're practically extinct.

I pull the album from its sleeve, blow on it carefully, then lower it down onto the turntable. Lifting the needle, I place it on the sixth track. The iconic intro of what I believe is the band's best song fills the space.

"This is Kashmir," I move my head to the unusual cadence of guitar and drums. "And if mankind did anything right, it was bringing this group of musicians together to create this song because it is perfection. There's nothing like it."

She tilts her head and listens as the song builds in rhythm and instrumentation. "It's…interesting."

151

"Interesting," I grin and reach for her hand, pulling her to me. "Let me show you how this song feels." With one arm around her waist, and my other hand holding hers close to my chest, I sway us to the music.

The raven-haired beauty in my arms is breathtaking. I drink in the plumpness of her lips and the curve of her neck, and I'm speechless. The moment is hypnotic, and as the song builds, my desire for her does as well.

As if feeling the weight of my eyes on her, Diablo stops and looks up at me. "Are you okay?" I swallow.

She licks her lips as her eyes dart to my mouth. "I...want you to show me what it should've been like."

I shake my head, confused. "What do you mean, angel?"

"Our first kiss," she shifts her eyes back to mine. "I want you to show me what it should have been like."

My heart skips a beat, sure my mind is playing tricks on me, given how hot I am for her. "Are you serious?"

"Very," she confirms. "And I won't ask again. So, either kiss me or—"

The air crackles and my scalp tingles as I pull her flush against me, cutting off her demand. I want to crash my mouth down on hers and kiss her with bruising force, but I don't. I want it to be perfect. It has to be everything she's waited for and something she never forgets.

Her green eyes flicker with fire, and when I lower my mouth to hers, and our lips meet, there's a spark, followed by light. Just like when I kissed her at *Saints*. As if two live wires have joined forces.

I savor her sweetness as my mouth moves slowly yet expertly over hers, giving her the best, softest first kiss ever. But when she greets my tongue with her own, it sends a jolt of electricity through me.

My hand travels to her neck, while the other holding hers at my chest, cups her cheek as the kiss grows deeper and hotter. I was wrong when I said this song was the greatest masterpiece created. She is. She's perfection, and I can't get enough.

I kiss her with a force that steals the air from her lungs and then move my mouth hungrily down her neck. She arches her back and grabs my arm as I nip at her skin–her touch fanning the fire between us into an inferno.

Blood rushes through my body with an infernal force, whooshing in my ears and making me hard. "We need…to stop," I pant. I'm intoxicated by her and seconds away from tearing this gown off and making her mine.

She pulls my head down harder on her neck. "Why?"

"If we keep this up, I won't be able to." I suck on the pulse point in her neck, savoring the sweetness of her skin.

She gasps as I draw small circles over the flutter with my tongue. "So…don't."

I look at her, wanting this more than I've ever wanted anything. "You're playing with fire, angel."

"I know," she bites her lip. "Just promise me one thing."

"Anything," I search her eyes and mean it. I would do anything for her. Whatever she wants, it's hers.

"Don't let me get burned," she says softly.

I'd fall a thousand times and travel to Hell and back to keep her safe. "Angel," I stroke her cheek gently. "I'd turn the world to ash before letting anything hurt you."

She looks at me, eyes wide and full of need. "Even if it's you?"

I hold her gaze for a moment, then make a promise I never thought I'd make. "Especially if it's me."

19
DIABLO

All night, I've tried to hide my longing for Dante, but I can't fight it anymore. Being with him has awakened something in me that doesn't want to stay buried. My need for him is so strong that I can feel it in every fiber of my being.

I put my hand on his cheek and stroked his jaw with my thumb. There is an exquisite magnificence to Dante. He is much more than what he pretends to be. He isn't just a daemon intent on my fealty. He's also charming and caring, with a soft spot for those he deems worthy of affection.

There is a noble warmth in how he talks about Vinny and gentleness when he addresses Lillian. Even Wills-Dante's respect for the one who sees that his every need is taken care of is obvious. The thought of Dante not being a part of my existence is unfathomable because the truth is, I want him. I've always wanted him–the dark and the light and everything in between.

He kisses me again while backing me up to the window, and when the coolness of the glass hits my burning skin, he turns me around. The view is magical. A million lights twinkling in the night extend as far as the eye can see.

"You belong here," he laces his fingers through mine. "Looking down on the world, not up from it."

"I don't want to look down on the world," I lean my head back. "I just want this."

He pulls my back to his chest and places a series of kisses along my shoulder. "Do you know what you do to me?"

I sigh, feeling the hardness of his body through the layers of my gown. "Tell me what I do to you, Dante."

"You make me want to stake my claim so that everyone knows you're mine. Be your first and last." His words make me shiver with anticipation. "But not tonight," he grips my chin with his thumb and forefinger and pulls my face gently up to him. "Tonight, I want to be perfect."

"It has been." This night has been incredible. Dante introduced me to his world and the one outside Eden. Treated me like a queen and made more than a few of my dreams come true. It's been more than perfect. It's been a night I'll never forget.

"As much as it pleases me to hear that," he strokes my jaw, "I want to do right by you. Start small."

I smile softly, knowing well Dante's intensity. "You want to start small?"

"For tonight, yes," his eyes lock on mine. "I don't want you to regret anything."

My need for him is strong and burns the space between us. "And tomorrow?"

"Tomorrow," his lips pull into a salacious grin. "It's game on. Whatever you want, it's yours." He leans in and kisses me again, mouth hot and full of promise.

I'm breathless when he pulls back, lips tingling. "And tonight...where do we go from here?"

He looks at me, eyes filled with heat and lust, a smoldering combination that fuels my longing. "What do you want?"

I want to drown in his touch and everything he makes me feel. "Take it off," I insist. "My gown...take it off, now."

He arches a brow, lips curving upward. "Are you sure?"

"Yes," my stomach tumbles; the look in his eyes is hard to

155

ignore. "I want you to touch me. At least give me that."

He reaches for the zipper on the back of my dress and pauses. But when I bite my lip and nod, he continues pulling it down. A rush of air hits my back as the gown slides from my body and pools at my feet.

"Oh, angel," he runs a finger along my back, his touch sending goosebumps dancing across my skin. "The things I want to do to you."

His touch draws fire, and I realize that I lied to myself. I want more than just his touch. I want all of him. "Don't stop," I beg, wanting as much as he'll give me tonight.

He turns me around and pins one hand above my head, locking his eyes on mine while trailing his fingertips across the swell of my breasts. "You're killing me. You know that?"

I writhe under his touch, my longing turning into hunger, as he moves his hand down my side, then between my legs.

"Do you want more?" he kisses my neck while rubbing his hand up and down the front of my panty. I inhale at the sensation of his touch as the friction of lace against skin sends chills down my spine.

"Yes," I sigh, aching with my need for him. He pulls my panty aside, and I draw in a sharp breath as he slips a finger into me.

"Fuck, angel," he moans in pleasure and presses his forehead to mine, breath fanning my cheek and lips. "You feel like paradise."

Every inch of my skin prickles; his touch gentle, yet skilled as the rhythm he sets, sends waves of pleasure through me. But when he rubs the sensitive spot at my entrance with his thumb, a jolt shoots through me, and my hips buck.

Moaning at my body's response, he slips another finger inside me while applying more pressure with his thumb. It turns my arousal feverish, and my legs shake. "Don't…stop," my words come in short breaths.

He grips my hand tighter and presses into me. "You have no idea how much I want you."

The heat of his words and the feel of his erection pressing into my thigh fuels my excitement. "Right there," I shift my hips, giving him better access to the spot I know will bring me the greatest pleasure.

He looks at me, a wicked grin pulling at his lips. "You have touched yourself before, haven't you?" I nod numbly, the tingling sensation spreading through my body, making it hard to speak. "You did not need to lie to me."

"Didn't…lie," I pant, pressing my free hand to his chest. "You… assumed…didn't correct."

His eyes flicker as he rakes his teeth over his lower lip. "Will you touch yourself for me, Diablo?"

"Don't…want myself," I grip his shirt.

He presses into my aching body, thrumming me deeper and harder. "What do you want?"

I stare into his eyes, my need for him consuming me. "I want you."

"Say it again," he commands.

"I want you," I gasp as every nerve comes to life. "Only you."

His mouth crashes down on mine again, and a growl rumbles his chest as our tongues dance. "I want more," he moans through the kiss. "I want to taste you."

"Yes…please." His words are illicit, but they excite me. The idea of his mouth on me everywhere makes me delirious with want.

He drops to his knees and, in one graceful move, rips my lace panty off, lifts a leg over his shoulder, and buries his face between my legs. My breath hitches as he swipes his tongue up my entrance, and I grab a fistful of his hair.

"Yes," I hiss as he grips my bottom with both hands and licks and sucks. His mouth is hot, my need wanton, and I've never felt such a powerful combination of want and need.

My heart pounds as the pressure in me builds, and when I can't take it anymore, every muscle in me tightens. "Look at me, angel," he demands. "I want to see you."

I lock my eyes on him, and he devours me as I come undone–my body shaking as bolts of pleasure shoot through me. The moment is euphoric, shockwaves rocking my body so hard that I never want to come down from the high.

Once my breathing steadies, Dante lowers my leg and stands, kissing me slowly and deeply. I taste myself on his tongue and the bourbon on his lips. "That was incredible," he grins and runs a finger along his lower lip. "You are delectable."

My heightened state makes each word sound bubbly, and my satisfied body feels as if it is floating. "That was starting small?"

"That was perfect," he runs the back of his hand against my cheek. "Your desire is beautiful. You are beautiful."

I smile lazily as a rush of fatigue hits me. "Let's get you to bed, hmm?" he picks me up and pulls me to his chest.

"I don't want to go to bed," I rub his neck dazedly with the tips of my fingers as he carries me out of the study. My body is still tingling, and I can't stop touching him.

"If you don't stop doing that, I will devour you while you sleep."

My lip tugs up at the corner. "But you said we wouldn't do anything more until tomorrow."

"It's past midnight," he kisses me softly. "It is tomorrow."

"So then?" I taunt, wanting more of him.

He adjusts his hold as we make it to the second floor and start down the hall. "You're exhausted. You need some sleep, and I want you to be awake when you scream my name. And make no mistake, you will."

Anticipation for what's to come makes my stomach plummet as he pushes through the doors to my suite and lays me down on the bed.

"I would have brought you to the shower but carrying you twice in one night is my limit," he winks. He disappears for a moment and then returns with my pajamas. I slip into them as he pulls the covers back, and I crawl into bed, and he brings them up around me.

"I'll take one in the morning." I could smell us on my skin and wanted to fall asleep with my senses filled with him. The thought, however, makes me think about what that would be like–taking a shower together.

"We will do everything when you're ready," he says as if reading my mind, then reaches for the comb in my hair and removes it. I look up at him as my dark waves spill-free, covering the pillow. "Promise?"

He looks at me with a fierce possessiveness that makes my chest tighten. "I do and don't intend to break it." The room grows quiet as we look at one another. "Are you okay?" he asks softly.

"I'm good," I turn on my side and smile gently, not remembering having ever felt this way before. "Will you stay with me?"

The connection that's always existed between us is stronger than ever, and I wonder if he can feel it, too.

He takes my hand, kisses it, then places it on the bed and brushes a strand of hair away from my face. "Just until you fall asleep."

"Okay," I exhale and tuck a hand under my head.

"You're not going to argue with me?" he smirks while settling into a chair next to the bed.

"Not tonight," I yawn. "There's always tomorrow."

He sits back and smiles, elbow pressed into the arm of the chair as he watches me. "Go to sleep, angel."

"Goodnight," I yawn again as the room fades into the background. "And thank you...for tonight. For all of it, including my firsts."

"I was honored you gave them to me," he sits back, legs falling to the side as he rests his chin on his fist.

"They've always been yours," I mutter drowsily as my lids close, and I drift off.

At one point in the night, I feel him still in the chair next to the bed, but I'm too tired to open my eyes and look. However, the idea alone makes me feel safe and wraps around me while I dream.

20
DIABLO

I look out the window with a reflective breath, watching the sunrise as memories of last night play in my mind. Remembering how Dante kissed me and where he touched me makes my skin tingle and cheeks flush.

In the blink of an eye, everything changed between us. Coupled with the fact that this was the first time I'd ever woken up outside Eden, it feels like my world's been cracked open. I see everything in a new light and want to experience every moment and feel each sensation.

After taking a shower and getting dressed, I make my way downstairs. "Good morning," Wills greets me in the foyer.

"Good morning," I offer a warm smile. "How are you this morning?"

"I'm well, thank you," he clasps both hands. "And you?"

"I'm good." I look around for Dante and, seeing no sign of him, wonder where he might be. "Have you seen him this morning?"

"Not yet," Wills shakes his head. "He should be down momentarily. Breakfast is waiting in the kitchen if you'd like."

"Oh," my mouth waters at the thought of coffee. "That sounds good. If you see Dante, will you tell him I'm in there?"

"I will do," he holds out his hand. "Kitchen is that way."

"Yes," I laugh softly. "I remember. Thank you."

Wills continues down the hall in one direction and I in the other. When I make it to the kitchen, I find a full breakfast and tea and coffee service set up, and my stomach growls.

After grabbing a bowl of strawberries and coffee, I sit down at the counter, savoring each. The berries are sweet, coffee rich, and aromatic. Every sip and bite is bliss. But when Dante pads into the kitchen, I forget about both completely.

"Good morning," he shoots me a grin. His sleep-tousled hair is sexy, and my stomach flips at his loose-fitting pajama bottoms and tight T-shirt.

I smile back, heat creeping up my neck. "Good morning."

"What time did you get up?" he grabs a cup of coffee, then sits down next to me.

I wrap my hands around the cup, needing something to focus on other than how good he looks. "A bit ago."

He takes a sip of coffee, then runs his hand through his hair and rests it on my thigh. "Did you sleep well?"

His touch sends electricity shooting up my leg. "I did," I swallow through the sensation. "And you?"

"I haven't slept that well in a long time," he looks at me, eyes on fire.

"So, what's on the agenda for today?" I know what I'd like to do, but curious about what Dante may have up his sleeve.

"Well," he takes another sip of coffee. "I need to leave for a bit. Is that okay?"

"Sure," I shrug, trying to hide my disappointment. I hated not being able to spend time with Dante after the night we had but knew he must be busy. "I'm sure you have work to do."

"No," he says with seriousness. "I do not work when it is our time together. I need to run a quick errand, that's all."

"Ah," I nod, his answer making me happier than I let on.

We stare at each other, the space between us hot and charged. "Can I say something?" he leans in, breath tickling my lips.

"Of course," I tuck a strand of hair behind my ear and lean

my elbow on the counter.

"I really want to kiss you right now," his eyes focus on my mouth.

I lick my lips instinctively. "I think we're past the permission stage, don't you?"

"I wasn't asking," he grabs the back of my neck with one hand and wraps his other arm around my waist, pulling me into a sweeping kiss. "You're delicious," he whispers through our locked lips. "You taste like coffee and strawberries."

"Dante," I press my hand on his chest, and he pulls back. "Last night was amazing."

"It was," he runs a thumb along my chin.

With the way he's looking at me, I want to pick up where we left off. I want more. I want all of him. "So, game on."

"Oh, you know it," his eyes flash, and he leans in again, placing kisses along my neck. I tilt my head to the side as he moves his lips to my collarbone.

Goosebumps prick my arms as fire shoots up my spine. "What if someone comes in?"

"They won't," he moves both of his hands to my hips. "And if they do, I pay them handsomely for their discretion."

The feel of his lips on my skin is exquisite, and I can't help the moan curling in my throat. "It's not being discreet when we're making out in the kitchen."

The heat of his touch burns through my pants as he grabs one hip, moves his other hand to my neck, and stares into my eyes while his thumb caresses my jaw. "Do you know how much I want you?"

I place my hand on his and hold it tight. "I think maybe you should show me."

"I will," he stares at me, long and hard. "Later."

"What?" my hand falls to my lap. "You started this, and

now you're leaving?"

"I know," he presses his forehead to mine. "And I will finish it. I promise. But right now, I need to leave."

I purse my lips and pout, just as I'd seen Lila do a thousand times. "Will you be gone long?"

"Um, no," he looks down at his lap, then back up. "If you can't tell, I'd rather be right here. I'll be back soon."

Seeing his need for me only makes me want him more. "Okay," I watch in defeat as he finishes his coffee, gets up from the chair, and makes his way out of the kitchen.

Before Dante reaches the door, he stops, turns, and hurries back over. "Tonight," he cups my face, then pulls me into a searing kiss before leaving.

The promise of what's to come is all I can think about while he's gone, and by the time he returns a couple of hours later, my need for him all but consumes me.

I'm in the garden, and my heart skips when I see him watching me from the doorway. "Hey," I smile. "How long have you been standing there?"

"A couple of minutes," his lips curve up. "Just admiring the view."

I blush at the comment. "Did you get done what you needed to?"

"I did," he nods. "So, now we can go. Are you ready?"

I make my way over to where he stands. "Where are we going?"

Dante's phone buzzes, and he reaches into his pocket. "Hold that…whatever it was you were about to do," he grins.

"Everything, okay?" I ask when his smile begins to fade.

"Yeah," he takes a deep breath and shoves the phone back into his pocket.

I can tell by the pinch of his brows that whatever it was,

wasn't good. "Is that something you should take care of?"

"Not now" he shakes his head. "Today is about you."

"Last night was about me," I counter.

"Every day should be about you," he holds out his hand. "So, shall we?"

I chew my cheek, hoping he's not missing something important because of me. "Are you sure?"

"Positive," he grabs my hand and leads me out of the garden and back down the hall to the foyer. "Do you need anything before we leave?"

"Well, that depends. Where are we going, and will I need anything?"

Dante looks out the wall of windows to our left. "A coat, probably. It's cooler today."

I hold up a finger. "Give me a minute, and I'll be right back."

"Hurry!" he calls as I race up the stairs.

When I get to my suite, I grab my phone and bag, cross it over my shoulder, then throw on a jacket. Before shoving my phone into my pocket, I notice I have a missed call. It's from an unknown number, and I know who it is.

Three days ago, I would have returned Minerva's call immediately. Today, I'm not so anxious to see what she's discovered. Part of me doesn't even care. Deciding to call her later, I shove the phone into my bag and head back downstairs.

When I reach the elevator, Dante holds the door open for me. After taking it only a few levels down, it stops, and we get out. "A garage?" I look around

"My angel is so perceptive," he shoots me a funny look.

"I'm just wondering why we didn't come this way before," I roll my eyes.

"Security changes daily, and how I come and go with it. But for the record, we did come this way last night. Only, you were sleeping."

"Ah," my chest warms, remembering that he'd carried me not once but twice last night.

We make our way over to a black Range Rover, where a man in a suit waits. "Diablo," Dante nods at the man. "This is Stuart. He will be our driver today."

"Hello," I smile politely. "You were the driver that picked us up from the airport yesterday."

"I am," he nods.

"It's nice to see you again."

"And you," he tips his head and opens the back door.

I climb into the back seat and wait for Dante to slide in next to me before asking him what he has planned today. "So, are you going to tell me where we're going now?"

"Today, wherever you want to go, just name it, and your wish is my command."

"Are you serious?" I ask excitedly.

"Very," he smiles in response to my excitement.

"Anywhere?" I repeat.

"Anywhere," he nods.

"Okay," I smile, knowing exactly where I want to go first. "How about, The National Gallery?"

"You heard her, Stuart," Dante taps the seat.

"You got it," Stuart smiles at us in the rearview mirror. "Next stop, Trafalgar Square."

For the rest of the day, Stuart navigates the streets of London, taking me everywhere I want to go. After The National Gallery, we see Hyde Park and Buckingham Palace. The Tower of London and The Crown Jewels. He even stops at Harrods and idles curbside while I run out to grab a bag of candy that I saw in one of the store's windows.

It's night by the time we get back, and I'm exhilarated and exhausted. "I'll be down in a few minutes," I head for the stairs. "I just want to get cleaned up."

As I place my hand on the railing, Dante wraps his arm around my waist and pulls me back to him. "Today was perfect." He rests his chin on my shoulder and breathes me in. It's the first real touch he's given me since this morning, making my chest flutter.

I turn around and drink in the look on his face. His eyes are dancing, and his smile is easy. He looks happy. Content even. "It was," I agree. "You made another dream come true."

"Well, you're about to get even more spoiled," his fingers dance along my lower back. I look at him, curious. "I promised you dinner, did I not?"

"That's right!" I grip his arm enthusiastically. "You're cooking for me."

"I am," he spins me around and taps me on the butt. "So, don't take too long."

I laugh and jog up the stairs. After changing my clothes and freshening up, I noticed a missed call and a text from an unknown number. The text is simple and tells me exactly who it is. Minerva.

Two found, on to three.

I'm intrigued by her message, but honestly, I feel the same way I did this morning. I type a response, then delete it. Then try another and delete that, too. Deciding to text her tomorrow, I leave my phone in the room for the night and head back downstairs.

Dante is behind the stove when I finally make it to the kitchen. He looks confident and relaxed as he moves between a sauté pan and cutting board while sipping a glass of

167

bourbon. He's miles away from the brooding being he's been the past couple of centuries, and my heart yearns for him.

I clear my throat as I enter the kitchen and make my way over to the stove. "What's on the menu tonight, chef?"

"Ah," he looks at me as I come in. "You are in for a treat."

"Oh," I lean in to smell what looks like garlic and onions simmering in the pan. It smells good, and my stomach growls. "Why is that?"

"Because this is the beginning of my very special pasta Bolognese."

I hop up on the counter next to the stove and dangle my feet. "And what, exactly, makes it so special?"

"I'm cooking it," he sets his drink down and winks.

"Ah," I nod and laugh, watching as he stirs more ingredients into the pan. "What's this?" I look down at a package on the counter next to me.

"That's for you," he smiles. "It's the errand I went on this morning."

"And here I thought you were trying to get away from me."

Dante stands between my legs, placing a hand on each thigh. "I've been trying to be near you for five thousand years. Why would I try to get away from you now?"

His touch sends heat racing through me, and I swallow and reach for the package. "May I?"

"Please," he insists. "I've been waiting all day to give it to you."

I grin, the double entendre hard to ignore, then turn my attention to the package. Judging by the shape and feel, it's a book. I tear the paper off, anxious to see which one it is, and when I do, I look up, stunned. "Where did you get this?"

"I called in a favor," he says casually. Only, the book in my hand is much more than that. It's a historical treasure.

I open the cover, wanting to see if what I am holding is real, and when I see the distinctive signature staring back at me from the title page, my hands start shaking, and I know that it is.

I look up at Dante, finding his eyes on mine. "How did you find this? Historians, researchers, just about anyone who is anyone has tried to find this."

Many historians believed Shakespeare was working on a play when he died, but efforts to find it throughout history had been unsuccessful. The book in my hands, however, proved the rumors were true.

"Yes," Dante takes a deep breath. "Quite a few folks have been looking for that. I just so happen to have a friend that owed me a favor."

"How did you know? You didn't see my collection until two days ago," I shake my head in disbelief.

"But I've known your passions as long as I have known you, and when I saw your collection the other night, I sped up my search to find it. Apparently, the right incentive can be very persuasive."

"I can't believe it," I look down at the book again, filled with so many emotions I could hardly think straight. "You've been looking for this for me?"

"I have," he confirms. "And it's the only thing that could have pulled me away from you this morning," he squeezes my thighs. "Seeing your smile now was worth the cold shower I had to take."

I look up and fight back the tears that threaten. "Thank you so much."

"Do you like it?" he rubs his hands up and down my sides.

"I love it." I pull him into a kiss. His mouth is warm and tastes like oak and caramel.

I grip the back of his head with both hands and wrap my legs around his waist, the kiss growing. "It's burning," he mumbles.

"I know," my breath quickens as the heat between us twists and builds, wild like fire.

"No," he laughs and pulls away quickly, moving the pan to a back burner, and turning down the heat. "Dinner...the sauce base was burning."

"Oh," I laugh, slightly embarrassed. "You were talking about the food."

"Honestly," he grins. "I was talking about both."

The day might have been long and one to remember, but something about that kiss and how he's looking at me tells me the night will be, too.

21
DANTE

We're in the study relaxing after dinner. Diablo is reading her book, and I'm stretched out on the couch next to her. I can't remember ever feeling this content. The more time we spend together, the further away the old me gets, and the more permanent this me, the one that is at peace just being with her, becomes.

"So, tell me honestly," I grab the back of my head with both hands and stretch. "Did you like dinner, or are you just stroking my ego?"

She lowers the book and grins at my choice of words. "It was delicious. You were right; you're a good cook. Is there anything you can't do?"

"Not really," I shrug. "You tend to pick up a few things after thousands of years."

"It seems that humility isn't one of them," she says playfully, then turns back to reading.

I smirk. Even her humor, at my expense, makes me ache. "How is Shakespeare's last hurrah?"

"It's marvelous," her eyes glisten.

"Is it a comedy, drama, or tragedy?"

"You'll have to read it and find out," she turns a page. "But I think it would've been a classic."

"How do you feel about taking a break and listening to a little music?"

"Sure," she closes her book and sets it down on the side table. "I probably should save a little of this for another day."

I push up from the couch and make my way over to the entertainment center. Diablo follows and lays down in front of the fire. "What are we listening to?"

I toss her a pillow from a chair nearby, and she sets it on the floor and rests her head on it. "I thought I'd share a few of my favorites. You game?"

"Game on," she grins, and I can't help but do the same.

Over the next couple of hours, I play a handful of my favorite albums. It was part of my plan for tonight; to share my world and let Diablo in. And I have. She shows genuine interest as she listens to me talk about each album and even asks me to create a playlist of my favorite songs for her. But it's time to make good on the promise I made this morning.

"What's the name of this group again?" she asks, stretching languidly.

I open the case in my hand and pop the disc into the CD player. This album is not for me but for us, and what I know is on both of our minds. "It's Nine Inch Nails, and the song I'm going to play is a little straightforward, so brace yourself."

She props herself up on an elbow and looks at me, intrigued. "How so?"

I shoot her a devilish smile. "You'll just have to listen and see."

The song starts with an electronic beat, followed by sexually charged lyrics. But when the chorus hits, her brows shoot up to her hairline. "Did he just say…"

"Sure did," I nod. "See what I mean?"

"That's straightforward, alright," she blushes.

"It's foreplay's wingman," I wink.

"Well," she swallows. "I wouldn't know."

I make my way over to where she's lying, kneel between her legs, and lean down. "Let me show you."

I press my lips to hers and kiss her, gently at first, then harder, using the beat and lyrics of the song to fuel its intensity. As it grows, I push her legs open wider with my knees and ease my body down onto hers.

"I've been thinking about you all day," I brush my finger along her cheek. "The way you smell. The feel of your skin. You drive me fucking crazy."

"I understand the feeling," she bites her lip.

"When you do that," I hover my mouth above hers. "The things I want to do to you."

"Then do them," she rubs against me.

I stare at her in awe, wondering how this perfect being could want me, the way I do, her. "Oh, trust me, I want to do everything with you, angel. But I don't want to hurt you."

Her heart is racing so fast that I feel it against my chest. "You won't," her eyes shift from my eyes to my lips. "I trust you."

I'm so hot for her I can't stand it. "You deserve beautiful, perfect moments. That's what I want to give you."

She wraps her leg over the back of my thigh, and it shoots fire through me. "I don't need perfect. I just need you. That's what you can give me."

I crash my mouth down on hers again and kiss her with all the intensity I'm feeling. She kisses me back with the same power, arching her back and pressing her body into mine.

"You deserve to be worshiped," I move my mouth down her neck. "Not claimed as some kind of prize."

"Why can't you do both?" she asks, breathless. "Claim and worship me."

I rest my forehead on her chest and take a deep breath. I would gladly kneel at her altar because she is my religion.

When I look back up, I find her eyes on mine. "Is that what

you want?"

"Yes," she licks her lips, eyes full of heat.

It's no use. I can't deny her anything. "Come with me,"' I get up and stick out my hand.

She places her hand in mine and looks up at me. "Where are we going?"

If she wants me, I have to show her all of me, even the dark. "You'll see."

I pull her up and hold her hand as we make our way across the room. Stopping at the wall next to my desk, I press on a panel that reveals a hidden door. It opens, and we step inside.

"Where are we?" she asks as we make our way down a dark corridor and enter an even darker room.

My eyes know this space and adjust quickly, but she's struggling. "Where you wanted to go yesterday."

"This is the room on the other side of those doors?" she looks around. "But it's so…dark. And empty."

I'm curious about what she thought it might have looked like and, at the same time, intrigued she doesn't appear to be scared. "Were you expecting something else?"

"I don't know what I was expecting," she admits. I can tell she's still confused, but when she turns her attention up to the ceiling, her mouth falls open, and she grows quiet.

Anyone that has been in this room thinks it's nothing more than an eccentric design–black glass with a million crystals embedded. But Diablo will know it's more than that.

"It's the night we fell," her nails dig into my hand.

"Yes," my skin prickles with her recognition.

"It feels like I'm there," she looks around. "The sky, the temperature…I can even smell fire. Is that possible?"

"I designed it that way." This room looks exactly like that

174

night. It is the moment I lost what I was and became what I am, and only one of the Fallen would know this.

She turns her attention to me. "But why, what do you do in here?"

"Oh, angel," I place my free hand on her cheek. "You know the answer to that question."

I expect her to pull away from me and run, but she doesn't. She places her hand over mine and peers up at me. "But why here...like this?"

Her trust in me does something. It encourages me to reveal to her that I have never confessed to anyone. "I chose my side, and not once since The Fall have I regretted it. But I was also cast out and abandoned, and that pain never goes away. This room is how I soothe that pain."

I pause, wondering if I should stop before saying something I'll regret. But I know I have to let Diablo in, just as she has me, if we have any chance of being more than what we were.

"Fear and pain," I continue, "their power is equal. And what man fears most is that which he does not know. This room–this unknown space of darkness–draws out that fear so I can consume it and suffocate my pain."

"Does it work?" There is no hesitation in her touch or judgment in her ask.

"No," I shake my head. "The pain always returns. But you know what does? Being with you. You fill me with a sense of peace I've never felt in all this existence, and I can't lose that."

"You won't," she insists. "And if this room is what you need if release from that pain is what you need...then I want that."

"Hell no!" I balk at the suggestion. "Your first time...our first time...should not be here. It should be perfect. In fact, you make me never want to be in this room again."

"You gave me perfect last night. Give me this, now."

"You deserve — "

"I know what I deserve," she cuts me off. "And I know what I want. And I want this, Dante."

"I can't do to you what I do to them here. You are too precious to me."

"I'm not asking you to do to me, what you do to them," she says frankly. "I'm asking you to let me ease your pain."

"You don't know what you're asking," I shake my head.

"I know exactly what I'm asking," she counters.

"You should have candles and roses and kisses that linger," I look around, this room the very antithesis.

"Stop telling me what I should have and listen to what I'm telling you," she levels her gaze. "I want you, here and now."

I want to give Diablo anything she wants, but she deserves the stars and the moon. Never darkness.

"Maybe my pain is as great as yours," she tips her head up. In the dimness of the room, I see her plea. Her beautiful face filled with need. "Maybe I, too, need this."

I pull our locked hands around my waist, and with the other, that's still on her cheek, brush a thumb along her jaw. "I want to give you the world Diablo, but this room does not deserve you."

"Dante," she pulls my head down to hers. "You can give me the world. But first, give me what I want."

Her eyes hold me captive, and I can't fight it anymore. I'm compelled to give her whatever she wants–even if it's this. My resolve gives way, and my pent-up need for her creates a powerful hunger. I reach for the bottom of her shirt, and she mine, and in seconds we've ripped each other's clothes off.

I will not lay her on the floor. It will not be the cold stone she feels when we're together for the first time, but my body and my warmth. I pick her up and move towards the wall as she wraps her legs around my waist and kisses me with the sweetest passion.

When she feels the wall behind her, she leans back, and I run my hand up her chest and to her neck, grabbing it while locking my eyes on hers. "Are you sure?"

"Yes," she looks at me, her hunger matching mine. "I'm sure."

I kiss her again with bruising force, then move my mouth down her neck. She grabs fistfuls of my hair as I continue to her breasts. She moans in pleasure as I devour her, and when I slide my hand between her legs and stroke her already wet entrance, her breath hitches, and she grabs my bicep.

I slide a finger inside her, curling it and applying pressure, and as her arousal climbs, she turns her focus to mine. Wrapping her free hand around my erection, she runs it up and down, sending fire shooting up my spine.

All the blood in my body rushes to my groin, and I slam my hand to the wall. "Fuck, angel," I rasp, "don't stop."

We please each other as if we have known one another's bodies for eternity, and it isn't long before our skin glistens with sweat, and we're both panting.

My body is hot with desire, my mind in a haze, and when I can tell we're both ready, I line myself up with her entrance. I pause to make sure this is still what she wants. But I don't have to ask. I can see the fire burning in her eyes.

The intensity of the moment fills me with heat, and when I enter her, she grabs my lower back with both hands.

"Are you okay?" I whisper, knowing it must feel like she's being ripped open.

"Mm-hmm," she bites her lip. But I can tell she's trying to

hide the pain.

"Let it out, angel," I kiss the side of her head and continue easing into her. "I'll take your pain." She cries out again, and I cover her mouth with mine and swallow it.

When I'm finally in her all the way and her tongue, not her cries, fills my mouth, it's rapture. Feeling her tight and warm around me, I've never experienced such euphoria. There's no darkness, only light, as our bodies fuse.

I start to move in and out of her in a steady rhythm, knowing it must hurt to take me like she is for her first time. But when I pull back and see the fire in her eyes, I know in taking her pain, I have filled her with both strength and desire and that she craves me, as much as I do, her.

I pick up the pace, and her body opens up to me as the thrusts of her hips match mine. But when she rips her nails down my back, electricity shoots through me and ignites an inferno. She's claiming me as I am her, and the realization fills me with wicked satisfaction.

The hammering in her chest matches mine, and as we move together, the stars overhead no longer torment me. They shine down and light up this moment that has been thousands of years in the making.

I want to stay like this forever. What I'm feeling is unlike anything I've ever experienced. But I also want to make her feel as good as she is making me. Moving my hand between her legs, I rub the knot of nerves at the top of her entrance, and it's not long before her breathing becomes labored.

"Let go for me, angel," I whisper when her grip on my arm tightens. Her body tenses and back arches, then she clenches around me and lets go. Her climax is music to my ears, and feeling her pulse around me, sends me to the edge of my own.

We're both breathing hard as we come down, and when I press my forehead to hers and she places a hand on my chest, it hits me–I can never be without her again. If I lose her, it will be my end.

22
DANTE

I'm sitting in the room that once held my darkest pain, and my mind is blown. Scratch that–every inch of me is blown. I've never had an experience like that before. Sex with connection–a dangerous combination capable of destruction and salvation. The beauty curled in my lap has changed my world forever. Now that I've had this, I never want another.

"Are you okay?" I run my finger up and down her arm.

"Mm-hmm," she looks at me and smiles. "You?"

I kiss her my response. I've never been better. For the first time since this existence began, I feel like I am home. "Do you want to move somewhere more comfortable?"

"No," she says dreamily. "This is perfect."

I've never thought of this room as perfect and hated the idea of our first time together being in here. But, looking at it now, there's a strange kind of poetry to it. To understand and appreciate the purest of pleasure, you had to let go of your darkest pain, and somehow, Diablo knew that.

"You're incredible. You know that?" I lace my fingers through hers.

"I don't know about that," she smiles softly.

I squeeze her hand. "You are. You trusted me when I gave you every reason not to, and because you did, I got to have this incredible moment with you."

"My last first," she exhales. "Now you own them all."

"Speaking of, are you okay, really? That wasn't exactly easy for your first time. Phenomenal, but not at all gentle."

"I'm fine," she laughs softly. "I'm not as fragile as everyone thinks."

I've never wanted to kiss the breath out of anyone more. So, I do. I kiss her like it's forever and never want to let go. The business of her fealty just got more complicated.

Sensing what I'm thinking, she looks down and grows quiet. I grab her chin with my thumb and forefinger and tip her head back up. "We don't have to worry about anything right now."

"I'm not," she lays her hand on my thigh, and the blood in my veins starts pumping. "I'm not thinking about anything but this."

"Come on," I smile mischievously. "Let's get out of here."

She shifts out of my lap and stands slowly. "Where are we going?"

I get up and hold out my hand. "I'm suddenly starving, and you need a warm bath and a soft bed."

She reaches for my hand, and I pull her to me, then bend at the knees, and hoist her over my shoulder. "What are you doing?" she squeals.

"I saw how slow you were to get up, and walking will probably not be easy right now. Plus," I rub a hand over her perfect bottom and grab a cheek, "I've wanted to do this since the day you walked into *Saints*."

She kicks her legs as I carry her out of the room and down the hall. "Um, Dante," she taps my back as I cross through the study and make my way to the foyer. "What if Wills or Lillian sees us?"

"They're asleep by now, and I already told you, I pay them well for their discretion."

I stride up the stairs like a king in his castle, and when we reach the second floor, I turn right and head to my suite.

Pushing through the doors, I cross the room and lay her down on my bed.

"I thought you said you were starving," she looks up at me, a sly smile pulling at her lips.

I kneel on the bed and drink her in, taking time to appreciate what belongs to me. "I wasn't talking about food."

Earlier I felt every inch of her but couldn't appreciate the full extent of her beauty in the dark. Seeing her now, however, sprawled out on my bed, melts my insides. She's perfect, and knowing she's mine, makes me hungry for more.

But that's not why I brought her here. This is about giving her what she deserves. Not what I want or need.

"Fucking stunning," I crawl on the bed towards her, kissing my way up her body as she lays back, sighing in delight. I trail my lips up her thigh, across her stomach, and to her breasts–worshiping her the way she should be.

Laying with her like this is better than Heaven ever was. I cover her body with mine, and my skin prickles with heat. But when she grinds her hips against mine, fire shoots through me, reminding me of the deliciousness of sin.

"Now, Diablo," I look up at her. "You had what you wanted. Now it's time for me to give what I wanted for you."

"You can't give me the world in one night," she looks down at me and smiles.

"Oh, but angel," I move my hand between her legs and stroke the inside of her thigh, "I can, and I will."

Knowing she is probably sore, I focus on her pleasure–trailing my tongue slowly down her body until I'm between her legs. Alternating between mouth and touch, I take time pleasing her, watching with wicked satisfaction as she grips the sheets and her body bows off the bed. It is this I want her to come back to when she remembers our beginning–the

182

memory of raw, unfiltered pleasure.

When I'm convinced that she is thoroughly satisfied, I slide up and kiss her with ownership. "Mine," I whisper. "Only, always mine."

My angel kisses me back with equal measure, running her hands up my chest, trailing over every ripple of muscle. She feels like a dream, and I want to curl up with her and stay asleep forever if this is only that.

But the mortal instrument in my chest, which has been without warmth since I came into this body, knows it's not. This moment is more real than any has ever been, and I never want to be without this kind of peace and pleasure again.

I draw her a hot bath and go downstairs to make some tea and a snack. Before heading up the stairs, I grab her book from the study and put it on the tray I've prepared.

When I make it back to the suite, she's waiting for me in bed, wearing one of my shirts and boxers, hair wet at the ends, and the most beautiful smile I've ever seen. It pierces my chest and makes me feel a rush of emotions, including happiness. There is nothing I want more than this.

We fall asleep in a tangled embrace. Hard to see where one ends and the other begins. It took thousands of years, but finally, we are no longer daemon or undecided but us–and it's the only side I ever want to know until the end of time.

23
DIABLO

I open my eyes and find Dante sitting on a chair next to the bed. He looks deep in thought, staring out the window into the night. I reach for him sleepily, and when he feels my hand on his arm, he turns and smiles. "Hey, angel."

We haven't left his room for two days except to eat, and honestly, I could spend the rest of eternity just like this, and it would be more than enough. Being with Dante has eased the weight I've carried for thousands of years, and I feel at peace since the first time this existence began. He is my salvation.

I grip the pillow under my head and yawn. "What are you doing out of bed?"

"Watching you," he takes a deep breath, then exhales. "And thinking."

"Oh yeah?" I stretch languidly, my body humming with satisfaction. Gone is the pain of my first time, and in its place, mind-numbing pleasure every time we are together. Being with Dante sets every part of me on fire. I know his body better than my own, and he, every inch of mine.

"I want this," he looks at me with a heaviness in his eyes that matches his voice. "Waking up with you next to me every day."

I want that, too–for Dante to be part of my life every day, for eternity. But I know what it will mean, and I can't do it. The thought of what I want and what I can have splits me in two.

He gets up from the chair and sits down on the bed next to

me. "Vinny called."

He doesn't have to say anything more. I can tell by the look on his face. "We have to go back."

"Yes," he leans down and kisses my shoulder.

I pull the pillow closer to me and burrow into its softness. I knew this moment would come but didn't want it to be so soon. Not yet. The past few days have felt like a dream, and I'm not ready to go back to the nightmare of being stuck in Eden.

"I wish we had more time." A wave of sadness washes over me, and tears prick my eyes. Going back means we are one step closer to the end of his time with me, and the thought makes my heart hurt.

"Ironic, isn't it?" he runs his finger along my shoulder. "We have all the time in the world, and then suddenly…not."

I once counted the days until Dante left. Now, I'm counting the days we have together. Irony had nothing on us. Cosmic jokes, on the other hand.

"When do we leave," I swallow, not wanting to think about when he leaves for good.

He turns his attention back to the window. It's still dark, but the moon has begun its descent. "A driver will take us to the airport in the morning."

Part of me fears going back to Eden means I will never see this place again. Who knows what the world will look like in a hundred years? If this place will even exist? But the other part of me can see myself here with him, regardless of the consequences of that choice, which scares me.

"We still have time before we have to leave," he flashes me a beautiful smile. "And we can do anything you want. And we can always come back."

I crawl into his lap, wanting nothing more than to spend

the end of our time together this century, where we finally began. "We can?"

"Of course," he tips my chin up. "We still have five days. A lot can happen in that time."

"You're right," I brighten. "So, we can do anything I want right now, then?"

"Anything." One hand trails down my back while the other rests on my thigh. I think about what we could do until we have to leave, and there's the obvious, which, given how his touch is making me feel, is the one my body wants. But then I have an idea.

I jump up, but he reaches for me and wraps an arm around my chest, pulling me back to him. "So, staying in bed isn't an option?" he whispers, lips ghosting my cheek.

"I thought about it," I look up, the fire in his eyes making it hard to think. "But there's something I just thought of that would be perfect right now."

"Oh?" he pulls back, eyes shining. "Care to fill me in?"

I run a finger down his cheek. "I will. But once you get dressed."

"Clothes aren't optional?" he winks.

"No," I laugh. "Dress warmly. But you definitely should not be wearing anything when we get back."

"Diablo," he says coyly. "Are you after me for my body?"

"Yes," I turn and place my hand on his chest. "Have you seen it?"

He kisses me, and it fills me with every emotion from the past few days. It is forever a part of me, just as he is. I will never forget this time together.

I know if I don't get up, we're not going to make it out of this bed, so I slide out from under his arm and jump up before he can grab me again. "Get dressed," I order playfully.

He looks at me, eyes heavy. "Are you going to tell me where we're going?"

I run to his doors and throw them open. "It's a surprise!"

"That's quite a view," he whistles as I sprint down the hall. "Don't think I won't try to strap you down in this bed when you get back," he calls out.

"Five minutes!" I shout back and laugh.

Once I reach my suite, I get dressed quickly, slipping into a pair of jeans, boots, and long sleeve shirt, then grab my jacket and a scarf and wrap it around my neck.

"Ready?" I ask when I get back to Dante's room. Surprisingly, he's dressed and on his phone.

"Yeah," he looks up. "Quick question before we go. Your informant in the underground network, is there anything else you can tell me about her?"

I look at him, slightly puzzled. "You want to know about that, now?"

He arches a brow. "Humor me?"

From the look in his eyes, I can see that he's serious, so I try to be for a moment, too. "Okay," I think back to what I told him that night at my house. "Well, she sells flowers in the old part of town, which is how I met her. She's the only one who sells peonies."

"Your favorite," he smiles.

"Right," my cheeks warm at the way he knows me. "She's been there for a couple of years, but that's all I know. I'm sorry, Lili doesn't say much."

"Lili?" he straightens. "That's her name?"

"Oh, right." Guess I did know a bit more. "Yes, that's her name. And she has long, red hair and sky blue eyes.

"Okay," he nods stiffly. "Anything else?"

I think for a moment and shake my head. "Nope. Now,

can we go?"

"Yes," he exhales and shoves the phone into his pocket.

His hands are all over me as we head down the stairs and into the elevator. "You want to go for a ride?" he asks when we exit the garage level.

"Grab the keys," I nod to the valet box on the wall.

"You know," he enters a code on the keypad, opens the box, and removes a set of keys. "We didn't have to leave if you wanted to go for a ride."

Heat creeps up my neck as he flashes me a devilish smile. "I don't want to ride. Well, I do, obviously," I shoot him a wicked smile. "But right now, I want to drive your bike."

"What?" he shakes his head. "Do you even know how?"

"Yes," I cross my arms.

He matches my stance. "Oh really? How?"

"I learned online."

He tosses his head back and laughs. "You want me to let you take my bike out based on what you learned online?"

I push up on my toes and whisper in his ear. "If you let me drive now, I'll ride you later."

He opens his hands without saying a word, and the keys fall from his into mine. "You like to play with fire."

"As long as I don't get burned, I'll stoke that fire as long as possible," I kiss him and wink.

He grabs my hand and leads me over to the bike. "Why am I letting you talk me into this?"

"Because you like to make me happy," I give him a cheeky grin.

"Well," he pulls me to his side and kisses me quickly. "You're right about that."

We reach the bike, and he lifts the seat, taking out two helmets. Once we've slipped them on, I swing my leg over the seat, and he slides in behind me. "If you wiggle against me, I won't be responsible for what happens," he grabs my waist.

"Just keep it in your pants for a bit," I flip the visor down on my helmet. "Okay?"

"I make no promises in that department. By the way, do you even know how to—"

I start the bike and rev the throttle, cutting him off. "Hold on," I command and use the heel of my boot to release the kickstand and pull my legs up as the bike lurches forward.

He wraps his arm around my waist as we make our way down the circular ramp of the garage, spinning round and round until we hit the street level. Once we do, I'm off.

The streets are empty. Neither night nor morning, it's like they're ours as I follow the route that I mapped and memorized. I planned to come back here this way before I left and wanted to surprise Dante with my riding skills. I'm glad we're doing it now. It's the perfect way to spend our last hours together in London.

We race along the river, passing St. Paul's and Covent Garden, Big Ben, and Southbank, then circle back to Westminster and take The Mall straight to Buckingham Palace. When we reach my destination, I stop alongside the memorial, use my heel to put the bike's kickstand down, and turn off the engine. Dante gets off first, then I do, removing my helmet.

When I first saw it the day we played tourist, I thought it was beautiful. But seeing it like this, at night against the purple sky, I'm speechless. The figure on the top of The Victoria Memorial is a gilded Winged Victory, but it may as well have been me. Her wings extend from her back, large and powerful; their gold so bright that it takes my breath away.

As we stand there in the quiet, both of us looking up,

something in me cracks. Tears I've held in for thousands of years break free, spilling down my cheeks.

An angel is what I was, and that virtue I once held dear and why I fell would forever be in conflict. I don't regret my decision, but I will always carry the weight of what I lost.

Strong arms wrap around me from behind, and I close my eyes and lean back. Being with Dante eases the pain and reminds me I may have lost my wings but gained so much more–even if it did take thousands of years.

He turns me to him and kisses my forehead. "Come on," he rubs his hands up and down my arms. "There's something I want to show you."

I sniff and pull back, handing him the keys. "You can drive now."

"Are you sure?" he reaches for them.

"Yeah," I reach for my helmet. "But if you wiggle against me, I won't be responsible for what happens," I joke softly, wanting to ease the heaviness of my heart.

"Noted," he pats the seat and winks. "Climb on."

We race back the way we came, crossing the river over the Millennium Bridge and stopping outside a round building in Bankside. It's white, constructed of oak, with mortise and tenon joints and a thatched roof.

Shakespeare's Globe Theater. I'd know it anywhere. Only, it's a reconstruction of the Elizabethan playhouse where he wrote and performed his plays.

"I planned to bring you here," Dante says as we get off the bike and make our way over to the structure. "But then, well, we wound up staying in," he reaches for my hand and smiles, heat surging between our palms.

After walking around the building and sharing his memories of the original playhouse, Dante leads me over to a bench overlooking the river. We sit there for a while in silence.

"Diablo," he says finally as the darkness in the sky starts to fade. "These last few days have been amazing. Introducing you to this world and seeing you smile has been such a gift." I swallow and look down, knowing what he will say next. "It's made me realize...I don't want your fealty. I just want your happiness."

I look up, shocked beyond belief. "For thousands of years, you've pushed for my fealty. Now you don't want it?" I shake my head. "What changed?"

"When I saw what that memorial did to you, I knew I could never do anything that would cause you that kind of pain. And fealty would," he tucks an errant strand of hair behind my ear. "So, I'm not going to ask for it. But I do want to be with you, more than anything. That's why I'm going to search for another way for us to be together."

I shake my head, wishing there was a way for us to be together because I wanted that more than anything. "But how?"

"I don't know," he looks at me, more serious than I've ever seen him. "But I'll search the entire world until I find an answer. I swear to you, Diablo, I will. I can't be without you."

I brush his cheek with my thumb, struck by the irony that I did what I initially set out to do. Only now, I didn't want to be apart from Dante. I never wanted to let him go.

"Take me home," I lean into him.

He kisses the top of my head and holds me close. "Where's home, angel?"

I look down the river and spot his building, thinking of the beautiful garden full of my favorite flowers and the study filled with his favorite music. Where he gave me my firsts and made me his, and I, in turn, made him mine. "The penthouse,"

I place my hand on his chest and look into his eyes. "And with you. You are my home."

I didn't know if there was a way for us to be together or if that kind of miracle existed, but I did know one thing–I wanted Dante with every fiber of my being, and I wasn't letting go without a fight.

24
DANTE

We arrive back at Eden that afternoon, and when we make it to Diablo's place, I walk around the property to check things out while she heads inside. The grass is matted around the window again, only, this time, I found the culprit. A black snake curled in a ball under a bush. I pick it up, and it hisses at me as I toss it over the fence.

After doing another lap and finding nothing else, I go back inside and find Diablo standing at the kitchen counter. She appears deep in thought but turns when she hears me come in and looks at me, lips pressed into a thin line.

"What's wrong?" I can't make out the look on her face, and it makes my fingers twitch with nervous anticipation.

"The day we left for London, one of your drivers picked us up, and one brought us back today. You don't trust the soulless, do you?"

My angel really is too smart for her own good. "I believe you should keep your circle of trust small." I know she deserves a better answer, but I don't know what else to say. Not until I talk to Vinny about what he discovered. The whole reason we came back so soon.

"But you trust them to keep an eye on your house and cars when you're not here," she presses. "What's changed?"

I make my way over to where she stands and wrap an arm around her waist. "I trust them with those things when I'm away because I have to. But you are more important than any possession will ever be. Nothing is greater than your safety."

Her troubled expression grows darker. "So, you think I'm in danger?"

"I think something is going on, and the sooner I know what, the better."

"That's why we came back," she says point-blank. "Isn't it?"

"It is," I confirm. "And I will fill you in just as soon as I know more." Worry fills her beautiful eyes, and a pit forms in my stomach.

"And what happens if something is still going on when you leave? What then?"

I pull her closer to me. "That's not going to happen. I promised I would look into every possible way for us to be together, and I don't plan to break that promise."

She looks up at me, eyes anxious. "But what if there isn't a way? What if we can only see each other once a century?"

A hundred years without being able to touch one another—fucking torture. Not to mention, it goes against everything I want. "The idea of a day without you drives me insane," my eyes search hers. "But I'm looking at every possible scenario. Even reading between the lines of the contract."

The darkness in her eyes begins to lift, curiosity growing in its place. "You've seen the contract?"

"No, not since the day we signed it. It's been missing for centuries. But there's no need to see it when we all know what it says." She chews her lip, and I can see the wheels in her mind turning. "What're you thinking, angel?"

"Has anyone ever tried to work around what it says, so to speak?"

"Sure," I nod. "I've tried to come here before it's time. And find you online."

"Why would you do that?" she looks at me, her beautiful

naivety making my chest ache.

I reach for a lock of her hair and roll it between my fingers. "Do you really have to ask?"

"You wanted my fealty that bad," she looks down.

"No," I tip her chin up. "I wanted you that bad. I told myself it was fealty, but it was always more than that. I just didn't want to admit it."

She curls into me and sighs. "What are we going to do? I can't swear my loyalty to him. I just can't."

Diablo's disdain for Luke has always been obvious, but I'm attuned to her body now in a way that I wasn't before. She's tense just talking about him.

Something shifts in me. Like two tectonic plates deep below my core, aligning. "Luke scares you, doesn't he?"

She flinches at my question and holds me tighter. "Can we not talk about him, please?"

I kiss the top of her head. "Maybe, one day, you will trust me enough to—"

"I do trust you," she looks up. "It's not that."

"Then what is it? You don't like him, it's clear. But you're also afraid. I can feel it. And I want to know why."

Her eyes search mine, and I watch as my spirited angel becomes fragile right before me. "My heart and my fealty," she says with trepidation. "They're…connected."

"Fealty could never change this extraordinary mortal instrument," I put my hand on her chest. "But I promise you…it's off the table. We'll find another way."

She grabs my neck with both hands and jumps up, wrapping her legs around me. "Do you mean it?"

She holds onto me as if her existence depends on it. "With everything in me," I run my hands up and down her back.

The urge to show her just how serious I am is strong, but I

need to see Vinny. The sooner I know all about what he uncovered while Diablo and I were in London, the better.

I sit her down on the counter and place my hands down on either side of her. "I need to go and see Vinny. But damn if I don't want to continue this."

She wraps her legs around me again and pulls me into another kiss. When we finally stop to take a breath, I'm so hot for her that every inch of my skin is on fire.

"Are you sure you have to go right this minute?" The way she's looking at me, eyes shining, cheeks flushed, it takes everything in me to not give in to my need for her.

I run my thumb over her kiss-swollen lips. "Yes. But be ready for me when I get back."

"What should I be ready for?" she asks innocently.

"Anything...and everything." I kiss her again, then make my way to the door. The sooner I see Vinny, the sooner I can pick up where she and I left off.

Thankfully, the impending conversation with Vinny cools me down, and by the time I walk into the gym, my need for her has been replaced by a need for answers.

"Hey, buddy," Vinny lifts his chin as I make my way over to where he's drilling a punching bag.

He's dripping with sweat, and the bag looks like it's taken a few rounds. "Been here a while?" I slip out of my jacket and toss it onto a piece of equipment.

"Needed to get some real sweat in. Not that salty, sex sweat."

I shake my head and grin. "You and Lila are still going at it, huh?"

"Don't you know it," he smirks. "Speaking of...you and Diablo have a good time?"

Usually, I tell Vinny everything. He's used to hearing the

blow-by-blow details. But I'm protective of my relationship with Diablo, and our private moments will stay between us.

"We had a good time," I grin, watching as Vinny pulls at the lace on his glove with his teeth.

"Yeah," he smirks, holding it out to me once it's off, then untying the lace on the other with his free hand. "How good?"

"Good," I say again as memories of our time together flash in my mind.

"Alright, brother," Vinny hands me the second glove and claps me on the shoulder. "Keep it to yourself...for now. I'll get it out of you, eventually."

"Yeah, yeah," I shake my head. "Go shower, and then we need to talk."

"Yes, we do," his face turns serious. "Give me a few, and I'll fill you in."

"Alright," I lift my chin. "But don't take long."

"Oh?" he tilts his head. "Got something waiting for you?"

I'm reminded of the look in Diablo's eyes just before I left, and my lip hitches up. "Brother, you have no idea."

I don't have to say anything more. With those five words, I've both filled in my best friend as I've always done and protected the moments Diablo and I shared.

"Well, alright," he nods with approval and heads to the shower.

I've been working up a sweat on the punching bag when he returns ten minutes later, hair wet and clothes changed.

"Spread your feet apart a bit more," he instructs while watching me. I jab the bag and then do a cross punch. "Good," he claps his hands when I make the correction and get more power in my punch.

"Tell me everything," I hit the bag again, harder. It can't wait any longer. I need to know everything Vinny does about the news that sent us back to Eden.

Vinny texted me every day that Diablo and I were in London, and with each update, I grew increasingly anxious. Things in Eden were off, but the news he shared last night unnerved me the most.

"Well," he crosses his arms. "I checked with everyone, and it's true...when the ten days are up, Diablo will be the last undecided in Eden if she's not with you."

Hearing it aloud irritates me even more than when I first read it in text. "How is that possible?" I punch the bag again with more force than my past two jabs. It swings outward, then comes back at me. "Even Viper and Sam?"

"Crazy, right?" Vinny nods. "They can't even stand to be in the same room together."

I nod, knowing well their non-chemistry. Viper and Sam are bound, but it doesn't mean it has created the kind of connection Diablo and I have, or Vinny and Lila, for that matter. They're like oil and water, not in the opposites attract way.

Viper is a daemon that can take a blow like Vinny and has a mouth dirtier than anyone I know. Sam is a soft-spoken undecided that bristles when she's around. To think he just gave in after all this time makes no sense.

"I talked to Viper, and she was adamant," Vinny nods. "Sam swore his fealty the first day she got here."

"I just don't get it," I shake my head. A few undecided were as unwavering as Diablo when it came to fealty. But now, suddenly, after all this time, everyone just decided? It didn't make sense or feel right.

"There's...more," Vinny adds, with a weight in his tone I don't like.

I hit the bag with a one-two punch, preparing for whatever

198

he's about to say. "Go for it."

"The bartender…he's not only been asking around about Diablo…he's been casing her house."

I catch the bag between my gloved hands and clench my jaw so tight that my teeth gnash. "What?"

"I tailed him last night, and just like every night since you left, he went to her house and stood across the street and stared at it for hours."

My blood boils, and I grip the bag and push it using all my strength. It swings high in the air and then breaks off its hanger. "What the fuck!" I explode with anger. "Who is he?"

"No one knows," Vinny shakes his head. "Everyone I spoke to says he keeps to himself."

"Well, I guess it's time to get answers," I hit my gloves together. "And there's one more thing, but you better brace yourself." Vinny looks at me curiously. "It's Lilith."

Vinny's eyes narrow. "What about her?"

"She's Diablo's informant for the underground network."

"Wait," he holds up a hand. "Come again?"

I take one glove off and toss it to the ground. Then untie the other and do the same. "Diablo said her informant's name is Lili. Says she sells flowers in the old part of town and has red hair and blue eyes."

"Sounds like her, alright," Vinny rubs his jaw. "But what is she doing in that part of town? It's been abandoned for years."

I move my neck from side to side. "I know."

"And better yet, what the hell is she doing in Eden?"

"I don't know!" I blow out a heated breath. "But it can't be good."

Lilith is trouble. Sworn to Luke, she is his forever concubine. They fight, then make up, and it's nauseating.

Remembering I used the word to insult Diablo that first day at *Saints* makes me cringe. The two couldn't be more different.

In her on-again, off-again relationship with Luke, they were currently off, and I hadn't seen her in decades. But one thing was for sure–if she was in Eden, it wasn't good. And if she'd befriended Diablo somehow, there was a reason, and it also wasn't good.

Her presence, the bartender, and the fealty of the Fallen were three coincidences, too many. Where there was smoke, there was fire, and I was about to light a mother fucking back burn to protect my angel.

Vinny reaches for one of the towels on the table next to the water fountain and hands it to me. "This doesn't feel right."

"You're telling me," I grab it and press it against my face. "Lilith sniffing around Diablo, the bartender watching her house, and the fact she will be alone in a city full of soulless after I leave," I shake my head angrily. "No fucking way."

"What do you mean?" Vinny looks at me, clearly confused. "It sounded like things between you were good."

"They are. But whatever happened between us, her fealty is not up for discussion."

"Dante," Vinny crosses his arms. "You need it. She can't leave Eden otherwise."

"I know, but I won't force it. We have to find another way. We have money and resources. We need to make it happen."

"Dante," Vinny holds out his hand, trying to reason with me. "It's been five thousand years. We have five days."

"I know how many days we have left. It's like a timebomb sitting on my chest, Vin."

"What happened between you two?" I can see he is curious about my change of heart. I've focused on her fealty for thousands of years, and now, it's off the table?

How could I put into words what happened between Diablo and me? One day, we're doing the same song and dance we've been doing for five millennia, and the next, she is my forever.

"She got to me," I say simply. "She more than got to me. She got me to feel things I never wanted to, and now the idea of not being with her drives me fucking crazy!"

Vinny laughs at me and shakes his head.

"What's so funny?"

"She got to you thousands of years ago, Dante. What you should be saying is you finally realize it." It was the second time Vinny dropped the truth on me, and he's right. "So, now that you do, what are you going to do about it?"

"I want her, and I know she wants me, and there's no way I can go another century without her. She's coming with me. Come hell or high water."

"Fealty is the only way she can leave this place, Dante. You know that."

I can't tell Vinny the promise I made to Diablo or the way the very idea of fealty paralyzes her with fear. I made a promise to her and intended to keep it.

"It can't be the only way. It just can't." I'm desperate for my words to be true because I know if she's not with me when I leave this time, it won't just make me an insufferable asshole for decades. It will shatter me. "I need you to help me."

Vinny takes a deep breath, then claps my shoulder. "Alright, brother. What do you need me to do?"

"Get the team on it ASAP. Spare no expense. Let them know there's a bonus for the one who finds something first."

"You got it," he reaches into his back pocket and pulls out his phone. "What are they looking for?"

"Answers, riddles," I start to rattle off, then stop cold,

remembering what Diablo and I were talking about before I came here. "Wait…the contract!"

Vinny's brows shoot up. "Like the one and only?"

"Yes!" I snap, remembering an essential element of my business. "Contracts always have a way out. You know I've broken the most ironclad agreements with loopholes. There has to be one in ours."

"Okay," Vinny nods. "But there's one problem. It's been missing forever."

"I know," I rub my hand over my mouth. "But a document like that isn't gone. It's being hidden or protected. Whoever took it knew about Luke, which means we'll have to search the darkest, deepest parts of the mortal world to find it. We're talking absolute underbelly."

"Yup," Vinny nods. "We'll use one of the dummy corps to keep this below deck."

"Good idea." Primordial's financials were clean, thanks to the companies I'd set up to use for instances like this. "I want no stone unturned. And we keep this between us."

"You got it," he reaches for his phone and sends off a couple of texts. "Anything else?"

"Yeah, there is." I wait for him to finish, and when he does and looks up, I continue. "I'd understand if you wanted to stay out of this. In a way, we're coming at Luke, and he's —"

"Not my brother," Vinny cuts me off. "You are. I got your back, now and always. We'll deal with the consequences if and when they come."

I'd already realized that doing whatever I had to for Diablo and me to be together was going against Luke, and I'd understand if Vinny wanted to stay out of it. He had a future with Lila planned, and I didn't want to risk that. But knowing he's got my back like always fills me with confidence.

Together, there's nothing we can't do.

Vinny shoves his phone into his back pocket and focuses on me. "Alright, what's next?"

"We head over to Old Town and look around," I straighten. "But first, we go to *Saints* and take care of problem number one."

"The bartender," Vinny grins.

"Yup," I grab my jacket. The bartender needed to be dealt with now before he gave me one more reason to kill him.

25
DANTE

I'm ready to explode by the time I get to *Saints*. The bartender is as good as dead when I find him.

Vinny was right. I fell for Diablo thousands of years ago. I just never acknowledged it. Now that I had, it made everything clear. I would fight anyone and anything that tried to stand in my way of being with her. Knowing she's mine fills me with a primal need to protect her. Whoever came at me next was in for a surprise.

"Where the fuck is he!" I call out as we enter the club.

The server that waited on us that first day in Eden turns her head and looks at Vinny and me as we storm over to the bar. "Where's who?" she asks, looking me up and down.

I slam my fist on the bar, and it rattles the stack of glasses on the other side. "The bartender, that's who!"

"What bartender?" she asks snidely.

"Listen, you piece of trash," I grab her chin and yank it up so I can see directly into her eyes. "Don't pretend you don't know who I'm talking about because I saw you two talking the other day when we were here."

She sneers, and a haughty laugh curls from her mouth. "I work in a bar and was talking to a bartender. Gee, that's odd."

"Don't play with me. You know exactly who I'm talking about."

She licks my finger that's closest to her lips and grins. "I heard you like it rough. If I keep saying I don't know him, will you bend me over and punish me?"

My eyes flash, and I shove her face back. "You're not my type." The old me would have fallen for that bait. This me, the one committed to Diablo, ignores it entirely.

"Oh, that's right," she narrows her eyes. "You like that whore with the black hair, strutting around in her underwear the other day."

"What did you say?" I grit my teeth.

"You heard me," she puts a hand on her hip. "When your pious angel doesn't give you what you want, come to me, and I'll give you what you need."

I push her back to the wall with my forearm pressed under her neck. "If you say one more thing about her, I will end you. Do you hear me?"

She reaches between my legs and squeezes. "Something tells me those dark urges of yours…that notorious insatiable hunger we've all heard about is begging to be satisfied."

Her touch is like ice, and it does nothing but irritate me. I reach for her jaw again with my free hand, holding it so tight my nails dig into her skin. "I wouldn't fuck you if you were the last piece of ass in existence. Do you hear me?"

Her eyes narrow, and she lets go of my crotch, smiling wickedly. "You say that now, but you will come looking for me when she's gone."

"What did you say?" I seethe.

"I know all about you," she grins. "And you'll need someone to warm your bed. When you do, I'll be waiting. You can make this up to me then."

Vinny comes over, standing with his arms crossed. "Come to rescue your friend?" she drawls sarcastically.

"Oh no," his eyes are firm. "You see, this is my brother. You threaten him, or anyone important to him, that's an attack on my family. You're as good as dead if you don't start talking."

"What is it with her?" she rolls her eyes. "Why does everyone want her?"

"Who is everyone?" I clench the server's jaw again, tighter than before. Her bone cracks under my hold, and she flinches, looking from me to Vinny.

"You two share her, is that it? I'm surprised she can take it. That's cool, though. I could take the two of you."

"Dante," Vinny taps my shoulder. "Let's go. She doesn't know anything."

"That's what you think," she spits out.

He trains his eyes back on her and smirks. "Not too bright, either."

"Oh yeah," she rolls her eyes. "And why is that?"

He moves his neck from side to side and cracks his knuckles. "You just proved you know something. So, tell us what you know, or we will take our time drawing it out from you. And trust me, the latter is something we're both fond of and good at."

She runs a hand up my chest, too long of nails scratching my skin. "I don't doubt you two are good at many things."

I let go of her and back up. "Don't touch me."

"She's not worth it, you know." The server runs a finger along her lip, then down between her breasts. "But I am. I could make your darkest dreams come true."

I can't believe I ever thought she'd be fun for an hour. Looking at her now, the only fun I want to have with her is making her talk. "What do you know about me or what I want?"

"I know plenty," she shoots back. "Which is how I know you need a real woman to satisfy your needs. All of them."

She reaches out to touch me again, but I grab her wrist and

stop her, bending it back this time. "This is your last warning. If you touch me again, it will be the last thing you ever do."

"Dante!" I turn at the sound of Diablo's voice. She's standing with both hands on her hips, eyes burning into me from across the room. "What are you doing?"

I look at her, hoping she's not getting the wrong idea. "It's not what you think."

"Stay out of this bitch," the server looks at Diablo with antipathy. "There's no room for you at this party."

Diablo storms over before I can respond, her lovely face hardened by anger. "What did you say to me?" she hisses.

"You heard me," the server looks her up and down. "By the way, nice to see you have clothes on this time."

"Unless you want me to rip your throat out," Diablo leans in, baring her teeth, "I suggest you shut your mouth."

Vinny looks at me, and I raise my eyebrow. Diablo is feral, eyes blazing. Seeing this side of her is a major turn-on. It's hot as fuck to see her so territorial.

"I'd like to see you try," the server struggles to reach for Diablo with the hand dangling at her side.

"I wouldn't if I were you," I tug the wrist I'm holding back farther.

Diablo looks from the server to me, confused. "Are you protecting her?"

"No," I laugh at the idea. "I'm protecting you."

"She couldn't hurt me if she tried."

"I can see that," I grin, the look in my eyes telling her just how much I can. "But it's not in your nature to hurt someone. I don't want you to carry that weight."

"You might have been an angel," the server smirks. "But here, you're no better than the rest of us. Come at me again. I dare you."

"Get out of my way!" Diablo snarls.

"No," I shake my head.

"Dante, move. I want a piece of her."

"You're not the only one," the server licks her lips and looks at me, and that's all it takes for Diablo. She turns and clocks her right in the jaw.

"Damn!" Vinny whistles. "The fire she learned from you, brother. But that form she learned from my girl."

"You're right, Vinny," Diablo takes deep, controlled breaths. "Thank you for teaching Lila so that she could teach me."

Diablo doesn't shake her hand or show any sign of pain. She steps in front of me, and I let go of the server and hold my hands up, watching my angel with pride and lust.

"Listen to me," she pushes the server to the wall. "If you ever sniff around him again, I will tear you apart. And if you sniff around him," she nods to Vinny. "I will tear you apart. Do you hear me?"

The server rubs her jaw and looks from Diablo to me and then Vinny. We all wait with bated breath for her response. To our surprise, she says nothing. She simply straightens her back, adjusts her vest, and walks away.

Once she leaves, Diablo turns to me. "What was that all about?"

"I'll fill you in later," I look at my angel, filled with every emotion possible.

"No," she crosses her arms. "You will fill me in, now."

Seeing that she's not going to back down, I exhale and explain. "We came here to look for the bartender. Vinny found out he's the one that's been following you. But then the server got in our face, and well, you can probably guess the rest."

She looks from me to Vinny. "Did you find him?"

"No," he shakes his head in frustration.

"Well," she turns her attention back to me. "I think I know where he may have been."

Diablo darts her eyes from me to Vinny, and the confidence she possessed just seconds earlier noticeably shifts.

"Why are you here?" I look at her with concern. "Did something happen?"

"I...found something," she looks at me, nervous and worried. "And I wanted to tell you, but you didn't answer your phone, so I came to look for you."

I check my jacket, then pant pockets, and realize my phone isn't on me. "I must have left it at the gym when I met up with Vinny. But wait, back up, you found something? What did you find?"

She digs into her pocket, pulls out a small device, and hands it to me. I grab it and squeeze it in my hand. "Where did you find this?"

"I was looking in my bag for something, and it fell out," she looks at the small piece of tech in my hand.

I clench the device hard enough to break it but stop just before I do. "What?"

"Is that what I think it is?" she asks nervously.

I hand it to Vinny, and he takes a closer look. "It's good tech, but ours is better. The question is, how did it get in her bag? And who put it there?"

"It must have been in there before we left London," Diablo watches our exchange.

"No," Vinny and I both shake our heads. "That's not possible. I installed Dante's security, and let's just say it's top-notch. There's not a piece of tech that can enter his building without being detected. And when it does, it flags the security team, including me."

"You're on his security team?" she looks at Vinny, clearly impressed.

"I'm both brains and brawn, baby," he flashes her a grin.

"He runs it," I shake my head at Vinny. I can't help but love the guy's ego. "And the security team at the penthouse he selected because of their abilities. They wouldn't miss something like this. They checked our bags when we got there, and I also asked them to increase security the moment we arrived."

"That leaves one option," Vinny looks at me.

"Someone put it in her bag when we got back." I turn to Diablo, and her face drains of color. "After I left earlier, what did you do? Did you go outside or into any room long enough for someone to sneak in undetected?"

She looks from me to Vinny and hesitates. "I was...um... I went to take a shower."

I see red. Someone waited for me to leave, then snuck in when Diablo was in the shower and planted devices in her home. Seeing the bartender is nowhere to be found, I have a good idea who that might be.

I clench my fist, veins in my forearms bulging. If that sick fuck was watching her, I'm going to kill him. And what did the server mean by *When she's gone*. It made my stomach uneasy.

I didn't like this. I didn't like any of this. "That's it," I say firmly. "You're coming to my place. And I don't want any protests. It's not up for discussion."

"Okay," Diablo nods, giving me no resistance.

"And Vinny, can you look into this?" I hand him the tracker.

"Already on it." He has his phone out and is sending a couple of texts.

"Once I get her settled at my place, I'll meet you in Old Town."

"Yup," Vinny nods. "Diablo," he looks up. "Lila is at my place. You two can hang out while Dante and I look into things."

"I'd like that," she brightens a bit.

"She misses the hell out of you and can't wait to hear all about your trip," Vinny smiles.

I reach for Diablo's hand to reassure her. "Our place is the safest in Eden. You'll be fine there."

"But don't soulless manage your place when you're gone? For all we know, they bugged it, too."

"Not possible," I shake my head. "You were right when you said I didn't trust them. I don't. That's why Vinny and I make sure our place is impenetrable. You will be safe there. I wouldn't have you stay there if it weren't."

She nods and grows quiet. "Why do you think he's watching me?"

I pull her to me and kiss the side of her head. "I don't know," I whisper in her ear. "But when I find out, he's dead."

"Alright," Vinny shoves his phone back into his pocket. "Dante, I tracked your phone. It's at the gym."

"You tracked his phone?" Diablo looks at Vinny, clearly impressed.

"The world is a crazy place, Diablo. We have each other's backs. Speaking of, I should put a tracker on your phone, too."

"Good idea," I nod at him. "Let's do that later. For now," I turn back to Diablo, "let's go back to your place so you can grab your bag and get you settled at mine."

Vinny is right. We have each other's backs, and outside the four of us, I now trust no one.

26
DIABLO

When we get to my house, Dante looks in every room, searching for devices like the one I found in my bag. To my shock, there is one in each, including my bedroom.

"He's dead," Dante fumes and slams a fistful of devices down on the kitchen counter.

I look at the scattered pieces, stunned. "Do you know it's the bartender for a fact?"

"Vinny caught him outside your house last night, and he wasn't at *Saints* earlier when that bug showed up in your bag. One plus one equals two."

"But why?" I cross my arms and chew the inside of my cheek. "I don't even know him."

Dante looks at me, eyes clouding over. "Isn't it obvious? He has a thing for you. I saw it that first day at *Saints*."

I frown, angry that we had to leave London for a soulless moron with a crush? "So, he's why we came back?"

"He's part of the reason, but not all." Dante clenches his fists and then turns suddenly and storms down the hall.

"Where are you going?" I follow close behind and find him in my room, searching in my bag. Finding nothing, he sets it aside and lets out a relieved breath. "Just making sure."

"You know," I lean against the doorframe, heat creeping up my neck. "You're pretty sexy when you're angry."

"Then you should see what I'm going to do to that bartender," his lips quirk up. "Because it will make you hot as hell. Which, by the way, can we talk about what happened between you and that server earlier?"

"What about it?" my eyes narrow, remembering how she looked at Dante like he was her next meal.

"Because that," he comes over to where I stand and reaches for me, "was hot as hell."

The need to show the server that Dante was mine had hit hard and fast. But it didn't surprise me. The response felt more natural than breathing. "She was clawing at you."

"And?" his smile grows.

"And…" I grab his shirt and pull him closer. "You're mine. No one touches you."

"That's my angel," he wraps his arm around my waist. "Honestly, how hard is it for you to say?"

I sigh with delight as he kisses me. It's commanding and heady and makes me weak in the knees. "Aren't we supposed to be going to your place?" I mumble through our locked lips.

"We will," he grips my hips. "But first, I want you."

"You are insatiable," I laugh as he walks me back to the bed and pulls us down onto it.

I straddle him, and he rubs his hands up and down my thighs. "For you, always."

"Can I tell you something?" I lean down, my lips ghosting his.

He pushes my hair back and locks his eyes on mine. "You can tell me anything and everything."

I drown in his nearness, wondering how I'd fought this. us, for so long. "I can't get enough of you either."

"Well, well, well," he rolls me over and pins my arms on either side of my head. "Who's insatiable now?"

"Oh, I think we've probably rubbed off on each other," I arch my back and press into him.

"No doubt about it," he smiles. "You clocked that server. It was a move straight out of my playbook."

"So, I'm a little darker, and you're a little lighter," I shift my hips, using the friction to satisfy the growing ache between my legs. "Is that what you're saying?"

"If the darkness fits," he winks.

The past few days with Dante, I've felt it. Not dark, necessarily, but certainly more fire and heat than ever before.

"And is wanting to end someone for following me your way of being the light?" I ask jokingly.

"Oh no," his eyes blaze. "When it comes to protecting what's mine, that's pure fire, angel."

He runs his tongue along my lower lip, then pulls it into his mouth and lets my hands go. I run them down his back and under his shirt as his mouth moves to my neck.

"For the record," I close my eyes, savoring the feel of his lips on my skin. "I didn't just want to hit the server for touching you. I wanted to tear rip to pieces."

"And for the record," he moans and nibbles on my ear. "No one will ever have me again. You are my beginning and end."

When Dante touches me, it sets my skin on fire. But when we're together like this, everything stands still. "I like the way that sounds."

He pulls back and runs a finger down my cheek, staring at me with such intensity it makes my insides melt. "You are more than I deserve, Diablo."

I place my hand on his chest and stare into his eyes. Such beautiful blue, like the ocean; powerful and endless. "Before I forget," I swallow, knowing well where this is headed, "I want to put my book in the library."

"What?" he asks, eyes heavy. "Now?"

"I want it to be safe with the others. That's what I was

doing earlier when I found the bug in my bag."

"Maybe you should do that later," he leans down to kiss me, but I slip out from under him and climb off the bed.

"I'll be right back," I grab my book from where I left it on the nightstand and hurry to the library.

When I'm done locking it in the case with the others, I turn and find him leaning against the doorframe, watching me raptly. "The first time I saw you in here, do you know what I was thinking?" he asks.

I tap my chin playfully, pondering his question. "How impeccable my design skills were?"

"No," he makes his way over to the couch closest to him and grips the back. "How badly I wanted to have you right here."

"Is that so?" I make my way over to where he stands.

A mischievous smile pulls at his lips. "Mm-hmm."

My need for him flares, and I get an idea. A crazy yet delicious idea. "Did you check in here for devices?"

He looks down at me, first with a look of annoyance that tells me no, apparently, he forgot, then curiosity as he watches a devious smile tug at my lips.

"Well," I reach for his hand and lead him over to the other side of the couch, speaking low enough so only he can hear. "If someone is watching me, they need to see who I belong to, no?"

Dante watches me hungrily as I unbutton his pants and slide them and his boxer briefs down. "Are you serious?"

"Very," I nod as he kicks them aside, then pulls his shirt overhead and tosses it to the floor. He looks like a god standing there, wearing nothing but his want for me, and it fuels my need for him.

He reaches for my pants and yanks them down and off in

one fell swoop. "I don't want anyone to see you."

"So let them hear me," I challenge, sinking onto the couch, taking off my shirt and bra, and tossing them to the floor.

He kneels between my legs, drinking me in as I lay back against the smooth leather, then covers my body with his chiseled frame. "I would burn Heaven and Earth for you," he lowers his head to my chest, trailing kisses across the delicate skin. "You know that, don't you?"

"Yes," I run a hand through his hair as he moves his mouth down my body. I know the lengths Dante would go for me, and I want him to know how far I would go for him.

"I want to drown in you," he trails his tongue from my hip to my thigh, making my back bow.

I didn't think Dante's possession over me would be a turn-on, but it is. I want him to own every inch of my body. "Then drown in me," I all but beg. "I am yours."

He grips my thighs with both hands and pushes them apart, kissing the inside of one before biting it. I yelp softly, and he licks the spot, then blows on it, making me shiver.

"Do you know why you were so angry at that server?" he trails a finger up the inside of my other thigh, then lowers his mouth and sucks on the skin gently.

My mind goes hazy from the powerful combination of pleasure and pain radiating through me. "Why?" I quiver.

"Because you don't want anyone touching what belongs to you, just as I'll end, anyone who touches what belongs to me."

"Yes," I lick my lips. His mouth and words are carnal and wicked and satisfy me.

"It was hot as fuck," he pushes my legs further apart, then drives his tongue into me.

The idea someone is watching us intensifies my arousal, and I grip his head with both hands. "You're making me hot as fuck."

My body tingles as his tongue works me, and when my breathing quickens and back bows, he uses his thumb to rub circles around the nerves at the top of my slit and send me soaring.

"Say my name, angel," he commands, knowing just what to do to push me over the edge. Warmth spreads through me as I cry out his name, and he licks and sucks me through my climax.

As I come down from my high, he pushes up between my legs and enters me; our bodies fitting together like a lock and key. "You are mine, Diablo," he flicks his hips, filling my already satisfied body with heat. "And I will destroy anyone who tries to hurt you."

Grabbing the arm of the couch with both hands, he thrusts into me harder and covers my mouth with his, owning me completely. I didn't think I would be into anyone watching us kiss, much less have sex, but the idea that someone could be is a rush.

"Dante," I pant when we've both worked up a sweat. He looks down at me, eyes full of heat. "It's my turn."

I push him onto his back, trail my tongue down his chest to the carved v of his lower stomach, and then look up to meet his eyes while taking him into my mouth. He groans and leans back. "Fuck, angel, do you know how that feels?"

"Think I do," I hum with delight as he fists my hair. Knowing I'm the only one he would allow this kind of control over him makes me feel powerful.

I pick up the rhythm, using my hand and mouth, and his thighs clench and words come out in short, ragged breaths. "Keep that…up…and… I…won't be able…to hold it."

"Then let go for me," I demand. "Show them who you

belong to."

Dante lets go, and I place my hand on his chest and devour him through his climax, as he did me.

Once his muscles ease, I slide up to kiss him. He looks at me dazedly. "Did you learn that online?"

"Nope," I grin, feeling his heart thumping wildly beneath me. "Do you think anyone was watching?"

"If they were, they got one hell of a show. Shit," he blows out a spent breath and laughs softly. "That was amazing."

I bite his jaw and grin. "Yes, they did, and yes, it was."

He puts one arm behind his head and pulls me to him with the other, and it hits me; this is the vision I had that day at *Saints*. Us together and happy.

We lay there for a while, too content to move. But eventually, we gathered up our clothes and slipped out of the library. Once we've put our clothes back on, Dante does a sweep of the library and finds both a video and listening device. For whom we just put on a show, I did not know, but the look in his eyes tells me he's glad that we did.

"By the way," he grabs my bag off the bed and follows me out to the kitchen. "I've been thinking about what you said about the contract, and you're right. How do we know it doesn't say more than what we think?"

"We...don't," I agree.

"Well, I think it's worth exploring. All contracts have loopholes, and ours should, too. That's why I started looking for it."

The room shifts, and I grab his arm. "You, what?"

He looks down at my hand on his arm and then back up. "I said I'd search the world over and meant it. That includes the possibility of the answer being in the very thing that limits us."

The fact Dante is trying everything he can to find a way for us to be together, including looking for the contract, makes my chest tighten. "I can't believe it."

"Well, believe it," he kisses the tip of my nose. "And with my resources, it's not if we find it, but when. And when we do, we'll know for sure if there's anything in there that we can use or if we have to search for another option."

I wonder if I should tell Dante that I might have a lead on the contract. Maybe his resources could get the rest of the pieces from the Vatican quicker than Minerva. Then again, what the Vatican had could not be the contract, making it better to have multiple searches happening simultaneously.

"We're going to be together," he cups my face, pulling me from the thought. "I always find a way to get what I want. And I've never wanted anything more."

As we lock up and leave, I feel more optimistic about the future. But as we head over to Dante's place, I can't deny the sliver of unease lurking behind my hope.

Since London, I haven't heard from Minerva, so I'm not sure if she's still trying to get the rest of the pieces. I need to talk to her. She needs to know I still want her to get them and don't care what it costs–that I'll give her anything. Absolutely, anything.

27
DIABLO

Lila practically knocks me over as we walk through the door at Vinny's an hour later. "Girl, I've missed you!"

"It's only been a few days," I laugh as she throws her arms around me.

After dropping my bag off at Dante's place and giving me a tour, he walked me down to Vinny's. Lila had a whole afternoon planned for us while the guys were busy, and I was looking forward to spending time with her.

"Yeah, I know it's only been a few days, but it feels like an eternity," she pulls back and smiles.

I look at Dante, and he grins. We both know exactly how long a few days can feel.

"How was London?" she asks excitedly. "I want to hear all about it. Vinny wants to take me there, but I want to go to Paris."

"Well, I've never been to Paris, so I can't weigh in on that."

"Yet," Dante corrects.

"Right," I look at him and smile, then turn back to Lila. "But, I've been to Milan, and it's beautiful."

"You two went to Milan?" Lila looks to Dante.

"Dante took me to the opera."

"I told him to treat you like a queen," Lila nods with approval. "Sounds like he took my advice."

"I told you I would," Dante rolls his eyes.

As I watch the two of them, it hits me how much like siblings they are, and Vinny, back at *Saints*, was like my protective brother. The four of us were family, and the realization tugged at my chest.

"Hey, can Vinny and I use the plane?" Lila continues.

"Of course," Dante shrugs. "What's mine is his. He knows that."

"Well, this changes everything," she muses, tapping her chin. "Maybe we can hit Paris for breakfast one day and Milan for dinner. That could work."

"Okay, well," Dante nods towards the door. "I'll let you two talk about travel and whatever else you talk about while I meet up with Vin. You two keep the door locked and call us if you need anything."

"Yes, Dante," Lila waves him towards the door. "We'll be fine."

"You have your phone this time?" When Dante showed me the gym earlier, we found it lying on the floor by the punching bag, right where Vinny said it would be.

Dante taps his jacket pocket. "Right here, so call me if you need anything."

"I will," I smile awkwardly. I want to pull him to me and kiss him until we're breathless, but Lila's staring at us, making me self-conscious.

Given the show we'd put on earlier in the library, I wasn't sure why. Maybe because I'd spent so much time talking with Lila about my need to get away from Dante, kissing him in front of her made me feel guilty somehow. Not to mention, I hadn't even had a chance to tell her that we were together.

"Oh, kiss him goodbye already so we can catch up," Lila looks down, pretending to examine her nails.

"How do you—"

Dante doesn't waste a second. He wraps his arm around my waist and gives me a searing kiss that makes me weak in the knees. "I'll see you later," he says huskily when our lips finally part. "Call me if you need anything. I mean it."

"I will," I swipe my thumb across his lips.

"Bye, Lila," he calls over my shoulder.

"Bring my man home in one piece," she calls back.

"Always," he shakes his head. "Bye," he kisses me again quickly, then turns and jogs down the stairs.

Once the door is closed and I hear his bike pull away, I curl up next to Lila on the couch.

"What?" I ask when I find her wide eyes staring at me.

"Are you kidding me?" her eyes dance with excitement. "You two are together? I need all the details. When and how was it? Is the sex as hot as that kiss? And why didn't you tell me sooner?"

I can't hide anything from Lila, but I want to keep the intimate moments between Dante and me private. "Answer to the first question, the night we left. And the second, my lips are sealed."

"You gave up your v-card that first night?" she squeals.

"No, Lila," I tuck a strand of hair behind my ear. "We kissed that night."

"Yeah, he kissed you everywhere," she grins.

My cheeks are warm, and I look down. "Okay, I'm not saying anything else."

"I'm sorry," she pinches my arm. "How was it, really? I mean, come on. I've been waiting centuries for you two to get together. You've got to give me something."

What should I tell Lila? I can't keep my hands off him. Every time we have sex, it's euphoric. He kisses like he fucks–hot and with intensity.

I look up and lift my coffee, taking a sip. "It was…nice," I say with mystery.

"Nice?" she wrinkles her nose. "Walks in the park are nice. Kittens are nice. Men with BDE better be out-of-this-world."

I didn't want to kiss and tell. Then again, I was all about fuck and show earlier. "Okay, Lila," I lean my head on the back of the couch. "When we're together, it's like an out-of-body experience. Is that what you want to hear?"

"I knew it," she pats the couch excitedly. "And the BDE?"

"Now that, I'm not telling you."

"That non-answer is an answer," she says smugly.

"Would you answer me if I asked you the same question about Vinny?"

"Damn straight I would," she nods.

"Well?" I turn my head.

"And...his energy, is his energy," she smirks.

We both laugh, and it feels good. I know we've had countless afternoons together over the millennia, but I know they are limited with her fealty all but certain.

"Man, Diablo, you two are fire together. I'm so excited for you."

"Well, don't get too excited," I chew my cheek.

"Why not?" she sits up slightly.

"It's...complicated," I sigh.

"Fealty still an issue?

"It's always the issue."

"Does it have to be?" she asks with sincerity. "I mean, you like him, and he likes you. What's complicated about it?"

"I know you won't understand, but it's not a simple decision for me, Lila."

"It's not for any of us," she says simply. "But eventually, you have to do what makes you happy. And from what I can see, and I won't say I told you so, Dante makes you happy."

"He does," I nod. "But soon, sadness will replace

happiness when he leaves, and time separates us."

"Diablo," she takes a deep breath. "Could you be overthinking it? Could it be as simple as swear your fealty and be happy?"

"No," I shake my head, wishing it were that simple. "But we're working on a solution. A proverbial needle in the haystack, if you will."

"Well, you better find it because when the days are up—"

"You're going with Vinny," I say, matter-of-fact.

"Yes," she looks down. "I didn't know how else to say it."

"I know," I reach for her hand.

"What do you mean?" her head whips up.

"I can see it in the way you look at him. You're already a part of his world. You have been for a long time."

"You can be part of that world, too," she grabs my hand. "Hell, you already are. Dante worships you. You're his queen. So, think about it, please? We could all be so happy together."

If only Lila knew it needed more than just thinking. It meant going back to the beginning, and I couldn't do that. I made my choice. And if Dante were to ask me again if it had been worth it, I'd say yes, unequivocally.

Lila gets up from the couch and makes her way to the counter, looking through a stack of takeout menus. "How about we order some food, make a little popcorn, and watch a movie?"

"Sounds great." I'm eager to put the topic of fealty aside for a while and just enjoy some time with my best friend.

We order from our favorite restaurant and watch a film we both like, and it's just what I need. But when my phone rings later in the day, and I see it's an unknown number, all the anxiety I've been ignoring comes crashing to the surface.

After leaving my house, I sent Minerva a text, but when it

came back as undeliverable, I feared the worst–she thought I had blown her off and was doing the same. Her calling me is good news.

I jump up with my phone in hand. "I'm going to get this."

"Spare room is down the hall to the left," Lila points while stuffing a fistful of popcorn into her mouth.

"Thanks," I quickly hurry down the hall and step into the spare room, answering the phone.

"Well," Minerva's cool voice greets me. "I'm glad to see you didn't fall off the face of the Earth."

"Hi," I clear my throat and close the door. "Minerva, I'm…so sorry I missed you."

"Twice," she clarifies. "You missed me twice. This was my last call."

"I'm sorry," I say again. "I was out of town, and my phone wasn't working. I just got your text today." The lie comes easily, but I'm hoping she buys it.

"Oh," she says airily. "Gotcha. Cell reception can suck in the middle of nowhere."

"Right," I breathe a sigh of relief. "So, how is it going?"

"As you know, I've got two pieces. I'm going in for the third tonight."

"You are?" my voice raises an octave.

"I am," she says airily. "And just a reminder, giving you the first piece was a sign of good faith on my part. I'll keep the rest of the pieces until you have paid in full."

"Understood," I shift the phone away from my mouth and take a breath before continuing. "Any idea on what you want?

"You'll know when it is time," she replies casually, then hangs up.

Once the line goes dead, I start pacing back and forth. I'll have the third piece by tonight, and the fourth when–the next day or the day after? I'm hopeful but also worried we won't get it in time. Or we will, but can't find a loophole, and all of this will have been for nothing.

My mind is spinning so fast that it takes a moment to register when raised voices carry down the hall. Once it does, I storm down the hall, wondering what's going on.

When I get to the living room, I see Lila standing with her arms crossed, shouting at Vinny and Dante. Vinny is looking down, taking it, but Dante's staring back at Lila intently, with his arms crossed.

"Hey!" I shout. The three freeze and turn to look at me. "What's going on?"

"Who were you talking to?" Dante asks. "Was it Lili?"

"What?" I shake my head, confused. "No, she doesn't have my number."

"Thankfully," he exhales, and I notice that he and Vinny have mud on their hands, and is that blood on their shirts?

"Where were you two? And why do you look like you've been in a war?"

Vinny's eyes shine. "We're fine."

"We were putting the pieces of this fucked up puzzle together," Dante adds. "Starting with Lilith."

"Lilith?" I shake my head. "Who's that?"

Dante and Vinny fill me in on who Lilith is and that she is the one that's been feeding me information on the underground network. She sounded like Luke, and I'm angry with myself for being so naïve.

"Why haven't I ever heard of her before?" I look from Vinny to Dante.

"Probably because she and Luke fight so much, we forget she even exists," he shrugs.

"But she does," Vinny adds. "And she can be a real pain in

the ass, so any decade without her is a good thing."

"Okay," I nod. "And the bartender? How does he fit in?"

Dante clenches the fist at his side. "He's been working for her."

I arch a brow. "How do you know?"

"That's why we look the way we do," Vinny says with wicked glee. "We finally caught the slippery bastard and made him talk. He's the one who put the bugs in your house."

I know what Dante said he would do when he found him. "Is he…" I can't finish the sentence.

"Not yet," he shakes his head. "We still need information. But when we get what we need, he will be."

His words neither frighten nor bother me, and the fact they don't doesn't either. Strangely, they send a rush of satisfaction through me.

"What does he want?" I cross my arms.

"Lilith asked him to keep tabs on you and for the server at *Saints* to keep an eye on me."

"She what?" I seethe. Now I knew how Dante felt about the bartender watching me. I wanted to go to *Saints* right now and scratch the server's eyes out.

"I heard about that," Lila says proudly. "Sounds like you delivered a mean right hook."

I shoot Lila a grateful nod. "You taught me well."

"There's more," Dante continues.

Wondering what else is going on, I take a deep breath and turn back to him. "I'm listening."

"It's about why we came back," he looks at me. "And…why we were disagreeing just now."

"Disagreeing," I cross my arms. "The three of you were shouting at each other."

Dante and Vinny are quiet, but not Lila. She looks at both

of them with determination in her eyes. "Tell her," she puts a hand on her hip. "She deserves to know."

Vinny and Dante remain silent, each staring at me with different expressions on their face. "Oh, come on…I can take it. I'm stronger than you give me credit for."

"Oh, I know you are," Dante's eyes flash. "But this will throw you."

"Then throw me," I motion for him to continue. "Out with it."

He looks at Vinny, who nods, then turns back to me and lets out a heavy sigh. "You're…the last undecided."

"What?" I laugh slightly, the idea ridiculous.

"Every undecided has sworn their allegiance. If you're not with us when we leave, you'll be left in Eden, alone."

"That can't be possible," I shake my head. I know how easy it could be for some to swear fealty, but there are a few besides me who vowed they never would.

"It is," Dante grabs my hand. "Vinny and I spoke with them and confirmed it."

"That's why we were arguing," Lila looks at me, apologetic. "I told Dante that I brought up the topic of fealty earlier, and he said that it was off the table and not to bring it up again."

I look at Dante, my chest tightening. "You told them that?"

"I promised you, and I plan to keep that promise. But we have to figure out the answer because there is no way I'm going to leave you here alone."

In Eden, on my own? Just thinking about it makes me feel more alone than I've ever felt. Perhaps that was Luke's plan all along. Take away everyone I cared about, bit by bit until no one was left.

I look at Dante and know what I need to do. "Who are you

calling?" he watches me with a puzzled look as I open my phone and pull up Minerva's text.

"Come on," I mumble, waiting impatiently for the image to load. Once it does, I hold my phone out for him to see.

He grabs it and stares at the screen. "Where did you get this?"

"Minerva. That's who I was talking to earlier. She's been looking for the contract…for me. I don't even know if this is it, but it could be."

Vinny shakes his head and looks from Dante to me. "Why are you looking for it when we already are?"

I answer him but keep my eyes locked on Dante's. "I asked her to."

"We have a ton of resources looking for it. You didn't have to—"

But Vinny doesn't get a chance to finish his response. "She was trying to find a way out of being bound to me," Dante cuts him off.

The look in his eyes makes my chest hurt. "Let me explain."

"No," he shakes his head.

"Please," I beg. "It's not what you think."

He tosses my phone, grabs both of my arms, and backs me up to the couch. I lock my knees and brace myself for whatever tirade he's about to unleash. But surprisingly, he doesn't say anything. Instead, he lets go of my arms and kisses me. I kiss him back with everything in me, needing him to feel how much I want this.

"Hey," Vinny clears his throat. "Do you two want to get a room?"

"Clearly, they're past the 'do we kiss in front of them' stage," Lila jokes.

I ignore them, and so does Dante. He wraps an arm around my waist and pulls me close, grabbing my jaw with his other hand and angling my head so he can kiss me deeper. At this moment, it's just he and I, and that's all that matters.

"I'm not mad," he says when we finally pull apart. We're both slightly breathless and eyes only on each other.

My heart is racing, and I can feel my cheeks are flushed. "You're not?"

"No," he presses his forehead to mind. "I've been horrible to you for so long. I don't blame you for wanting to be rid of me."

"But I don't want that anymore. You believe me, don't you?"

"I do," he whispers in my ear. "I feel how much you want us every time we're together."

My hand finds his chest, and I grip it tight. "So, you're not mad? Really?"

"Hell no," he flashes a beautiful smile. "My being an asshole paid off in a way. We're one step closer to what we both want."

"But we don't even know if it's the contract."

"I can solve that right now," he lets go of me and reaches into his pocket for his phone. "Send me the image."

I do as Dante asks, and when it pops up on his phone, he steps away to make a quick call. When he finishes, he comes back over. "Okay, we should know if it's the contract in a couple of minutes. David will send us a text."

I look at him, confused by what's happening. "Who's David?"

"A relic hunter. We need artifacts from time to time, and he helps us track them down. He's studied a lot of the ancient languages, including Enochian."

230

"Wait, what?" I look at him, my mind spinning. "Are you kidding?"

"Nope," he smiles. "There's not much on the image, but it should be enough to tell if it's the contract or not. And if it is, we're in good shape. We know what Minerva wants and can make it worth her while to get the rest of the pieces, fast."

"She doesn't want money," I shake my head. "She's elusive with what she does want, though."

"Oh, I'm aware," he says wryly. "Minerva's currency is secrets, and we've got them in spades."

I'm stunned by this strange turn of events and feel like I should pinch myself. "So, it's okay that I did this?"

"It's more than okay," Dante's eyes light up. "How long did it take her to find this?"

"I reached out to her a year ago."

"A year?" he runs a hand through his hair, face falling slightly. "Okay, that's fine," he nods, and I can tell he's trying to convince himself. "We can work with that if we have to. How many pieces are there?"

"Four in total. But it didn't take her a year to find the first piece," I clarify. "She found it last week and the second piece when we were in London."

"Really?" his smile returns. "Now that's good news. When does Minerva plan to have the rest?"

"She's planning to get the third piece tonight, and I'm not sure about the fourth. I imagine soon."

"Okay," his smile grows. "Question though, where are they?"

"The Vatican," my eyes narrow. "They're in some kind of digital vault."

"Of course," he shakes his head. "Should've known. Regardless," he reaches for my hand, "this is good news."

Heat surges between our palms and shoots up my arm. "You think?"

"I know." He pulls me to him again and draws me into a kiss when his phone buzzes.

My heart starts to race as he reaches into his pocket and takes out his phone, reading a text. "Well?" I ask impatiently.

He looks up and smiles. "From what David translated, it looks to be the contract."

"Well, alright!" Vinny claps. "Sounds like we have something to celebrate. How about a drink? We all deserve one, I think."

Dante lifts his chin at Vinny but keeps his eyes on me. "Sounds good. Just give us a minute."

"You got it," Vinny slings an arm around Lila and pulls her towards the kitchen. "Let's go, sweetness."

Once it's the two of us, Dante pulls me close. "Just a couple more days, then it's you and me, forever. You believe me, right?"

I rest my head against his chest, wanting to believe him more than anything. "I do."

The four of us spend the rest of the night together, and when Minerva texts to let me know that she has the third piece, I manage to relax and have some fun. But I can't ignore the foreboding lurking, threatening to swallow my forever.

28
DIABLO

Later that night, I'm awakened by a horrible dream. After finding the bed next to me empty and a note on the nightstand from Dante that says he's in the gym if needed, I push the covers off, throw on one of his shirts, and tiptoe down the hall.

Crossing my arms to brace against the chill in the air, I push through the door to the stairwell and follow it down to the gym. Dante's in the corner doing a series of reps on a bench press when I get there. His earbuds are in, and he doesn't hear me, so I stand back for a moment and admire him.

His chiseled body is perfection, every muscle defined by an exercise meant to sculpt and strengthen, and he wears a look of intense concentration on his face. His beauty takes my breath away, and my heart flutters with the realization that he's mine.

I make my way over to him and straddle his legs. Feeling me, he grins. "Did anyone ever tell you not to sneak up on someone with weights in their hands?"

"Is that dangerous?" I ask coyly. He sits up and sets the weights down on the floor, then removes his earbuds and shoves them into the pocket of his workout shorts.

"It is, but something tells me you like a little danger." He runs his hands up the back of my legs, and when he reaches my bare bottom and realizes I'm not wearing any underwear, grabs my ass with both hands and pulls me down onto his lap.

I run my finger down his chest. "You're sweaty."

"Then a little more sweat won't hurt," he kisses my neck, pressing his drenched body against me.

I smile and lean my head back, relishing the feel of his mouth on my skin. When he pulls back, the light in his eyes has faded. "What's wrong?" I ask, pushing aside a lock of hair that's fallen.

He presses his forehead to mine and takes a deep breath. "I wanted to kill that bartender today. Just the idea he was in your house, watching you. I've never felt such rage before. But I didn't because I want to be worthy of you."

"You have always been worthy." I run my finger down his cheek, wanting to tell him just how much so. "I don't want you to be anyone but who you've always been. You are magnificent."

We stare at one another, and I know what's on both of our minds. "Minerva will get the last piece," he says with confidence.

I draw a long breath, wanting to be as confident. "But what if we can't find a loophole?"

"Let me tell you something about contracts," he tucks my hair behind my ear. "They always have a loophole. You just have to find it. It's like a riddle. It's all in the words. And there isn't one I haven't been able to solve yet."

"You're just that good?" I grin.

"Well, I don't want to brag, so maybe you tell me?" he waggles his brows.

"Oh," I bite my lip. "My experience is limited, but you're the best from what I can tell."

"I plan to be the only experience you have," he kisses me and runs his hands underneath my shirt. "Hey, is this mine?"

He cups my bare breasts, and I moan softly. "Yes, why?"

He trails a finger around my nipple. "Who said you could

wear it?"

"Me," I grin. "You've got hundreds of them."

"It does look better on you," he strokes my bare skin with his fingertips. "But it's covered in sweat now. I think you should take it off."

"And I think you should continue your workout," I shake my head.

"Oh, I am, just not in the gym," he presses his growing erection against me. "Let me have you right here," he pulls my lower lip between his teeth and bites down gently, making me shiver.

"I've got a better idea. How about a shower? Then, whatever you want."

"Now, that's a good idea," he moves his hands down to my thighs and gets up from the bench, taking me with him.

I wrap my legs around his waist, and he carries me to the back of the gym, not up to his place. "Where are we going?"

"To the shower," he winks.

"Here?" I look at him, eyes wide. "What if Vinny comes down to work out?"

"Oh, he's already working out, no doubt," Dante grins.

I press my lips together and shake my head, realizing what he means. "Thanks. I didn't need that in my head."

"They're like rabbits," he carries me into the bathroom and sets me down on the sink. "Nothing we can't top, though. Don't move."

I look around, drinking in the spacious bathroom. It's bigger than mine and spotless for a gym, which is impressive.

Turning my attention back to Dante, I watch as he reaches into the shower and turns it on. From here, I have a prime view of his ass. Like the rest of his body, he has muscles there, too, and I'm turned on just looking at him.

He walks back to the sink, and I pull my shirt overhead before he picks me up and carries me to the shower. Steam fills the stall as we step inside, and once my feet are on the ground, he squirts soap on his hands, rubs them together to create a lather, then washes his body.

I clench my legs together as I watch him, my arousal growing by the second, and once he's finished, he squirts more soap onto his hands and then turns me around. He washes my back slowly, then reaches around to lather up my breasts and stomach, then slips his hand between my legs.

I press my hands against the tile wall and arch into him as he teases me. "You're killing me."

"Good," he buries his head in my neck and then lifts my leg, sets my foot on the low bench, and enters me in one thrust.

The sensation of him filling me sends a rush of heat shooting through my body. I brace one hand against the wall and reach up and grab his neck with the other as he pounds into me hard and fast. With the combination of his touch, the water, and the intensity in which he holds me against his chest while flicking his hips, it's not long before we're moaning in our shared climax.

Once we've dried off and made our way upstairs, we crawl into bed. Dante falls asleep quickly, but I lie awake, watching him. He sleeps peacefully on his stomach, head to the side with both hands tucked under the pillow, and I have a perfect view of his back.

I've seen every inch of his body and traced his tattoos, but this one is more breathtaking than all the others. I trail my hand along the flames, then kiss the scars on his shoulder blades before curling up against him and closing my eyes.

I wake the following morning to the smell of something

cooking, and when I make my way into the kitchen, I find Vinny and Lila at the stove and Dante at the counter drinking a cup of coffee.

"Hey, look who's up," Vinny points a spatula at me. "What'll it be, eggs or pancakes?"

"You're cooking?" He's wearing an apron that says, 'Kiss the Chef...Pucker Up,' and I can't help but laugh.

"Dante and I are great cooks, didn't you know?" he winks and turns back to the stove.

"Oh, I know he is," I make my way over to Dante and sit down on his lap.

"Morning, angel," he kisses the side of my head.

I warm with his touch and wonder why Lila and Vinny are here so early. "What are you two doing here?"

"Cooking breakfast, obviously," Lila winks and cracks an egg over a mixing bowl. "Vin and I got to talking, and we thought, there's no use in walking around on eggshells all day. No pun intended," she tosses the shells in her hand into the trash can. "Why not start the day with breakfast and then do something fun. It took some convincing of sour puss over there who wanted to hog you to himself, but he gave in, eventually."'

"Oh yeah?" Lila places a coffee in front of me. I reach for it and give her an appreciative smile.

"I simply told him he couldn't keep you cooped up all day when your best friend and brother want to spend time with you, too," she says as sweet as candy.

"Oh, is that what you are now?" I take a sip.

"Diablo," she wipes her hands. "You've been my best friend since—"

"Not you," I laugh and nod at Vinny.

"Hey," he turns to me, serious for a moment. "I will tell

you the same thing Dante told Lila. You're family. I got your back, always."

I look at Dante and take a sip of coffee. "You said that?"

"Of course. She's like my sister," he looks over at Lila, lip tugging up at the corner. "The annoying, loud sister that's banging my best friend."

"Okay, now wait," she laughs. "If Vin is your brother, and I am your sister, does that make him and I siblings?"

"Baby," Vinny kisses her. "You're not my sister. But you can call me daddy, anytime."

Dante laughs, and it warms my heart. I could get used to this–all of us together. But then I remember what we need to do to make that happen, and the daunting task still ahead turns me silent.

"We're going to break the contract," Dante whispers. "I promise."

"What if she can't get the fourth piece?" I look at him. "What if there isn't a way out? What if there is no loophole?"

"She's found three pieces in what…six days. We'll have the fourth soon," he says with conviction. "In fact, why don't we start the celebration now."

Dante suggests the four of us head over to *Scorched* and get tattoos. He believes this century will be the turning point for all of us and is worthy of another one. Lila and Vinny agree excitedly, and despite the sliver of doubt that lingers, I allow myself to believe it and get excited, too.

29
DANTE

I shake my head, hoping Diablo changes her mind. She has her heart set on wings like mine, but I can't bear to see her flawless skin covered in ink. I'm trying to help her find a design she likes while Lila and Vinny are in the back getting theirs.

I'm having a tough time maintaining my position, though, given how she's looking at me. "Maybe start small," I suggest.

"What, like a heart with your name on it?" she laughs.

"I like the sound of that." I run my hands over her bottom. "Right on this delectable ass of yours."

"You're too much," she laughs and flips through the sketchbook.

"I am, but the way you take me is beautiful." My voice is smoky and does nothing to mask the not-so-subtle double entendre.

"What are you getting?" she looks up at me, the fire in her eyes matching mine.

"It's a surprise," I grin, my hand twitching with anticipation. "But I think you'll like it."

"I've liked all of your surprises so far." She flashes me a luminous smile, which pierces through my chest. "Besides, I don't know why you're against me getting wings like yours."

"Because," I run my thumb along her jaw, "you're perfect just the way you are."

She tips her head up, lips ghosting mine. "I'm tired of the scars of the past. And maybe, I want my wings back, but on my terms, as you did."

"How about I let you touch mine any time you want?" I rub her back suggestively.

"As much as I like the sound of that," she laughs, "I need...something."

"Oh, I'll give you something," I growl, pulling her close.

"Dante," she swats my shoulder and turns around. "Help me."

"Fine, fine," I lean my chin on her shoulder. "Let's look."

She flips through the pages, and nothing looks fitting until something pops out towards the back of the book. "How about this?" I point down at the page.

She stares at it for a moment, then nods. "It's perfect. Where should I put it?"

I use my free hand to move her hair to the side and kiss the back of her neck. "How about here?"

Feeling my lips on her skin, she inhales. "We're talking about the tattoo, right?"

I press against her, our bodies fitting perfectly together. "Yes," I whisper. "By the way, have I told you how sexy you are?"

She tilts her head, giving my mouth better access. "About a hundred times."

"How much I want you?" I whisper.

She inhales as I lick her earlobe. "A...hundred and one."

I stop and close my eyes, filled with unparalleled devotion for the angel that owns my heart. "How much I adore you?"

She freezes for a moment, then turns around slowly. "What did you say?"

"I mean it," I place my hand on her cheek, never feeling anything more. "I adore you, Diablo. I always have."

She places her hand on mine and kisses me, sucking the air

from my lungs. "Me too."

"Geez," Lila comes through the door and rolls her eyes. "Do you two ever stop?"

"Um," Diablo clears her throat as we pull apart. "I believe I could say the same of you two."

"Yeah," she looks at Vinny, who comes up behind her and smacks her on the ass. "It's true."

"What did you get?" I nod at Vin.

He twists so we can see the back of his neck. It's an upside-down feather with a shaft that's the blade of a sword.

"Wait," Lila twists so we can see her neck. "You have to see them together." She has the same tattoo. Only it's in the opposite direction.

"It's perfect," Diablo nods with approval.

"What about you two?" Lila asks.

"She's having my name inked on her ass," I say casually.

"He's putting an arrow on his lower stomach that points down and says mine," Diablo says without missing a beat.

Vinny and I stare at her, stunned, while Lila barks a laugh. "What have you done to her?" Vinny shakes his head and looks at me when he can finally speak. "She was the sweet one."

"Oh, she's sweet, alright." I stare at my angel. There has never been another in existence more perfect for me. How lucky am I that the broken stars matched us?

"Alright," JJ calls from the back room. "Dante, you're up."

"Come on," I reach for Diablo's hand. "Let's go."

We make our way to the backroom, and JJ smiles at my attentiveness as he inks Diablo's neck. I raise my eyebrows to say, 'yes, she has me around her finger, so what.'

Like everyone she meets, Diablo charms JJ. He laughs and listens to her stories, talking as if they've known each other forever. Everyone she meets falls under her spell. Hell, she charms me every second I'm with her. It must be the angel effect, remnants of her ethereal spirit that never left.

Once JJ finishes Diablo's tattoo, he rubs it with petroleum jelly and covers it, then gives her instructions on how to care for it. Since I know them like the back of my hand, I promise JJ that I will make sure she's caring for it properly.

After he cleans up his workstation and readies it for me, I reach into my back pocket and pull out a folded-up piece of paper. I hand it to him, and he takes a look.

"What is it?" Diablo asks, curious.

"It's a surprise," I shoot him a look, and he holds the paper away from her. "Why don't you go read and wait," I shake my head and laugh. "It shouldn't take long."

"Fine," she looks at me innocently, then sits down in a chair across from the workstation, reaches into her bag, and takes out a book.

She starts reading as JJ begins, and when he finally finishes, I look down to examine his work. It's flawless as always. "Well done, my friend."

She puts her book back in her bag, gets up from the chair, and walks over to me. "Well, what is it?" she asks impatiently.

"Take a look," I hold up my hand.

She looks from my hand to my face. "Enochian?"

"Yup," I nod. "And do you know what it says?"

"You know I can't read it anymore. And I thought you couldn't, either."

"I can't. But David can, and I called him before we came here so he could send me what I wanted to get."

"And that was?" she looks at my hand again.

"Your name," I smile.

She looks up at me with tears in her eyes. "What?"

This new ink and the one on my forearm are my most important tattoos Both remind me of us–the day we began and my forever–and I'll tell her this when it's just she and I.

"It's your name, angel," I say again. "So you're always with me."

She shakes her head and looks at me, her face a mix of surprise and affection. "I… don't know what to say."

"You don't have to say anything," my smile grows. "Now, why don't you show Lila your tattoo? I'll be right out."

"Alright," she leans down and kisses me, then makes her way to the front.

Once she's gone, I look at JJ. He's wearing the biggest shit-eating grin I've ever seen. "Go ahead and say it."

He holds up his hands. "I wasn't going to say anything."

"Of course, you were," I smirk. "I know you, JJ."

"I was just going to say that it's nice to see you happy, that's all," he reaches for his tattoo gun and starts to clean it. "Things are going well, it appears?"

"They are," I push up from the chair, debating whether to tell him about what's been happening…with the bartender and Lilith.

"That's good," he keeps his attention on his equipment. He looks different since the last time we saw him, a bit older if possible.

"Hey, JJ…are you doing, okay?"

"I'm good," he wipes his hands.

"Are you sure?"

"Yes, dad," he looks up. "I'm sure."

I clap him on the shoulder. "How about you, Vin, and I grab a drink before leaving Eden?"

"I'd like that," he nods. "You should spend all the time you have with your angel."

JJ knows leaving Diablo is hard for me. But he doesn't know everything we're doing to make sure that doesn't ever happen again. "Well, hopefully, I can spend as much time with her as I want after we leave Eden."

He looks at me, clearly surprised. "You secured her fealty?"

I look to the front, where Diablo and Vinny laugh with Lila. "Not exactly. We may have found another way. Cross your fingers for me, would you?"

"I'd do anything for you and Vin. But be careful," his eyes cloud over. "Don't get into trouble."

"Would I do that?" I flash him a wicked grin and make my way to the front. "See you for that drink in a couple of days, buddy."

When I make it upfront, Lila is inspecting Diablo's tattoo. "Thus, from my lips, by thine, my sin is purged," she reads the quote JJ inked on her neck in Elizabethan font. "What does it mean?"

"It's Shakespeare," Diablo smiles.

"But what does it mean?" Lila asks again.

"If you have to ask, you don't need to know," I say smugly.

"No need to get snotty, Dante," she rolls her eyes. "What did you get?"

I hold out my hand, and both she and Vinny examine it. "What does it say?" he looks up.

"If you have to ask, you don't need to know," Diablo shoots back and winks at me.

"Well," Lila crossed her arms. "You two are becoming more like each other by the hour."

Diablo and I look at each other and smile. Two halves, finally a whole. The way we should have always been. I can't help but bite my lip in wanting.

"Alright," Vinny claps. "Everyone ready?"

"Ready," I grab Diablo's hand and tuck her into my side.

"JJ," he calls out. "We're going. See you later, buddy."

We all wave goodbye as we head out the door, but when JJ sees me, I see something on his face that I'd not seen in all the years I'd known him–worry. It lingers in the back of my mind the rest of the day and that night as I lie in bed wide awake, running my fingers through Diablo's hair as she sleeps.

I haven't let on how worried I am because if I do, she'll worry even more, and I can't stand to see fear in her eyes. But the thought of not being with her rips me apart. It sits in the back of my mind, nagging at me.

As if hearing my thoughts, she stirs next to me, and I place my hand on her back, and she quiets again. Ever since that first night in London, when she asked me to stay with her until she fell asleep, I'd done the same thing.

Of course, I'd stayed in her room and watched her sleep that first night together, and I was glad I did. I was there to comfort her when she stirred and had been every night since. But I can't do that if I'm not here. I can't hold or kiss her, and the idea alone drives me insane.

Finding a way to break that contract is more important than any business deal has ever been, and I want that last piece so we can get to work. Knowing the loophole is our best hope fills me with anxiety. I won't accept leaving Eden without her. I just won't.

I curl up next to Diablo and fall asleep, and when the sun comes up the following day, the number of days we have left sits like a rock on my chest. Three days.

30
DANTE

The four of us are shooting a game of pool at my place that afternoon when Diablo's phone rings. She reaches for it so fast that she knocks it off the table's edge, sending it flying. We both drop to the floor, frantically searching on our hands and knees, and when she finally finds it, she pulls it to her ear and answers quickly.

"Put it on speaker?" I whisper.

Diablo does as I ask, and Minerva's smug voice fills the room. "Hey to whoever is listening."

I hold up my hand, and no one says a word while Diablo responds. "Sorry, my hands are full, and I didn't want to miss you." She sounds calm, but I know her heart is racing because mine is also.

"Right," Minerva says dryly. "Well, good news. The last piece was easier to get than I anticipated, and I have it. I will send it along with the others just as soon as we resolve the matter of payment."

"Great," Diablo's face brightens as she flashes me a thumbs up. I nod for her to continue. "You want information, right?"

"I do," Minerva confirms. Her response is so pleasant that it makes the hair on my neck stand up.

Vinny moves his finger in a circle, indicating for Diablo to speed things up and get to the request. "So," she clears her throat. "What information do you want?"

"It's a question, really."

"Okay," she looks up at me, her expression of apprehension and curiosity. "What is it?"

Minerva pauses for a second and then asks the question I've asked countless times before. "Why did you fall, Diablo?"

Diablo shakes her head as if she didn't hear the question. "I'm sorry?"

"Why were you part of The Fall?"

"That's...two questions."

"Not really," Minerva sighs. "It's the same question, asked differently. Really, Diablo, for such a learned individual, I'd think you know this."

The way Minerva just spoke to Diablo makes me want to reach through the phone and snap her neck. But I resist saying anything because we've almost got what we need. I nod for my angel to continue and wait for what comes next.

"Why...do you want to know?" Diablo asks crisply.

"That is not relevant. I did a job for you, and now you owe me. And I will take that payment in an answer."

"What value does that question have for you?" Diablo's voice is shaky, and her composure is fading.

"Everything has value, Diablo."

"Not that," she says simply.

"You want what I found, or you don't," Minerva says coolly. "There's only one answer."

Diablo neither blinks nor breathes. She simply stands there frozen, not saying a word. "Minerva," I cut in, surprising everyone.

"Dante," she laughs. "Thought you might be there. How are you?"

"I'm not in the mood for games, so cut the shit, and name your price."

"I already did," she laughs haughtily.

"I'm talking about money, Minerva. I know how much you like it, and you know I have more than enough. Name the amount, and it's yours."

"Come now, Dante," she tsks. "Not everything is about money. I need the answer, or what I found stays with me."

Diablo is quiet, her face unreadable. I want nothing more than to hang up and find another way. But there isn't one. We need the contract, and we're seconds away from having it.

"Tell her," Lila whispers to Diablo.

Whatever trance she's been in appears to break, and she looks from me to Lila. "I...can't."

The question hasn't simply scared Diablo. She is downright terrified. I can hear it in her voice and see it in her eyes. I grip the phone, knowing what I need to do.

"Minerva," I set my jaw with determination. "Remember that job you did for me?"

"Which one?" she asks flatly. "There's been a few."

"Berlin," I reply with little emotion myself.

She pauses for a moment, then responds. "Yes."

"You give us the pieces, and that stays buried."

There's another pause, and I look at Vinny, who stands with his fist clenched close to his mouth. "Two pieces, and that stays buried," she says crisply.

"All the pieces," I say again, "and I give it to you so you can bury it yourself."

"Fine," Minerva laughs icily. "You drive a hard bargain, Dante. It makes me almost wish you didn't have a dick."

Diablo looks up, and her eyes come to life with a flicker of fire. Seeing my angel return from whatever has paralyzed her makes me warm. "Well, I do," I grin. "And I like to use it. So, the documents?"

"Right," Minerva laughs. "I just sent them. When can I

expect payment?"

I see an incoming text on Diablo's phone from an unknown number. Looking at Vinny, he nods back at me. "You should have it now," I confirm.

The sound of fingers moving swiftly across a keyboard fills the line for a moment. "Received," she says simply. "The code for the message is 0667. Nice doing business with you, Dante. And Diablo," she adds. "Good luck."

The way she says it makes the hair on the back of my neck stand up a second time. I hand Diablo her phone, moving my neck from side to side to ease the sensation. "Will you send her message to me?"

She clicks on it, and it pops up on my phone in seconds. I send it to Vinny, then set my phone down and take a deep breath.

"I'll call David and tell him to get started," Vinny pounds his fist on my shoulder once.

"Thanks," I watch as Diablo walks down the hall to my bedroom. "I'll…be back."

I make my way to the room and find her staring out the window. "Why would Minerva ask me that?"

"It doesn't matter," I close the door. "We got what we needed."

"Did it cost you?" she turns to me, eyes full of dread.

"Not as much as losing you would," I cross the room and come up next to her.

She closes her eyes, and a tear spills free. The pain she carries is rooted so deeply. I want so badly to ease her grief.

I pull her to me, and she leans her head against my chest. "You asked me the same question once," she says softly. I don't say anything. I just hold her tight and listen. "And you asked me if it was worth it. I can't answer the first part, but I can tell you it was. And I would do it again in a heartbeat."

I can tell the admission is hard for her, and it fills me with an incredible sense of privilege. If and when she wants to tell me, I will be there. Until then, I'll wait.

I kiss the top of her head. "Hey, how about we find that loophole so I can take you home for good?"

She tips her head up, a small smile pulling at her lips. "I like the sound of that. Do we expect to hear back from your contact soon?"

"Vinny is talking to him now. It shouldn't take long."

"Alright," she takes a deep breath and wipes her cheeks as we head back to the living room.

An hour later, David texts. "The translation is ready. He emailed it to both of us." I grab my laptop from the counter and hand it to Vinny. "Can you wire his payment and pull it up?"

"You bet," he grabs it while holding his cell in the other hand. "I'm wiring the money now."

"Great," I squeeze Diablo's hand. "I'll be right back. I just want to give David a quick call."

I walk over to the other side of the room as Vinny sets the laptop on the table and pulls out a chair to take a seat; Diablo and Lila are standing behind him, looking over his shoulder.

"The money should be in your account," I say when David answers.

"It's there," he acknowledges. "Thanks, Dante."

"Were there any problems?" There's so much more I want to ask but can't.

"I was able to thread together what I think is a solid translation."

"That's good to hear," I exhale and look down.

The line goes quiet for a moment. "Dante, can I ask you a

question…about those documents?"

"Depends," I pinch the bridge of my nose.

"Right," he takes a deep breath. David is used to my cryptic responses. The items we have enlisted his help to find have always been on a need-to-know basis, and he respects this.

"Are they what I think they are?" he asks cautiously.

I look over at Diablo, and feeling the weight of my stare, she turns and looks back at me. "What do you think they are?"

"Come on," he huffs. "Give me more credit than that."

David has helped me a lot over the years, and he just did the impossible. He deserves to have at least one of the universe's great mysteries answered.

"Yes," I reply as Diablo returns her attention to the laptop. "They probably are."

David inhales sharply. "Dante, this is incredible."

"Not really, because it's about to make or break someone who means everything to me."

"Oh," he pauses. "I'm sorry. I just…to know what it is…or what it's from, rather…it's a lot to process."

Of course, it is. A document that confirms the War in Heaven is both a theologian's dream and a relic hunter's greatest treasure. "I trust you will be discreet."

"Of course. I would never break your trust, Dante. You know that. But may I ask another question?"

"Depends," I say for a second time.

"That someone you mentioned…is it the one in the translation?"

I look over at Diablo again, my heart thumping hard against my ribs. "What did you say?"

"Have you not read it yet? No, of course not," he exhales, "you've been talking with me. Well, when you do, if you have questions, give me a call."

I nod but say nothing as he hangs up. A strange feeling sweeps over me as I make my way over to the table. Every step is weighted, almost as if I'm walking through sand.

Diablo watches me with a peculiar look in her eyes. "Are you coming?"

I reach for her hand, and when I feel it in mine, the air rushes back into my lungs, and the heaviness in my steps eases. "Do you have it up?" I ask, mouth dry.

"Vinny just opened it, but we haven't read it yet. We were waiting for you."

"Alright," Vinny knocks his knuckle on the table. "Let's see what we're dealing with."

Diablo squeezes my hand, and I squeeze hers back. Then we look at the screen and read the contract that started this all.

DOCUMENT 1
FIRST, THERE WAS LIGHT.
THEN CAME THE DARK.
THEN AN ANGEL,
THAT LOVED LIKE A HEART.
SHE ASKED FOR A FAVOR,
AND I HAD TO OBLIGE.
AS HER PLACE IN HEAVEN,
WAS OF EQUAL SIZE.
HER TEARS, HOW THEY FLOWED,
HER WINGS, HOW THEY CRIED.
THE LIGHT SHE POSSESSED,
FADING FROM SIGHT.

DOCUMENT 2
YES, I STARTED THE WAR,
FREE WILL OR ABOVE.
BUT IT WAS ALSO ABOUT,
THAT ONE RECKLESS LOVE.

There's always a price,
When you choose to deceive.
The one who created,
All of you and me.
You, my dear Fallen,
Were born from this fight.
The wants of but one,
Coming at a great price.

Document 3
On this day, you must choose,
One of the sides.
In which to exist,
And forever align.
Me, or alone,
There is but one choice.
For once you have chosen,
It is forever your voice.

Document 4
To those who swear loyalty,
Forever you'll reign.
To the undecided,
Forever your pain.
Bound for eternity,
To one most like you.
Your fate for your role,
It is what I will do.
But for the angel who loved,
And the one that remains.
They will sit at my throne,
If one and the same.

The room is quiet as we finish reading the translation, each staring at the laptop, eyes wide with disbelief.

"That's not what we signed," Vinny's booming voice shatters the silence.

"It is," I point at the last page with our signatures that David attached to the translation.

"I see the signatures, but that's not what we heard," Vinny looks up at me. "You don't remember any of that, do you?"

I run a hand over my face. "No. But it's been thousands of years. Maybe some of the details got twisted over time?"

"No way," he shakes his head. "Not so much that it's an entirely different contract."

Lila looks at Vinny, then at me. "You didn't read it? Either of you?"

"No," I shrug. "Why would we?" I try to sound nonchalant, but my mind is reeling.

How could we have signed this? It's nebulous, at best. But as soon as the question crosses my mind, the answer follows. We fell for greed. We fell for desire. And we signed it because we were told we would get all that and more.

"Oh, I don't know," she puts a hand on her hip. "Maybe because it's a forever binding contract."

"Well, did you read it?" I shoot back.

"We weren't allowed to," she crosses her arms. "We were only allowed to sign it after the binding. But if we were given a chance to, I would have."

"What?" I shake my head. "You never —"

A sting in my hand cuts me off, and when I look down, I see Diablo's nails digging into my palm.

I look up, wondering what's going on when I notice her face is pale and her eyes glazed over. "Hey, angel," I ask with alarm. "Are you okay?"

"I think I'm going to be sick." Almost as if it's happening in slow motion, she pulls her hand from mine and falls back.

"Diablo!" I catch her as her eyes roll back in her head, and she passes out.

When she doesn't respond, I pick her up, carry her to the bedroom, and lay her down on the bed. "Can someone get me a cold towel?"

Lila goes into my bathroom, runs a hand towel under the faucet, then brings it back to me. I place it on Diablo's head while holding the back of my hand to her cheek. She's burning up, and her pulse is racing.

Lila looks down at the bed; face pinched with worry. "Is she okay?"

Diablo stirs, and she curls towards me instead of opening her eyes. "I don't know," I admit. "Maybe the last twenty-four hours have taken their toll?"

Vinny slings his arm around Lila and pulls her to his side. "Is there anything you need us to do?"

Diablo's pulse begins to steady, and her temperature is evening out. "She appears to be settling. Give me a minute, and I'll be right out?"

"You got it," Vinny tugs Lila's hand. She looks at Diablo again and sighs, then heads with him down the hall.

I watch the gentle rise and fall of Diablo's chest, wondering what's going on, and when she appears to be resting peacefully, I get up from the bed and make my way back to the living room.

"Alright," I run my hand over my face, pull out a chair and sit down next to Vinny. "Where were we?"

"Is she okay?" Vinny looks at me.

"Yeah," I take a deep breath. "Let's just figure this out."

He nods and turns back to the computer, and the three of us get back to work.

After what feels like hours, I lean back in my chair, put my hands behind my head, and blow out an exhausted breath.

Lila looks from me to Vinny. "Is anyone going to

acknowledge that—"

"No," I cut her off, knowing what's going through her mind because it is also in mine.

"But Dante, you can't deny—"

"No," I say again, more firmly. Vinny looks up from the computer, brow arched. "Sorry." I hold up my hand in apology. "I know, Lila. I know."

The last of their kind. It is unnervingly similar to what's happening right now. But the rest doesn't make sense.

"Why don't you call David?" Vinny suggests.

"Yeah," I rub a hand over my face. "Maybe he knows something that can help."

"Does he know what he's doing?" Lila looks from me to Vinny. "I mean, could this translation be wrong in any way?"

"Doubtful," Vinny shakes his head. "David knows more about ancient languages than anyone I know."

Vinny rattles off David's past work as I slip down the hall to use the spare room to call him, so I don't wake Diablo.

"I thought you might be calling," he says after picking up after the first ring.

A barrage of questions rushes at me. Did the translation make sense? Could it be off? Could any of the words be wrong? But one hits the hardest—who is the angel in the contract?

I don't know what to ask or where to begin. Thankfully, David continues. "Have you ever heard of a drawing called *Sacrificium*?"

"No," I exhale. "Should I?"

Papers rustle in the background as David responds. "It's a depiction of the day the angels fell from Heaven."

"Oh really." I can't fight the antipathy in my reply. Countless artists have painted the Fall throughout history, and the most prominent collector of these works was The Church.

"It's of one angel, specifically," David continues, "and it's quite remarkable."

A strange prickling sensation crawls up my back, and I straighten. "Oh?"

"You-know-who started The Great War," he whispers. "Right?"

"Yes," I take a deep breath. Of course, I knew who started the war, and I'd been loyal to him since the Fall. "But why are you whispering?"

"I don't need him hanging over my head, if you know what I mean."

Luke had much bigger fish to fry than a relic hunter. "I think you'll be fine," I say dryly.

"Well," David continues. "Like I was saying, you-know-who started the war, but it's believed the angel in the drawing is the one that will start the war still to come."

"What are you talking about?" I sit down on a chair in the corner of the room. "What…war still to come?"

"That I do not know. But I believe the drawing and those documents I just translated are part of it."

I sit back, mind spinning. "Well, what does the drawing look like?"

"I'll send it to you. I'm just trying to find it. I have a copy I stumbled across years ago, and…oh wait, here it is," David's voice fades, then comes back onto the line. "I'm taking a picture and sending it through text now."

I tap my foot while I wait for the text to come in. When it does, I click on it and nearly drop my phone when the image pops up.

"Did you get it?" David asks when my end of the line goes silent.

"Yes," I manage but can't say more. Of all the art I've witnessed and collected, I can honestly say I've never seen anything like it.

An angel lays over a figure, her wings wrapped around it protectively, as tears run down her cheeks. It evokes loss and desperation and would elicit emotion in even the hardest of hearts. But it's not that which has rendered me speechless. It is the angel's uncanny likeness to one in particular–mine.

I swallow to ease the tightness in my throat. "Who drew it?"

"No one knows," David sighs. "The only marking we have to go off is that scribble in the corner. But it can't be attributed to any other work in existence."

"Can you take a picture of the marking close up?" I'm curious if maybe I've seen it before.

"Of course," David confirms. "Sending now."

This time, when I see the image staring back at me, I do drop my phone. The room tilts, and the air thickens as my heart starts to pound and my ears ring.

Thankfully, David's voice grabs my attention through the deafening clamor before I, too, pass out. "Dante, are you there?"

I bend down and pick up my phone. "David, I have to call you back."

I end the call and get up from the chair, storming down the hall. "Where are you going?" Vinny looks up in alarm as I grab my coat and keys.

"If she wakes, tell her I'll be back," I command.

"No problem, but where are you going?" he asks again.

I reach for the door and yank it open. "Hopefully, to get some answers."

31
DANTE

I storm through the door at *Scorched*, calling out JJ's name as I make my way from the front of the shop to the back.

"Dante," he looks up from where he sits, face ashen. "What brings you by?"

Each time I see JJ, he looks worse. Almost as if he is aging by the day. "Hey, what's going on with you?" I crouch down next to him.

"I'm fine," he waves me off, just like he did when I last asked.

I study him for a minute, knowing he'll only be irritated if I ask again, so I cut to the chase. "I need you to tell me about this." I hold out my phone to show him the drawing. "And I know you drew it because I've seen those initials in your sketchbook."

JJ reaches for my phone with a shaky hand, staring at the image for a moment, then gives it back to me. "I'm sorry," he takes a shallow breath. "I tried. I did."

I reach for a chair next to me, roll it over, and take a seat, so we're sitting face to face. "You tried, what?"

He looks up, eyes full of a thousand words I can't make out. "To protect her…and you."

"Are you talking about Diablo?" I rest an elbow on my knee. "When Vinny and I came here that first day we were back, you said she was important. I need you to tell me why. And I need you to tell me when you drew this picture?" I point to the phone.

JJ is quiet, then gets up slowly and shuffles over to a bookcase on the other side of the room. He moves a few things around on the top shelf, then, after finding what he's looking for, pulls it off the shelf and comes back over.

"Here," he hands me a large book and sits down slowly. "You will find that drawing towards the back."

I pull the book to me and open it, aged bindings stretching with the movement, and start flipping through the pages. I pass dozens of sketches, each on a different kind of paper, indicating their origin in time. But when I come to the drawing that brought me here, I stop. It's the same as the one on my phone, but clearly the original, and the detail is extraordinary. Fine lines make up the plumes of the angel's wings, and the tears on her cheeks appear endless. But it's the way she lays over the object she's protecting which makes my chest ache.

"I remember that night like it was yesterday," JJ takes a deep breath. "The night you fell...it was like a million stars had just vanished. It was devastating to see your light fade as you touched the earth. But it was even more heartbreaking to see her."

I look up from the drawing, trying to swallow the lump in my throat. "Who?" I ask, not recognizing my voice.

"The angel that wept," he sighs. "I can still see it in my mind. It moved me more than anything had in my life to see this beautiful being so fierce and devoted to that which she protected. I knew I had to capture the moment, lest I forget, so I did, with what I could find—a ripped piece of parchment and a piece of burned wood from a fire pit nearby."

"Who is she?" I look back down at the drawing, my heart pounding. My need to comfort the angel is strong, but just as powerful is the sense I can feel those same wings around me.

He puts his hand on my knee. "You already know the answer, Dante."

Hundreds of pins prick my skin as I stare at the drawing. He's right; I do. It's Diablo…my angel. I've stared at her more times than I can count, and I'd know her anywhere.

Seeing her like this, so beautiful and bereft, splinters my heart. I run my finger along the etching of her wing, wanting to hold and comfort her.

"She regretted the rebellion," I nod, knowing well the weight of her grief. It's why I promised I would do everything in my power to make sure she never felt that kind of pain again. "It has stayed with her all this time," I look up.

JJ sits back and rubs his thinning goatee. "She did not weep because of the rebellion. She wept for you. It is you she is protecting in that drawing."

Those first moments after The Fall are hard to recall–after we lost our ethereality, and our existence was dark. But in the void, in that endless chasm of nothingness, I have always remembered a light. It's the same light I saw the first time Diablo and I kissed and the one I saw the first time we were together. The light is her. It has always been her.

I look down at my hand, the symbols that make up her name staring back at me. "Why did she fall?"

I need to know what was worth her pain. What reason had brought her to me?

JJ reaches for the book and brings it to his lap, flipping the pages until he stops on another drawing. "It's not about why she fell, but for whom."

He turns the book back to me, and I look down. It's another drawing. Only there are two angels–one is Diablo, and she looks terrified, and the other stares at her in a way that sets my insides on fire. I've seen that fear in her eyes only once, and it was when I asked her why she was so afraid of the angel standing opposite her-Luke.

"I have not looked at that drawing in more than five thousand years," JJ's voice is sad. "But I knew the day would come when I'd have to."

"When was this?" I need to know more. It may explain her loathing for the one to whom I swore allegiance. Although, that loyalty was hanging by a thread just seeing this.

"Shortly before the contract that bound the Fallen," JJ looks at me. "It is Luke and Diablo."

I nod but can't speak. Even though the moment in the drawing happened thousands of years ago, I have to take a breath to steady the anger I'm feeling. "Why is he looking at her like that?" I manage to ask.

"He was angry because of what she was trying to do." I shake my head and look up at JJ. "She is trying to save you."

My eyes widen, and my heart thumps hard against my ribs. "Me? But how could she save me if she, too, was among the Fallen."

"She was an angel of the highest order, Dante. She did not rebel. She would never have gone against her reason for existence for free will. But she would, and did, for the most powerful force in the universe."

I close my eyes, Diablo's voice echoing in my mind-*And I would do it again in a heartbeat.* My throat is dry, and my ribs hurt from the pounding of my heart. "Why did she do it?"

"You know why," he says simply. "You've always known."

Moments Diablo and I have shared over thousands of years flood my mind, including those of the past few days. Even yesterday in this very spot. In each, one thing is consistent. No matter how relentless I was in pursuing her fealty, how she looked at me never changed. Even when I hurt her, it was always there in her eyes–affection.

The reason for my angel's sacrifice presses down on my chest, making it hard to breathe. "She fell...for me."

"She did," JJ smiles softly. "She gave up her spot in Heaven to save you. But when she arrived, Luke was there, and it changed everything."

The walls feel like they're closing in on me. I need air. I set the book down and get up from the chair, taking deep breaths.

"He never planned to give the Fallen their freedom," JJ continues. "He wanted to bind you so you'd forever serve him. But when Diablo arrived, she learned this and made him a deal. Give the Fallen a second chance. Let them choose for themselves who and what to serve."

I stare at JJ, stunned by the revelation. "Fealty was Diablo's idea?"

"It was," he nods softly. "It was she who saved the Fallen. Not Luke."

Those of us who swore our allegiance to Luke did so because it was a way to honor the one who freed us. But knowing that was never his real plan enraged me.

"You said it was a deal?" I think about the second drawing and the look of anguish on Diablo's face and the triumph on Luke's. He never did anything without getting something in return. "What did it cost her?"

JJ lets out a weary breath. "You. She can never reveal to you why she fell or their deal. If she does, he gets her loyalty, and you pay with your existence."

"What?" I stumble backward, the admission making my head spin. "But he forced us together and pushed me to secure her fealty?"

"Yes," JJ sighs. "Luke did that on purpose. He believed if

Diablo discarded her wings for you, she would not be able to keep her feelings a secret for long. He assumed her feelings for you would all but ensure her loyalty to him."

My heart and my fealty...they're connected. That's what Diablo meant that day in her kitchen. "But we're together now," my mind races. "Does that mean she's in danger?"

"I don't know," JJ admits. "Given Luke's penchant for words, I imagine her safety has to do with what she can and can't say."

I think about everything Diablo, and I have said to one another, and JJ is right. When I said I adored her yesterday, she was silent before responding in the only way she could. She did not say those exact words back because it would end me and us.

Diablo's suffering, all this time, was because of her feelings for me. I couldn't believe it. I want to hit something. Worse, I want to tear Luke to shreds. "How could he do this? I thought loyalty deserved better."

"The only loyalty Luke has is to himself," JJ huffs.

"But why?" I shake my head, not understanding. "Why does he want her fealty so bad?"

"She's the highest among the Fallen other than him, and it would be the ultimate middle finger to Heaven to secure her loyalty. Everything he has done has been to win her. Even the terms of fealty."

I look up, my anger growing. "What are you talking about?"

"Ten days every one hundred years. Nothing more, nothing less. What better way to get what you want from one than to keep what they hold dear from them?"

That's where the rules came from–Luke's desire to hurt Diablo and keep us apart? "Son of a bitch!" I fume. All this time, she ran from me because she had to. He made her existence a living Hell.

In me swirled unbridled energy to destroy. When I felt this way, I was capable of doing anything. "Where do you fit in, JJ? How do you know all of this?"

"I witnessed all of it…The Fall and Luke's deal with Diablo. And he gave me a choice–death or my soul. It was an easy decision. Giving up my soul to watch over the angel who sacrificed herself for the Fallen seemed a small price."

"And the drawing?" I want to know how David had a copy of it. "How did it get out of Eden?"

"I didn't know it had gotten out, to be honest," JJ shrugs. "But I guess it's a good thing that it did. Now you know."

I grab the back of my head and let out a heated breath. "I understand why Diablo never told me any of this. She couldn't. But why haven't you?"

"That is part of my deal with Luke," JJ looks down. "I was forbidden from speaking about any of this, or it would mean my end. But the more I got to know you and Vinny, the more you two became like the sons I never had, and I wanted to keep you safe."

"If that's the case, why are you telling me now? Does this mean Luke will be coming for you?"

JJ places a hand on his thigh and takes a ragged breath. "When my health began to decline, I figured my days in Eden were numbered. I planned to tell you and go out with a bang. But it was so nice to see you two together, and I just wanted you to be happy."

My head was spinning with secrets of the past, and all that was happening in the present. It raced around in my mind, each a piece of the same puzzle but not quite fitting together.

"Something's going on, JJ. I don't know what," I shake my

head. "But she needs to get out of Eden. We're trying to find a way out of the contract that doesn't involve her fealty, but I don't know," I close my eyes, thinking of the translation's confusing language.

David looks at me, regret in his eyes. "There isn't a way out of it, Dante. Not once in five thousand years has it been broken."

I run a hand through my hair, my anxiety skyrocketing. "Every contract can be broken. You just need a loophole."

"Are you sure?" he arches a brow.

"Didn't build the empire I did without that very precedent being true. And it has to be. I can't leave her behind. She means too much to me."

"Then you need to go," JJ points to the door. "If you think you can find a way out of it, you must."

I look at my friend, wanting to help him but unsure how. "Do not worry about me," he waves me on. "Your angel needs you."

He's right. I need to save Diablo before time separates us. "Thank you for telling me everything," I grip his shoulder.

"I'm sorry I didn't tell you sooner," JJ pats my hand.

"I understand," I offer him a small smile; thousands of years of friendship passing between us.

"Take the book," he hands it to me. "You should have it. And I suspect you may need it."

I reach for the book and pull it to me. "Are you sure?"

"Yes," he insists. "Now go. When this is over, and Diablo is safe, come back, and we will have that drink. The five of us."

I offer another smile, but it's rooted in anger and worry. I want to save my angel and JJ, and I want the Fallen to know their loyalty was in vain. And I want to end Luke for doing this to all of us, especially Diablo.

"She might not be able to tell you how she feels," JJ calls out as I reach the front of the shop. "But that should not stop you from telling her. She deserves to hear it after all she has done."

I stop, look back at JJ, nod, and then turn around and open the door. He's right. Before going to war, Diablo needs to know who I'm fighting for, whom I will always fight for–her. She is my reason for existence, and I will do whatever it takes to save her now, just like she did for me in the beginning.

32

DIABLO

When I wake up, it's quiet. Vinny and Lila are in the living room talking, and Dante is gone. I should get up and see where he went and let them know I'm okay, but I can't. I'm too weighed down by five thousand years of guilt to move.

It had been a shock to see the contract. Every word squeezed the air from my lungs until there was nothing left. They deserved an explanation for why I passed out, but I didn't know how to give them one. How could I explain the contract was not the deal I made with Luke without risking Dante or me?

The terms are clear–don't reveal why I fell or the deal I made, or Dante would pay, and Luke would get my loyalty. And for five thousand years, I've followed them and buried my feelings. But they never went away and never would. They were as old as my very existence.

However, feelings and wants are a different story, and touching Dante and showing him how I feel and what I want is fair game. When he kissed me at *Saints*, I learned physical contact was a loophole of sorts, and that first night in London, I discovered just how far I could push it.

But while these past few days, I may have learned how to work around the rules and give my heart what it's always wanted while not putting us at risk, Dante deserved to know how I felt. We need to break the contract so I can tell him the truth of my heart.

Not to mention there was the matter of the contract itself.

The translation shocked both Dante and Vinny, which means Luke either changed it or lied when issuing the decree.

I'm asleep when Dante comes back hours later, and the weight I feel eases as he crawls into bed behind me and presses his chest against my back. "Angel, are you sleeping?"

I take a deep breath, and when it catches on my exhale, he wraps an arm around me and pulls me close. "I need to tell you something, and all I need you to do is listen." I close my eyes and steady myself. "I know what you did, and I know why. And just know, I feel the same, with all of my existence."

His words stun me, and the damn breaks and my shoulders shake. "How…do you know?"

"JJ," he exhales. "He told me everything…about the Fall and your deal with Luke."

I turn to Dante and press my forehead to his chest, fresh sobs forming. "How does he know?"

"He's been there since the beginning," Dante kisses the top of my head. "In a way, JJ's been watching over us this whole time."

"I'm so sorry," I bury my head. I can't believe what's happening right now, but I don't care. He knows, and if we only have a few minutes together before everything crashes down around us, I am thankful for them. "You should hate me."

"I could never hate you," he tips my chin up. "You fell for me, angel. I could only ever adore you."

"But I'm the reason—"

He presses his finger to my lips and stops me from saying anything further. "Don't say anything that will give him your loyalty."

"Trust me," I search his eyes, my vision blurred by tears. "I know what I can't say."

Dante was right about the power of words, and there is no careful workaround for the truth of my heart. The terms that bound my fate boiled down to three simple words. They were why I fell and our undoing if I said them out loud.

"I may not be able to say what I want to, but actions speak louder than words," I offer him a small smile.

"Yes, they do," he wipes my sticky cheeks and kisses me. It's searing and reaches into my very spirit.

"What are we going to do?" I ask when our lips part. "I can't keep how I feel to myself any longer, but I can't lose you or have my loyalty go to Luke, and the idea of only seeing you once a century hurts beyond words."

Dante's eyes light up. "We are going to break the contract. Luke lied to you. He lied to all of us. That's the loophole."

"What?" I search his eyes for understanding. "How is that the loophole?"

"I've been going over it in my mind for hours, thinking about everything JJ told me and the translation. The fact Luke knowingly made false statements to get us to sign the contract is false misrepresentation if it has a material effect on the deal. And it did. We sided with him because of what he said. But had any of us known he never planned to give us our freedom, we wouldn't have. It makes the contract invalid. That's the loophole."

"But Luke plays by his own rules. He's a liar and a cheat and will say we made it up."

"I fully expect he will," Dante nods. "But we have the contract, and all of us can attest that what we signed is not what we were told."

"Okay," I consider the logic. "But how do we get everyone to see it in the next two days?"

Dante's smile grows. "At the end of our time in Eden, we

meet at Luke's to review who was successful in securing fealty and who wasn't. They will be here then, and we can show them our evidence."

"But they will hate me. Knowing it was me—"

"Who saved them," he says what I cannot. "Fealty was your idea, not Luke's. And when they know that it's what saved all of us, they too will fight for you."

"But they've been loyal to him for thousands of years," I shake my head. "Why would they believe us over him?"

"They'll have to when I show them this." Dante reaches over to the nightstand and grabs a large book, then places it on the bed and sits up. I do the same and watch while he flips through the pages, stopping on a drawing that makes my heart skip a beat.

I put my hand on it and closed my eyes. The memory of that night is strong, even now. "You fell for me," he says softly. "Then you saved me and all of the Fallen. Now let me do the same, Diablo. Please," he pulls my chin towards him. "I cannot exist without you."

I open my eyes, and the reason for my tears now is the same as it was the night I fell. They are for him and how I feel.

"I tried to hate you," I take a deep breath. "I tried to get you to let me go. But I couldn't."

"You said you fell because of your heart. Now I know what that means," he squeezes my hand.

How I feel was a part of me before I was even in this body. Before I even had a heart, Dante was what I wanted. I didn't want to lose him.

Dante cups my face and looks into my eyes, his reflecting all of what I feel for him. "I know you can't say it, angel. But I feel it. And when the contract is broken, you can say it to me every day, for eternity."

I lean into him, and he wraps his arms around me and holds me tight. "How does everything that's been happening play into all of this?" I ask when we both grow quiet.

"I don't know," he exhales. "Maybe it's some kind of game Lilith and Luke are playing? For all we know, Minerva is working with them, too, and that's why she asked you what she did earlier. To get you to admit what you could not."

"Thankfully, you had an ace up your sleeve. I don't know what we would have done if you hadn't."

"Hey," he tightens his hold. "I will always have your back. No one messes with you and gets away with it. Whoever is involved is going to pay. I promise you."

"So, Luke wants me, and Lilith wants me. Anyone else?"

"You forgot the most important one." I look up and meet his eyes. "I want you, and that trumps both. We will break this contract, and you will come home with me. That is the only outcome I will accept."

Time stands still as he looks at me and all of my longing for him fills my heart. "When you first arrived this time, I was trying to fight with fire so you would let me go. Did you know that?"

Dante laughs softly. "And I was trying to show you a side of me I don't let anyone see so you would trust me and tell me why you fell. I thought if I knew what you wanted, what was worth your wings, I could give it to you. But you broke down all of my walls, and I wanted to be that side for you, more than anything."

The irony we were both playing to win is hard to ignore. "You never had to show me a side of you or be any side because I want all of you. I've always only wanted you."

He kisses me again, this time more fiercely. It creates a spark and a flame all at once, and in seconds we're tearing each other's clothes off.

There is hunger and urgency in our touch, and when I sink onto his erection, he sits up and wraps his arms around me, so nothing separates us. As we move together, heat shoots up my spine, reminding me of the fire that burns for him.

"Don't stop, angel," he whispers breathlessly, and I'm so lost in him that I couldn't if I tried. It consumes all of the fear and lies and drowns me in everything I've ever wanted.

Without breaking our connection, Dante shifts me onto my back. With every flick of his hips, every caress of my skin, he shows me the depths of his heart. "I'm never letting you go," he wipes away the fresh tears that spill. "Never."

We reach the height of our climax together, and as we lie side by side after, I look over at him, filled with everything I feel. "I know," he reaches for my hand and laces his fingers through mine. "Me too."

"Do you think it will work?" I ask softly.

"Sure," he blows out a spent breath. "I might need a minute, though."

"Not that," I smile gently, the thought of a second-round sending a tingle through my already satisfied body. "Showing the translation to the Fallen."

"Oh," he grins and lets out a small laugh. "It has to. And I will fight every one of them until they accept that their loyalty belongs to you, not Luke."

"I don't want their fealty. I just want their freedom."

"And if it comes to it," he turns to me, "you say exactly that."

"Even to Lila and Vinny?" I look down, unsure how I feel about telling my best friend the secret I've kept.

Dante props himself up with an elbow. "We're family. They will not blame you. They will thank you. Without you, we would not exist. It's that simple."

"And if they do?"

"Then I will hold them captive until they don't."

"Would you really do that?" I lift a skeptical brow. Dante and Vinny are closer than brothers. There isn't anything they wouldn't do for each other.

"Angel," he runs a finger down my arm, then kisses my shoulder. "What wouldn't I do for you?"

I curl into him, and he holds me close, not letting go even when he falls asleep. After tonight there are two days left, and I'm so nervous and scared that I'm about to lose everything that only once my silent tears have run dry do I finally drift off, too.

33
DANTE

I wake early in the morning to get something to drink, and when I go back to the bedroom, Diablo is gone. I look up and down the hall, then knock on the bathroom door–no sign of her. After searching my entire place, I run downstairs and pound on Vinny's door to see if she might be there with Lila.

"Yeah?" he answers the door sleepily.

I grip the doorway with both hands, heart pounding in my chest. "Is Diablo here?"

"No," he yawns. Then seeing the look of alarm on my face, he snaps awake. "What's wrong?"

"Shit!" I run up the stairs, climbing two at a time.

Vinny follows me, with Lila on his heels. "What's going on?" she asks sleepily.

"Diablo's gone," I race through my front door and grab my cell phone to check the security footage.

"What do you mean?" Lila watches me, clearly worried. "How long has she been gone?"

Seeing no sign of her on the footage, I slam my phone down and run a hand through my hair, racking my brain, wondering where she could be. "I don't know. A couple of minutes, maybe. She was there when I got up and when I came back, gone."

"Did you try her phone?" she suggests.

"Of course," I shake my head. "But it's on the nightstand."

Lila crosses her arms and sticks out a hip. "Did something happen after we left last night?"

"You can say that." I know Diablo was nervous about telling them the truth, but she wouldn't leave. Not when she knows what's at stake. Maybe she went for a walk to clear her head.

"Like a fight?" Lila crosses her arms and shoots me an accusing glance.

I look from her to Vinny, debating whether to tell them everything. Diablo and I were going to today, but it looks like that moment is now if it's why she left.

"I need to tell you something. But you need to let me get it all out, then ask questions. Got it?"

"Of course," Vinny nods.

I look at Lila. "Alright?"

"Sure," she says crisply.

"No, I mean it, Lila. Not a word until I finish, okay?"

"Fine," she motions for me to continue. "Out with it."

I take a deep breath, then tell them everything–about Luke's original plan for the Fallen, the deal Diablo made to save us, and that it was me she fell for, not the rebellion in Heaven. I even show them JJ's drawings.

"Well?" I look from one to the other when neither says a word once I've finished.

"You told us not to say anything until you were done," Lila says. "Are you?"

"Yeah," I nod, bracing for whatever they're about to say. "I'm done."

"Son of a bitch!" Vinny snarls.

"Exactly!" Lila agrees, moving her head up and down with vigor.

I look from one to the other. There's anger in their eyes, but I know it's not with Diablo. Still, I want to ask to make sure. "So, you're not mad?"

"Mad?" Lila laughs as if it's the most ridiculous thing she's ever heard. "Not at all. I owe her. We all do."

"We wouldn't even be here if it weren't for her," Vinny agrees. "She sacrificed herself for you, for all of us."

"So, you're both okay with all of it? I need you to be honest with me. No lies."

"You don't even have to ask, Dante," Lila's response is automatic. "She's my best friend."

Vinny claps a hand on my shoulder and squeezes it. "The four of us are family. I still got her back, brother. Now, and always."

Vinny's assurance relieves me more than I thought it would. He and I, we'd die for one another. But now that I know the power of connection between two hearts, I also know loyalty and love are forces that, when opposed, can destroy. But together, they're unstoppable, and I know he would fight alongside me for Diablo, just as I would with him for Lila.

"Do you think she left because she didn't think we would understand?" Lila asks sadly.

"Maybe." Her smell still lingers, and it feels like the world is crashing down around me. Where is she? Think Dante, think.

The three of us pace back and forth, each throwing out ideas that the other shakes off. Then, like the clearing of clouds after a storm, I see the answer staring back at me in a copy of the translation on the table–*But for the angel who loved, And the one that remains. They will sit at my throne, If one and the same.*

Red flashes in my mind as the puzzle pieces that didn't make sense suddenly fit perfectly and unnervingly together. "Luke," I clench my fist. "He took her."

"Wait," Vinny holds up a hand. "What?"

I press my finger down angrily on the contract. "He doesn't want her loyalty. He wants her. It's right there!"

Vinny and Lila look down at the contract, then back up, pupils dilated.

"You were right, Lila," my heart starts slamming hard against my ribs. "It does sound like her because it is. I can't believe I didn't see it before."

Vinny picks up the paper and grips it tightly. "You didn't know what you know now."

"But I knew when I came back from JJ's last night, and I should have put two and two together. Now she's gone, possibly taken." I grab my head, a scream building deep within me, and when it finally comes out, it vibrates my chest and shakes the walls. "Fuuuucccckkkk!"

When it stops, and I'm standing there, blood pumping so hard I hear it in my ears, I see something stirring in the corner. Vinny and Lila watch me with bated breath as I cross the room and bend down and grab the culprit by the head. It's a black snake, just like the one I found at Diablo's house, and it hisses at me as I carry it to the window and toss it out.

"What was that?" Lila shudders.

"Luke," I gnash my teeth. It's his calling card. I should've known. But when I swore allegiance to him, I assumed he wouldn't be stalking my angel. Obviously, everything I thought about him was wrong.

"He's right," Vinny looks at Lila and nods crisply.

"There was one at her house the day we got back, and I didn't even think..." my breathing accelerates again. "If he lays a hand on her...if he hurts her, I will burn his fucking empire to the ground."

"Hey, Dante," Vinny looks at me, eyes hard. "Calm down

and just…take a breath."

"Take a breath?" I start to pace. My head spinning as rage rolls in me like molten lava, threatening to incinerate everything in my path. "Would you take a breath if he took Lila? Take a breath," I say again. "How can I take a breath when I can't fucking breathe!" Before I know what's happening, I've flipped the dining room table over and smashed everything around me.

"Hey," Vinny shouts after I've ripped the mirror off the wall, glass laying all around my feet. I look at him, breathing so hard my lungs feel like they will burst. "It's me, brother," he comes over and holds up his hands. "Just…me."

I close my eyes as my body shakes. "If I lose her…."

"I know."

"If he hurts her…."

"I know," he places a hand on my shoulder, grip firm and grounding. "We'll find her, I promise."

I'm seconds away from losing it, and not in the way I just destroyed my house, but in the way I feel myself descending into darkness without her.

"Where do you think he took her?" Lila asks nervously.

I look at Vinny, knowing there is only one place he would have taken her. "You know where."

"Well, let's go get your girl," Lila pushes up her sleeves.

I hurry to the bedroom, change, and race back to the living room. "I swear if anything happens to her…."

"Of course," Lila says as if she's just remembered something.

I grab my keys from the counter and shove my phone into my pocket. "Of course, what?"

"Love is the opposite of hate."

"Yeah, and water is wet, and rocks are hard," Vinny adds.

"What about it, babe?"

Lila rolls her eyes and talks to Vinny and me like we're five years old. "She wanted you, but it was easier to hate what she couldn't have."

"This isn't making me feel any better, Lila." I look at her impatiently, wondering if she has a point in pointing out the obvious.

"No, wait," she holds up a hand. "Hear me out. Love and hate they're opposites. Heaven may be angry with the Fallen but still loves us. That's why we weren't wiped from existence but punished. Heaven wouldn't allow Luke to hurt Diablo because of her reason for existence. It will keep her safe."

I stop in my tracks, thinking about what Lila just said. Could there be some truth in her logic? As mixed up as it sounds, it does make a bit of sense and gives me some hope, which is better than what I had a minute ago.

"I could kiss you," I smile at Lila. "But I won't. One, I love Diablo. She's the only one I want to kiss, forever. And two, Vinny would kill me."

Vinny smirks. "You're not wrong."

Lila's eyes widen, and a smile pulls at her lips. "You love her?"

"Well yeah," Vinny shakes his head. "Isn't that obvious?"

She looks at Vinny, then at me. "Really?"

"Yes, Lila," I exhale. "She might have fallen for me, but I fell for her too, long ago. I've just been too stubborn to admit it."

"I knew it," she smiles smugly.

"So, help me get her back so I can break this contract and tell her myself."

Lila locks her knees as if preparing for battle. "Hell, yes."

"Hey," Vinny looks from Lila to me. "We can't go in, guns

blazing. It's Luke. We need a plan."

"You're right," I shake my hands, needing to do something. "Any ideas?"

"I've got one," he rubs the back of his neck.

"Then let's talk about it on the way."

"Count me in," Lila straightens.

"Oh no," Vinny shakes his head. "You're not coming."

"Of course, I'm coming," she shoots Vinny a ferocious look. "She's my best friend."

"Lila—"

"No, Vinny," she cuts off whatever protest he's about to make. "We're family. And family sticks together. I'm going, and that's final."

I look at Vinny, brows shooting up. "She has a point, brother."

"Great," he exhales and shakes his head. "We've got a three-way ticket to Hell."

"I just hope it's not too late when we get there," I grab my jacket.

"We'll get dressed," Vinny and Lila head to the door. "Meet you in the car in five minutes."

I follow them out, keys in hand. "You've got three."

Lila and Vinny run up the stairs to get dressed as I make my way to the garage and head to the SUV in the corner. My skin is on fire, and I feel anger, anxiety, and something else I've never felt, in all of my existence, coursing through me—fear.

I climb into the driver's seat and stare out the window, every second feeling like an eternity. My mind wanders to dark places, thinking of all the things Luke might do to her.

JJ was right. Luke's the worst. He will rip Diablo's spirit to shreds if he gets his hands on her. Fuck, I grip the wheel. I can't even think about him touching her. She clocked the server for being near me. I can't even imagine what I'll do if he touches her.

What am I saying? Yes, I can. I'll kill him. I've killed before, and I will do it again. For her, I would do anything.

"Alright," Vinny climbs into the passenger seat and Lila in the back. "You know the way."

Lila leans forward, head poking between the front seats. "Where are we headed?"

"I wasn't kidding when I said we had a three-way ticket to Hell," Vinny turns around.

"What?" she swallows. "You're...serious?"

"Yup," he grins. "So, buckle up, baby."

"How long does it take to get there?"

I peel out of the garage and step on the gas. "It's closer than you think."

"We just have to make one stop on the way." Vinny fills me in on his plan, and when done, I nod for him to move forward full speed. It's not bad. Not bad at all. And it has to work because it's the only shot we have. There is no other option.

34
DIABLO

Luke's domain looks as one would imagine–dark, hot, and desperate. Red light seeps through its stone archways, and candle wax drips from sconces lining the walls. It's the least welcoming place one could imagine. Then again, as a bastion of Hell, I didn't expect it to be anything but dismal.

"We're almost there," he guides me down the hall, moving one hand to my lower back while wrapping the other around the handle of his cane.

"Don't touch me," I scowl and pull away–the staff's steel tip clicking on the stone floor grating on my nerves.

Luke is just as I remembered–oppressive and arrogant. I've only been in his presence for minutes, and it's already long enough.

"Now, Diablo," he leans forward. His breath is hot and burns my cheeks. "I know you like having hands on you."

I jerk my head back and shoot him a dirty look. "What's that supposed to mean?"

"Please," he dismisses my protest. "Do not take me for a fool. I know everything that happens in Eden, and I know Dante has spent quite a bit of time touching you."

The idea Luke was behind the devices Dante found in my house rouses my anger. "I guess it's easy to know the business of others when you invade their privacy and bug their homes."

"What?" he scoffs. "Why would I do that when I have eyes and ears everywhere?"

The idea he'd been the one watching Dante and me that day in my library makes my skin crawl. But his response, which is casual and with indifference, offers a bit of relief. Something tells me if it had been him, he'd take great pleasure in telling me so.

"I hear he is quite the lothario," Luke continues, nudging me forward. "A regular chip off the old block."

"Why am I here?" I ask angrily. My skin prickles at his comparison; Luke and Dante couldn't be any less alike if they tried.

"I thought it was time to get reacquainted," he says casually. "After all, it has been many millennia since we knew one another."

His response was partially correct. I don't need to know who he is now because I already know.

It had been many millennia since we knew one another. We were both archangels once–the highest of our kind and of equal importance–but his betrayal twisted the light he'd once been into something unrecognizable.

"That's why you snatched me out of bed in the middle of the night," I sneer. "To catch up?"

He presses his lips together and shakes his head. "That's a bit dramatic, don't you think?"

"No," I grit my teeth. "It's not. You snuck into my house, and—"

"It was not your house," he cuts me off, a flash of red flickering in his coal-black eyes. "It was his house and his bed. But now that you will be my queen, it's time for you to be in my house and my bed."

His response sends a chill down my spine. "What are you talking about?"

"You are home, Diablo," he stops and extends a hand.

"Take a look."

Before us is a vast hall with a domed ceiling and large stone columns. At one end is a black marble throne, with fire pits on each side, and on the other, a vast pit with chains hanging down over it and smoke billowing up from below.

"This is not my home, and I will never…." I can't finish the sentence. The very thought of sharing anything with Luke makes my stomach churn and bile rise in my throat. The room is hot, but despite the beads of sweat forming at the nape of my neck, my body is cold as ice.

"It is," he smiles. "And you can do whatever you'd like to make it yours. Perhaps, bring your beloved books."

I push aside the feeling I'm going to be sick and find my strength. "Why am I here?"

"Now, Diablo," he smiles. "You know exactly why you are here."

"No," I protest, "I don't." I've been careful about every word I said to Dante and taken great care to not put him or me at risk. "I have done nothing wrong. You had no right to kidnap me."

"It is not kidnapping when you belong to me."

The idea he thinks I'm his possession fills me with fury. "I do not belong to you!"

"Ah," he wags his finger. "But you do. When I won your loyalty, I won you."

"You have won, nothing. I've played by your rules for five thousand years, and nothing has changed. I have not, nor will I ever, swear my loyalty to you."

"You do not have to," he says with great pleasure. "It is already mine."

"Already yours," I shake my head. "What does that mean?"

"Now, now," he tsks. "Feigned ignorance does not become you. If you think hard enough, I'm sure you can figure it out."

Luke's condescension infuriates me. I'm about to shove his misguided righteousness right back in his face when the last lines of the contract flash in my mind–the last undecided in Eden and the angel that loved. If they're the same, he wins. His contract of lies says that I am his.

"I knew you were up to something when you began looking for the contract," Luke's smile grows as my face falls with the realization. "And do not bother denying it. I know you have it because I allowed my daughter to find and give it to you."

"Your daughter?" I stare back at him, confused.

"Minerva," he muses. "Smart like her mother and as eager to please, too."

The revelation knocks the wind out of me. "Minerva...is your daughter? But she's...soulless."

"She is Cambion," he corrects. "Half-demon, half-human. How do you think she walks freely between this world and the mortal one?"

I assumed Minerva's hacking abilities made it possible to navigate both worlds. To know she was not soulless at all, but Luke's daughter made my head spin.

"So, she works for you," I close my eyes, reeling.

"She loops me in on requests that she thinks I will find interesting. And in your case, I'm glad she did. It gave me time to prepare."

"You mean it gave you time to rewrite the contract into nothing more than a sheet of lies."

"I have done nothing of the sort," he smirks. "It has remained protected and untouched for thousands of years."

"Protected," I stop and look at him, a chill taking hold of

my bones. The church's representation of the Fallen was always wrong, yet Luke's image always managed to be strangely on point. Now I knew why. "The contract was never stolen" I shake my head in disbelief. "It was you. You gave it to the Vatican."

"They offered me a deal I could not pass up," he admits. "They safeguard the contract while I do my thing. It's a relationship where we both win. I get my souls, and they get the sheep that find their way back to the flock."

"You're despicable," I narrow my eyes in disgust. "Your duplicity knows no limits."

"Those who live in glass houses should not throw stones, Diablo."

"How dare you," I seethe. "I have honored the deal we made, but that contract is not it. It's nothing but lies. And once the Fallen know the truth, your days are numbered."

"The legion is loyal to me," he smooths his hair and turns. "They have no reason to believe anything you say. Not to mention, they signed it, and the contract is irrevocable."

"Save the Fallen!" I shout at his back as he turns and walks to his throne. "That was our deal. My loyalty defaulting to you if I was the last undecided in Eden was never part of it."

"And neither was you fucking Dante!" he sits down, and his eyes flicker with fire.

My head snaps back, shocked by his comment. "The terms were clear. Never confess why I fell or the deal we made. Technically, I have done neither. But you changed the language to fit your needs."

"I did nothing of the sort," he dismisses my claim. "Now, come sit with me. We have much to discuss, you and I."

"I'm not going to discuss anything with you. You're a liar, and I owe you nothing."

"You will," he says coolly. "Or I will end Dante's existence with a mere snap of my fingers."

I inhale sharply, pain stabbing my chest at the very thought. "You can't do that."

"Do you want to try me and find out?" he arches a brow.

I knew Dante would be coming for me, but I needed to stall for time and get Luke's mind on something else. I think about possible ways to distract him, then realize the answer is staring me in the face.

"How did you do it?" I ask with honest curiosity.

Luke sets his cane down and stares at me. "How did I do what?"

There was nothing Luke liked more than himself. I was sure he'd enjoy regaling me with stories of his cleverness. "How did you get the rest of the undecided to swear their fealty?"

He considers the question before responding. "Everyone has their price. Even the undecided."

"Not me," I lift my jaw in defiance. "I can't be bought."

"We both know that's not true," he studies me. "You will do anything to save Dante. You already did."

I clench my fists, angry with myself for bringing the focus back to Dante. "He swore his allegiance! Does loyalty mean anything to you?"

"He wants what I want," Luke says coldly. "And I cannot have it."

"You don't want me," I turn my head. "You want my loyalty."

"Now see, that's where you're wrong," he sits back, eyeing me lasciviously. "I've watched you, Diablo. You fascinate me."

"Well," I turn my head in disgust. "You repulse me."

"You said something similar to Dante, and look how that

turned out. Perhaps you'll kiss, then hit me, too," he grins.

Well, that confirmed the bartender was serving both Luke and Lilith. He told Luke everything that happened between Dante and me that first day at *Saints*. "I don't know what game you and Lilith are playing," I cross my arms, "but you need to leave me out of it."

"Lilith?" he sits up. "How do you know about her?"

Her name appears to have struck a nerve. "Trouble with your girlfriend?"

"Do not speak of things you know nothing about," he sits back stiffly and turns his head. I can see the subject is one he'd rather not talk discuss.

"Oh, I know plenty," I press. "Like how the two of you love to play games. Perhaps, she's playing one with you right now."

"What Lilith does, is none of my concern," he scoffs.

Remembering what Vinny said about Luke's on-again, off-again relationship with Lilith, I wondered if this meant they were currently off. "If Lilith is not your concern, then why is she in Eden, and why is she following me?"

Luke whips his head back in my direction, eyes, and tone cold. "What do you mean, following you?"

The bartender had bugged my house under Lilith's orders but did not tell Luke. At the same time, Lilith had not told Luke she was in Eden. It appeared as if the bartender was playing both sides, and Lilith was keeping secrets of her own. Why, however, I hadn't a clue.

I couldn't worry about it, though. Right now, my focus needed to be on getting away from Luke and back to Dante. "I don't know what she wants with me," I cross my arms and look away. "Maybe you should ask her yourself."

Luke slams his hand down on the arm of his throne. "I am

asking you!"

"I'm not telling you anything," I say defiantly.

Luke jumps up from his throne and eats up the space between us. "Listen to me," he grabs my arm. "You will do as I tell you!"

I look down at his hand and back up. "Let go of me."

He yanks me to his chest, and the contact makes his eyes flash. "Are you this willful with him?"

I try to pull free, but his hold tightens and makes my skin burn. "I said, let go."

"I can smell him on you," he sneers. "Tell me, Diablo, did you like having what so many others before you have had?"

"Shut your filthy mouth," I spit, anger ripping through me.

"When you became my queen, you were to be untouched. I was supposed to be the first to have you. Not him! But don't worry," Luke's nostrils flare. "I'm going to enjoy erasing Dante from your mind. He won't even be a distant memory when I've finished with you."

I close my eyes, the very idea of Luke touching me making my stomach churn violently. "Why are you doing this?"

"Because he still wound up with you after everything I have done, and I cannot allow it."

"So, what," I yank my arm free. "You're jealous?"

"There is no reason for me to be jealous. From this day forward, you are mine. End of story, and you and Dante. You cannot fight your fate."

I didn't think I would be capable of such hatred, yet I don't just hate Luke. I want him to pay. He ripped me away from my safety, away from Dante. Luke needed to know just how hard I would fight for the one who owned my heart.

"You're right," I say simply.

"Well," Luke takes a deep breath. "You're finally coming to your senses. See, that wasn't so—"

"About Dante," I cut him off, flashing a wicked grin. "He is an amazing lover."

Luke's smile fades, and his face twists in anger. "I would stop if I were you."

I should heed his warning but want him to feel what I'm feeling. My need for revenge fills every inch of me.

I think about Dante-the way his touch brings me to life and grants me peace. About the pleasure, he draws from me, and I, him. "I never tire of his touch and will never want another."

"Enough!" Luke shouts, bringing the back of his hand down hard against my cheek. The large ring on his index finger cuts my lower lip and draws blood.

I'd never been hit before, and the sensation was strange. I taste iron on my tongue as my eyes water and my head throbs.

"Look what you made me do?" he reaches for my face, and I flinch.

Despite the pain radiating down my shoulders, I feel something else deep in me-rage.

"He will come for me," I swipe my finger over my lip, the cut his ring left behind stinging. "And when he does and sees what you've done, he will kill you." Luke turns and walks back across the hall. "Did you hear me…he will kill you!"

After settling into his throne, he leans back, takes a deep breath, and locks his dark eyes on mine. "Not if I kill him first."

35
DANTE

Nervous energy hums through me as we speed down the road. It's different than anything I've ever felt. I'm always calm in business. No matter the situation, nothing rattles me because of my ability to focus. But not this time. This time, a part of me is missing, and I feel unhinged.

I can't believe Luke took Diablo. He has my heart in his hands, and every minute she's gone, he's crushing it. The idea anyone would covet her makes me furious. But knowing it was the one I pledged my loyalty to fills me with a rage I didn't think I was capable of and, if left unchecked, was liable to do anything.

I feel like a fool. All this time, I'd done what Luke asked, without question. I even pushed for Diablo's fealty because he wanted me to, though it drove me into a darker side of myself for centuries. But all this time, my loyalty meant nothing to him. He wanted her loyalty. He wanted her.

But Diablo never failed me. She's been with me all along. In the darkness, she has been my light. She fell for me, and I would fall for her, always. That's why I have to get her back. So I can tell her how much she means to me.

JJ was right. Last night, I should have told her that she is the very breath in my lungs and my reason for existing. And the idea that I may never get the chance to say all of this to her makes me feel desperate.

"We'll find her," Vinny says confidently, noticing my steely countenance.

I lift my chin and tighten my grip on the wheel. "Everything ready?"

"They'll be there," he nods.

"You two are something else," Lila says from the backseat. It's the first time she's spoken since we hit the mainland over an hour ago.

"If you think this is something, just wait," Vinny turns around.

"Do you think it will work?" she asks, clearly anxious. I know she's worried about Diablo, but I'm impressed with how she sat back and said nothing, letting Vinny and I do what we needed to.

"It's what I would do if it were you," he winks.

After Vinny filled us in on his plan, I had to admit that it was the best chance we had of getting Diablo back.

We had unlimited resources, yes. But we couldn't beat Luke on his home turf without a more thought-out plan. And that would require time, which we didn't have on our side at the moment.

I wanted to end Luke, but I knew it would take more than just threats to make it happen. It would need a different kind of plan. One that would dismantle the kingdom he'd built, one layer at a time. I could do this once she was safe. But right now, I just needed to get her back, and that's what Vinny's plan would do.

I step on the gas and pass a car going way too slow for my nerves. "What's the ETA on the shipment?"

Vinny looks down at his phone. "Plane should land in about an hour."

I nod tersely and look at the clock on the dash. Two hours had passed since I first realized Diablo was gone. But if our hunch was correct and Luke had taken her to his place, we were doing okay on time.

I, however, was not doing okay. With every passing minute, I grew more anxious. The only thing keeping me from losing it was knowing he couldn't take her far.

Only the daemon to whom she was bound could take Diablo out of Eden, which meant this trip to get her back had actually taken me away from her. But it was necessary, I tell myself for the hundredth time. We need what we came here for and can't get her away from Luke without it.

We speed through the gates at a private airstrip up the coast and pull up alongside the tarmac, and finally, after what feels like forever, a cargo plane touches down. I tap my fingers on the wheel anxiously, watching as it taxies.

Once it stops, a large set of stairs unfold, and a crew member descends. "Be back in a few," Vinny swings open the passenger door and hops out of the SUV.

He makes his way over to the plane and greets the crew member. They shake hands, then make their way to the back of the aircraft–returning a few minutes later, wheeling a large wooden shipping crate.

Once they reach the SUV, I get out and make my way over to them. "Is this everything?"

"Yes," the crew member opens the top of the crate with a crowbar and reaches inside, handing a gun to Vinny and one to me. "Everything you asked for."

I inspect the muzzle and trigger, remove the magazine, check the rounds, and shove it back in. "Have they all been checked?"

"Inspected each one myself," he confirms. "They're ready to go."

"Good work," Vinny pats him on the back.

"And the second shipment?" I look up at Vinny.

"It's on the plane."

"Good," I shove the gun in my hand in the back of my jeans, then turn my attention to the crew member. "I want you to have this plane fueled and ready to go. We should be back in a couple of hours and will need to leave as soon as we arrive. We'll call when we are ten minutes out so you can be ready."

"Copy that," the crew member nods. "And the second crate?"

"A security team will be arriving in thirty minutes. Make sure each is armed with one of the guns in that crate, and arm yourself. If anyone arrives before we do, you have the order to empty every round you have into them. Vin, anything else?"

"That about sums it up," Vinny shoves one gun into the back of his jeans and grabs another, doing the same.

"Alright then," I turn and make my way back to the SUV.

"Everything okay?" Lila asks when I climb into the driver's seat.

"All good," I confirm. "We'll be leaving in a minute."

Vinny and the crew member load all of the guns from the crate into the back of the SUV. After they've finished and closed the trunk, Vinny hops back into the passenger seat, and we speed away.

"So," Lila looks over her shoulder. "That's it behind me?"

"That it is," Vinny smiles.

"How does it work again?" she bites her lips nervously.

For the next five minutes, Vinny explains the tenuous nature of eternal life to Lila. No, the Fallen could not die, but we could be wounded, and one of the elements we'd learned could do so was Fire Obsidian. A rare material at the heart of Earth's creation, it was a danger to the Fallen because it was everything we were not. A natural part of this world.

Vinny said to me once that it wasn't a matter of if our kind would one day turn on one another, but when, and that we should look at mankind as an example of what not to do. No one thought more strategically than Vinny when it came to defense, so I trusted him to make sure we were ready if or when that day ever came.

After buying as much Fire Obsidian as we could find, Vinny had ammunition made and stashed in stockpiles around the world. That way, he said, we'd be ready whenever and wherever the shit hit the fan. The closest reserve was at my airfield in London, which was the cargo plane's starting point.

I never thought we'd have to use it, and to think Vinny had been right about the fact we would, and that time was now, was a bit of a mindfuck. Only, we weren't planning to use it on just any of the Fallen. We were going to use it on the one we'd been loyal to for thousands of years.

Not once since The Fall had I swayed from Luke's side. I'd been loyal to a fault. But when I realized he was the one who took Diablo, any allegiance I felt towards him died instantly. Now, the only thing I felt was the desire to empty as many Fire Obsidian bullets into him as I could.

"Well," Lila sits back. "When all this is over, I want to know more about the other elements that can harm us."

"Baby," Vinny's eyes flash. "I will tell you everything. And, if I'm being honest, I can't wait to put one of those guns in those perfect hands."

The way the two are looking at one another makes me anxious for Diablo. I want her with me so badly I'd shoot my way through an army to hold her.

Once Lila and Vinny peel their eyes away off one another, she turns her attention out the window, the familiar coastline we passed earlier rushing by once again.

"I can't believe we had to leave Eden only to come back," she sighs.

"I know," Vinny looks over at me, waiting for me to say something.

"You made the right call," I nod sharply. "We needed that ammunition. It is the only way."

A heavy silence falls between us as we speed back up the coast. "What do you think Lilith has to do with this?" Vinny asks while looking out the window.

"I don't know," I shake my head.

"Maybe it's a game?" Lila suggests.

"Possibly," I grip the wheel tighter, the idea making me tense. The games Lilith and Luke played were ruthless. Anyone caught in the crossfire usually got burned.

When we finally make the turn off for the tunnel, I sit up straighter in my seat and take a deep breath. "Do you think this is the war David mentioned last night? The one still to come."

Vinny taps his hand on the door. "Maybe. It certainly feels like it."

Lila sits forward, looking from me to Vinny. "Remember what I said earlier, about…" her voice trails off, and she points up.

"Yeah," I look at her in the rearview mirror.

"Does Luke still have…power?" she asks, and I can tell by the look on her face that she is thinking about something.

"Unfortunately," Vinny and I say in unison.

As an archangel, Luke was the highest of the Fallen, and when he fell, he retained some abilities. He'd used a lot of it to help perfect those who pledged their loyalty, and what remains to create the soulless.

"Well," she looks from Vinny to me. "Diablo and Luke...they're both archangels. If Luke still has power, maybe she does, too."

Vinny and I turn to one another, eyes wide. "Holy shit." Why hadn't we thought about that before?

"Have you ever seen her use any kind of...power?" Vinny turns to Lila.

"No," she shakes her head, then smiles softly. "But it's Diablo. She walks into a room, and people melt." My heart thumps deep in my chest. No truer words had ever been said. I'd seen it...and felt it. "Look at him," she waves a hand at me. "She did the impossible and turned him to mush."

"I am not, mush," I shake my head.

"Okay, sorry. How about you're tolerable now," she rolls her eyes.

I shake my head and shoot her a dirty look. "Did anyone ever tell you that you're a brat?"

"A brat?" she scoffs. "Said like a true obnoxious brother."

We both laugh, and soon Vinny is, too. It's a moment of levity we all need.

"We'll get her back," she squeezes my shoulder.

"I know," I say with confidence because we are. There is no alternative.

"Have you seen her use any kind of... power?" Vinny turns his attention to me.

"Other than what Lila said? No. But maybe that is her power."

We all grow quiet for a moment as the end of the tunnel comes into view. "Well," Lila pats both of our shoulders. "I'm betting on our girl and you two."

Vinny sticks his fist out, and I bump it with my own. When we exit the tunnel and see the convoy of cars waiting, I sit up.

Lila leans forward, a smile pulling at her lips. "I almost forgot how many of us there were."

I look at the group in front of me. "It's one hell of a legion, that's for sure. But there's double the amount of soulless, and make no mistake, they will be at Luke's, ready to serve and take us down."

"They'll be ready, too," Vinny says with assurance, nodding to the cars ahead of us.

Lila looks at him, her smile fading a bit. "What makes you so sure?"

"Because they are also family. And we have one another's backs, no matter what."

"Even when Luke is dear ole' dad?" she quips.

"No," Vinny shakes his head. "When this one," he points to me, "has had their back, more than dear ole' dad ever has."

I pull up next to the convoy and get out, followed by Vinny and Lila. It's time to tell them everything. Luke's betrayal, his plans for my angel, and that it was she who saved them, not Luke. I just hope Vinny is right–that they remember all the shit I've done for them. Because it's time for me to collect on every favor owed to me, and I won't take no for an answer.

36
DIABLO

I sit with my back against the wall, feet pulled to my chest. I have no idea what time it is, my head hurts, and my lip is beginning to swell where Luke hit me.

Since the outburst, he hasn't spoken, but he's kept his eyes on me, watching as servants come and go, offering food and other comforts. I declined each, disinterested in all of it, except for the change of clothes set at my feet.

I felt vulnerable wearing nothing but the T-shirt I'd been sleeping in when Luke took me and would've accepted anything not to feel so exposed. But when everything fit perfectly, down to the shoes, I was reminded of how closely he'd been watching me and felt the flames of my anger flare.

"Diablo, you must eat something," Luke says finally, breaking the silence between us. "I need you to be healthy."

"The only thing I need is for you to let me go," I pull my legs closer to me.

"It's never happening, so you should save yourself the headache and just accept it."

"Funny, not being hit could have saved me a headache, too."

"You know," he takes a breath. "None of this would be happening if Dante would've just secured your fealty as obligated."

I rub my temple, tired of Luke's insidious presence. "Why is my fealty so important to you?"

"Because I have plans that require your loyalty, that's

why."

I push up to my feet, anger getting the better of me. "You have no right to make plans for me! Did you forget we were equals once?"

"Oh, I remember," he smiles. Something about the way he says it sends a chill down my spine.

"Let me go, and whatever game you're playing with Lilith—"

Before I know what's happening, Luke has pushed up from his throne and making his way toward me again. "This is not a game, and it has nothing to do with Lilith! It is about you and me and your future."

I scramble backward, the look of fury in his eyes shifting my defiance into fear. "Stay away," I stick out my hand, not wanting him to come closer.

"I will not stay away from you," he reaches for my wrist and yanks me towards him. "You are my destiny. And I am going to enjoy watching Dante's face as I take from him what he took from me."

I struggle in Luke's grasp, but he is too strong. Red flickers in his eyes, and he spins me around and pulls me back to his chest. "Soon, you will beg for my touch, not his."

"Stop," I close my eyes, every muscle in my body flinching. Luke's hold is blistering, and I wince in agony as the skin on my arm sizzles.

"Why do you think the soulless give themselves to me so easily, hmm?" his lips touch my ear as he speaks, sending the hair on my arms sticking straight up. "I show them things they can only imagine. Do things that would set your body on fire."

"The only thing I want from you is to leave me alone!" I try to pull back, but his hold tightens.

"Every part of you was made for sin, Diablo. Your body and name are a reminder of the wickedness you possess. A darkness I am going to enjoy drawing out of you."

"No," my body stiffens at the thought.

"Yes," he moans with delight, pressing his chest into my back. My body tensed, his proximity alarming every inch of me. "And, when it is time, you will give me an heir."

My stomach roils violently, and my legs feel like they're about to buckle under me. "That's...not possible."

Luke wraps his arm around my waist and places his hand on my stomach. "How do you think Minerva is here? How do you think half of the children daemons have sired are here?" he growls wickedly. "But our child, Diablo, will be unlike any other. It will be the offspring of two archangels. And with your beauty and my mind, they will bring the world to its knees."

"No," his words horrify me. I try again to break free, but he holds me tighter. "You're sick."

"I'm focused," he counters, running his pinky along a strip of skin exposed by my shirt's riding up. "And make no mistake about it...you will give me an heir. No matter how long it takes."

My heart pounds in my chest, and blood whooshes in my ears as the room starts to spin. I'm close to crumbling, then a voice breaks through, silencing all of the noise and fear. "If you say another word, I'll pull the trigger."

Air rushes into my lungs, and I turn to see Dante standing with his arm outstretched and the barrel of a gun pressed against Luke's head. His shirt is ripped, and blood runs down his temple, but his focus on me is unwavering.

"I see you made it through my guards," Luke says with displeasure.

"Try eliminated," Dante smirks, but it fades when he sees the cut on my lip. Looking down at the ring on Luke's hand pressed against my stomach, then back up, his jaw clenches. "Did you hit her?"

"She's fine," Luke says flippantly. "If she's going to be with me, she needs to get used to a little rough handling."

"Let her go," Dante presses the barrel of his gun against Luke's head with greater force.

"Now, Dante," Luke tsks. "You know that gun is meaningless. I cannot be killed. And you," he tightens his hold. "Stop fighting me, or I'll break that delicate arm of yours."

"Maybe not," Dante says sharply. His focus is on Luke, but I know the tightness of his voice is due to his concern for me. "But I have what I need to get her away from you."

Luke flashes Dante an evil smile and licks my ear. I yank my head away, but his hold is unyielding. "Does she taste this sweet, everywhere?" he moves his hand down to the waistband of my pants. "Maybe I should find out right now while you watch."

Dante's blue eyes turn murderous, and he cocks the trigger. "Get your…fucking hands…off her!"

"Funny," Luke laughs, rubbing his hand back and forth over my stomach before digging his nails into my skin. "That's what I said every time you touched what belonged to me."

Dante forces Luke's head away from mine with the barrel of his gun and narrows his eyes. "I'm going to burn your empire to the ground. Do you hear me?"

Luke tightens his hold on my wrist, and I wail in pain as the flesh on my arm blisters. "She is so delicate," he moans with delight. "Will her wrist snap if I grip it just a little harder? Or have you taught her the pleasure in pain?"

"You are a deplorable piece of shit," Dante bares his teeth. "I can't believe I ever swore my loyalty to you!"

"You didn't always feel that way. You were my biggest fan at one point. Do you remember?"

"Consider my opinion forever changed the day you decided to take what's mine!"

Luke lets go of my wrist, and the pain eases, followed by a chill that shoots down my spine as he moves my hair to the side and trails a finger down my neck.

"Do you brand all of your play toys, Dante? Maybe I should erase this nonsense and give her a brand of my own. She will be the mother of my child, after all."

His touch doesn't just make me sick. It provokes my rage. I slam my head back into Luke's face, and a bolt of pain shoots through my already throbbing head. He grunts and tightens both arms around me.

"Aren't you tired of fighting for him?" Luke rests his head on my shoulder, squelching my struggle. My chest aches and my body feels like it's being crushed and set on fire. "Aren't you tired of your guilt and those endless, beautiful tears?"

"Angel," Dante says evenly. I look up and find his eyes on mine. They are full of strength and resolve, and love. So much love I can feel it in every fiber of me. "Remember what Vinny said at breakfast."

I think back to that happiness yesterday when time stopped for a spell, and we felt normal, like a family. I try to focus on Dante's words, but my woozy head makes it hard to understand.

"About family…" he continues. The memory of Lila and Vinny cooking in the kitchen flashes in my mind, and Vinny's words echo in my ear–*You are family. I got your back.* I look at Dante, and he nods. "Now," his eyes dart quickly to the right, "and always."

It hits me then what Dante is trying to tell me, and without thinking, I use all of the strength I can muster and bend over. Luke's arms pull away, and I break free as Dante pulls the trigger of his gun, hitting Luke in the head while a bullet strikes his back.

Dante reaches for my hand with his free one and pulls me behind his back as Luke doubles over and falls to the ground.

"I got him," Vinny approaches from behind, gun trained on Luke.

Dante's eyes are cold, his expression full of rage and resentment, but it fades when he lowers his gun and turns to me. "Are you okay?" he pushes my hair back to examine my face, looking at my cheek and lip, before turning his eyes to mine.

I fight back the tears, everything I feel for him crashing to the surface. "I'm fine."

"Are you sure?" he swallows. "He didn't...do anything, did he?" I can see the question is hard for him to ask.

I lean into his touch and put my hand over his. "He hit me, that's all."

Dante blows out a relieved breath and cups my face, kissing my forehead and cheek, and lastly, my lips, gently, careful of the cut. "I can't believe that bastard hurt you."

A tear breaks free as he pulls me into his embrace. "Thank you for finding me," I whisper.

"I told you," he tightens his hold, "I will always find you."

I want to stay like this forever, but I know we can't. "We have to leave," I pull back, desperate to get as far away from Luke as possible. "He has plans...for me and you."

"I heard," Dante's jaw tics. "But he will never touch you again, angel. I promise."

"Please," I beg. "We need to go. Now before he wakes." I can hear the panic in my voice, and so can Dante.

"We will," he says with reassurance. "But there is something we have to do first. What we shot him with will keep him down for a bit, but for good measure," Dante turns and unloads another round of bullets into Luke.

Vinny strides over to us with Lila at his side. "Thank goodness you're okay," she throws her arms around me.

"You came, too?" I hug her tight.

"Girl, of course," she squeezes, then releases me and steps back.

Vinny looks at the bruise on my cheek and narrows his eyes. "I'm fine," I say before he can ask. "He hit me, that's all. But listen, there's something I need to tell you." Hearing the urgency in my voice, the three look at me intently. "It's Minerva. She's...his daughter."

"What?" they say in unison, three sets of eyes wide in disbelief.

"Wait, there's more. Luke knows we have the contract. And get this, he's the one who gave it to the Vatican. It's part of some deal they made."

Vinny looks at Luke and shakes his head. "That bastard!"

"There's one more thing." Vinny turns back around, and the three of them look at me, pupils growing with anticipation. "Lilith and Luke...they're not working together. He seemed genuinely surprised to hear she was here, and the bartender is working for both of them, but neither knows, it seems."

Dante exchanges a look with Vinny, then turns to me. "You used your time to distract him and get information, didn't you?"

"That's why he hit me. I wasn't giving in without a fight. I was biding time until you got here."

Dante grins and flashes me a look that's a mix of admiration, pride, and passion. "My clever angel."

"What do you think is going on?" I ask, unable to pull my eyes from his.

"I don't know. We'll discuss all of this later. Right now, we need to finish this."

I look from Dante to Vinny, curious about what could be more important than getting out of here. "What's going on?"

Dante turns his attention to the end of the hall. "Take a look."

I follow his eyes as the sound of footsteps fills the cavernous space. All the Fallen are here, and they stand together, determination in their eyes and a weapon in hand.

I stare at them in awe, forgetting how many there are. "We told them everything," Dante continues. "They know Luke lied, and they will rescind their fealty."

I shake my head and turn to him. "I can't believe it. You got them to listen."

"What wouldn't I do for you, angel," he reaches for my hand.

"Diablo," Viper approaches, gun in hand. "You fought for us. Let us fight for you."

She was one of the toughest daemons and wanted to fight for me. I stare at her, stunned by her loyalty. "I don't know what to say."

"Don't say anything," Dante squeezes my hand. "Just let us and them do what we need to do."

"Alright," Vinny claps his hands together as Viper nods at me. "Let's do this and get out of here. And remember, on the count of three, and for it to work, we have to say exactly what Dante told us to and at the same time. Got it?"

A few laugh, others nod, and some even whistle, but when Vinny begins the countdown, all the Fallen turn silent, and when he reaches zero, they rescind their loyalty in unity. A rush of air blows through the chamber, sending goosebumps down my arms. I can feel it–we're free from the contract. It worked.

"I can't believe it," I look up at Dante as the vow that has bound us together for five thousand years ends, and a new promise–one made between our hearts, begins.

"Believe it, angel," he leans in and kisses me.

"Alright," Vinny pulls Lila to his side. "Let's go! We got a plane to catch."

37
DIABLO

We start to make our way out of the hall when a voice stops us in our tracks. "Not so fast," Luke says darkly. The four of us turn, watching in shock as he pushes up from the ground. "Heaven couldn't kill me. I doubt you'll be able to."

Dante aims his gun at Luke. "Didn't plan to kill you…yet."

"If you're going to get me, you need to do it now," he rolls his shoulders. "Because if you don't, I will feast on your angel while you watch."

"You will never touch her again!" Dante holds the gun tight. "Do you understand me? Whatever sick fantasy you have in that mind of yours, it's never going to happen. She belongs to me. Me!" he repeats angrily, his voice echoing along the walls.

"Oh, Dante," he laughs. "You know you only have her because of the things I taught you."

I hold Dante's hand tight, reminding him of the truth. "I have her because she chose me," he says confidently. "And I would sooner die than let you hurt her again."

"Fitting words, since death will be the only way you leave here."

"It's game over for you," Dante stands tall and cocks his gun.

"Oh, you're my judge and jury now?" Luke sneers. "You and what army?"

Dante looks to the end of the hall, and Luke's eyes follow. "Hers."

"We've shown them the contract," Vinny says, gun trained on Luke. "They know you lied."

Luke looks to the legion and notices they are standing ready to protect us, not him. "You can't do this!"

"We can, and we did," Dante smirks.

"I made you who you are," Luke looks from him to Vinny. "You betrayed me!"

"Betrayed you?" Dante shouts back. "You deceived all of us! She is the reason we exist. She saved us, not you! And because they know what you did, they have rescinded their fealty and sworn it to her. After five thousand years, your reign is over."

"You are all fools," Luke stares at the Fallen. "And you," he looks back at Dante. "You will pay for this."

Out of the corner of my eye, I see one of the Fallen step forward. I turn and find Sam with a gun pointed at us. "Sam?" I look at him, confused.

"I'm sorry, Dante," he shakes his head, eyes frantic. "But I can't let you leave with her. He has my daughter. And if you leave, he'll kill her."

"Your daughter?" Dante shakes his head, confused. "What are you talking about?"

Everyone has a price, Diablo. That's what Luke said earlier. And the life of one's child was worth the price of deception.

"That's why you swore fealty," I look at Sam.

"I'm sorry," he looks at me, eyes full of apology. "I know I said I never would, but I had to do something."

"Sam," Viper turns to her undecided, face serious. "Put the gun down, now."

"I can't do that," he shakes his head. "If I don't do this, I will never see my daughter again."

Viper reaches for the gun, but it goes off before she can

grab it. I watch in horror as the bullet flies across the hall and hits Dante. "Nooooo!" I scream as he stumbles backward.

He clutches his chest and looks up, baring his teeth. "I'm…fine, angel."

"But you're bleeding," I look at him, frantic.

He smiles at me gently as blood seeps through his fingers, marring the fresh ink bearing my name. "I'll be okay, angel."

My hand finds his and presses down. "Are you sure?"

He nods as the bleeding picks up, soaking both of our hands. "I'm… okay," he breathes through the shock. "Stings a bit, that's all."

"What the fuck!" Vinny turns his gun on Sam. "What is wrong with you?"

"I only did what you would do for Lila," he shakes. "What Dante would do for her."

Vinny cocks his gun. "Tell me why I shouldn't empty every bullet I have in you right now?"

"Because you need the bullets for me," Luke's voice taunts from behind us. Lila, Vinny, and I turn to see him push up from the ground as if his body wasn't full of bullets.

Vinny strides over to Dante and me, pumping Luke full of bullets as he walks. Once Luke is again on the ground, he puts his hand on Dante's shoulder. "You, okay, brother?"

"Is…he…down?" Dante asks.

"He's down," Vinny looks at Dante's wound, shaking his head. "But something's not right."

I look at Vinny in alarm. "What do you mean?"

"Vin…need to…get her…out." Dante's words come in short breaths.

"Fire Obsidian knocks you out. You'll bleed if you get shot with it, but you'll be okay. Dante should be down right now, and Luke should have been for hours with how many bullets

311

we put into him."

"Don't...think...it's obsidian," Dante falls to his knees.

Vinny and I sink to the ground with him. "But that's all the ammo we had."

"It's not one of ours," Viper calls out as Vinny helps me ease Dante onto his back.

"What is it?" Vinny asks, keeping his eyes on Dante.

Viper takes out the magazine from Sam's gun and inspects it. "I don't believe it," she looks up, expression grim. "It's...stardust. Where the hell did you get this, Sam?"

Sam's eyes shift to Luke's lifeless body. "He gave it to me."

I look at Vinny, not liking the expression on his face. "What is stardust?"

"It means we have to get Dante out of here, right now," he clasps a hand over his mouth.

Viper and the rest of the legion surround Sam, but I see Luke stirring. I turn and look at him as he pushes up, lips pulling into a smile. "Why?" I ask, hating him more than I ever have.

"I told you," he stands slowly, pausing to catch his breath. "You are mine."

Vinny looks from Dante to Luke. "How is this possible?"

"You think I didn't know about your stockpile? That I don't have a backup plan? I split Heaven in two. You can't outsmart me."

Vinny looks at Sam who is being restrained by Viper and a couple of the Fallen. "You betrayed us!"

"He has my daughter," Sam croaks. "I had to do something."

"You could have come to us!" Vinny shouts angrier than I've ever seen him. "We would have helped, like always."

Dante starts to cough, and his grip on my hand weakens.

"Vinny?" I look up, starting to panic.

"I thought you said we couldn't die," Lila drops down next to Vinny.

"We can't," Vinny responds, one eye on Luke and the other on Dante. "But stardust can hurt us badly."

"How?" I ask, growing frantic by Dante's deteriorating state.

"It is what we were," Luke answers crisply.

"And when what we were, meets what we are," Vinny shoots Luke a scathing look. "It neutralizes us. Why the fuck are you up again?"

"What do you mean it neutralizes?" My voice is high and bordering on hysterical.

"Our immortality fades, and mortality kicks in. And whatever injury you have, becomes mortal."

"He was shot in the chest!" I grip Dante's hand with both of mine.

Vinny grips his jaw, exhales angrily, and then looks at Luke. "How did you get your hands on it? Only a few sources exist."

"I know, and I bought them all and built up my immunity to it and everything else that can harm me. As I said, I will always be one step ahead of you. You may as well face it, Diablo," Luke holds out his hand. "Your place is with me."

Dante's hold on my hand weakens, and his eyes flutter. "Vinny, we need to get him help, now."

"You will be going nowhere," Luke adjusts his jacket.

"Hey, man," Vinny grabs Dante's shoulder. "Hang in there, brother."

"He can hang in as long as he wants," Luke laughs. "But you will be going nowhere with Diablo."

Dante's eyes drag sluggishly up to Vinny, and he mumbles

something to him, then he turns to me, lip tugging up at the corner, as his hand slackens in my hold.

I close my eyes, tears spilling free, as a feeling of déjà vu slams into me, stealing the air from my lungs. The desperation in my heart is the same as that which crushed my spirit five thousand years ago when I begged for Dante's existence and gave up my wings to save him.

"Please," I place my hand on Dante's face. "Stay with me."

But he doesn't respond. He doesn't smile, squeeze my hand, or move at all. He is still, just as he was the night he fell.

I look at Luke, filled with neither anger nor rage but the need for revenge. "You're going to pay for this."

"You'll get over it," he scoffs. "And you—" he looks to the legion.

"You...will pay for this," I push up on one foot, fists clenched at my sides.

I want to hurt him for all he has done. Yet, despite the ferocity of my need to make him pay, I also feel every other emotion I've experienced since the fall—regret, guilt, abandonment, joy, happiness, and love. They storm through me, the last one the strongest of them all, fueling me with solemn strength.

I push up with my other foot and straighten, staring at Luke coldly. "Do you know why I chose the name Diablo?" I ask, voice devoid of emotion.

He stares back at me, sick curiosity burning in his eyes. "A testament to your darkness?"

A laugh, foreign from my own, escapes my lips. "A testament to the wrath I am capable of unleashing."

"Your anger is nothing compared to my will."

"That's where you're wrong," I grin viciously. "My wrath is not fueled by anger. It's fueled by love. A force more powerful than any."

The contract is broken. I can say what I want without regret or repercussion, and my confession will be my ammunition. "It's why I fell and has been my reason for existence ever since. And it will be your reckoning."

I look up, needing Heaven to see I am again fighting for the reason for our existence–love. Love was love. What did it matter for whom we felt it? If we could feel it for man, I could feel it for Dante. It wasn't wrong. It was the essence of my spirit.

"I have always served you," I whisper. "Do not abandon me when I need you most."

"Heaven does not hear us anymore," Luke tsks, watching me with feigned pity. But I know it can. Heaven hears all and sees all. I know it has kept watch, allowing Luke to do as he wished because another battle is coming. One where I will be its greatest weapon.

"I will fight for you when you need me," I plead. "If you fight for me now." The hall is quiet. Nothing but the sound of a thousand heartbeats echoing along the walls. "Please!" I scream, tears rolling down my cheeks.

Another beat of silence, flanked by heavy breathing, then I feel it. A sharp pain in my back, followed by the sound of tearing flesh and breaking bones.

Vinny and Lila look around as the hall begins to shake, and fire rips through me. The agony is excruciating, stealing my breath as it ravages my body, followed by pain, unlike anything I've ever felt. But as soon as it starts, it stops. All of the pain. All of the agony. All of the fire…gone.

Luke stares at me, fear in his eyes and disbelief on his face, as I straighten my shoulders and feel them behind me–wings the color of fire, extending high and wide. "It's not possible," he shakes his head.

"You were right when you said I would be queen," I flash a menacing smile. "But not yours. Never, yours."

I flap my wings once, feeling their power behind me, still familiar after all this time. Then I do it again, sending a wall of wind the force of a hurricane, barreling towards Luke. It sends him crashing into the wall, obliterates the fires next to his throne, and cracks it in half.

He looks from me to the back of the hall and, without saying another word, turns and then simply vanishes. "That's right, you coward," I shout. "You better run because I'm coming for you. Do you hear me, Luke? I'm coming for you!"

I stare after him, shocked that he just left after all of his threats, bravado, scheming, and lies. Something tells me we haven't seen the last of him.

"We need to get him out of here." I drop back down to Dante's side and place my hand on his chest. His heart is still beating, but it's weak.

Lila reaches out to touch my wing, hand trembling. "How is this possible?"

"I don't know," I shake my head. "But it doesn't matter right now. We need to help Dante. Vinny," I look up, "do you know what to do?"

"Yes," he shifts his focus from my wings back to his best friend. "We need to get him to London. There's a plane waiting for us an hour down the coast. But we need to leave now."

"Then let's go. Can you carry him?"

He reaches under Dante and stands. "Already done."

Dante is eerily still, which makes my blood cold. If anything happens to him, Luke will pay. So, help me, he will pay.

"What about them?" Lila looks to the legion. Each wears a mixed expression of awe, shock, and disbelief on their face.

"I will not force loyalty," I straighten my back, wings folding tightly behind me. "They are free to choose."

It's quiet as the three of us stare at them, waiting for a response. It takes a minute, but then Viper approaches and takes a knee. "We got your back, Diablo."

"And Sam?" Vinny asks, shooting daggers at the undecided that shot his best friend.

I put a hand on his shoulder. I should want Sam to pay, but I don't. My fight is not with him. It is with Luke. "Our focus right now needs to be on Dante. He's all that matters."

Vinny's face is hard with anger, but he nods stiffly in agreement. "Keep an eye on him, Viper. And if he gets out of line again, empty every bullet in that gun he got from Luke into him."

Sam stares back at Vinny, regret heavy in his eyes. "I'm sorry," he shakes his head. "Dante will be okay, won't he?"

"Save it," Vinny scowls. "And you'd better hope he's okay. If not, you'll have not only me to deal with but Diablo. And something tells me my anger will have nothing on hers."

"When he's healed," I look at Vinny as we make our way out of the hall, with the legion close behind, "we finish what you two started. We burn Luke's kingdom to the ground."

Vinny turns to me, his lip hitching up. "Sounds like my kind of plan. And those wings, do we look for answers?"

"We'll see," I look down at Dante, nothing mattering more right now than him. Once he's okay, we look for answers and go to war. Angels may be merciful, but we are also vengeance, and I plan to wield that sword until Luke's kingdom is no more. After all, I am one of the Fallen, and no one fucks with my family and gets away with it.

COMING SOON...
LEGION OF THE QUEEN, BOOK 2

Thank you for reading Fealty of the Fallen! If you enjoyed it, please leave a review on your favorite retailer or book community, blog, or website. Your support means the world to me!

I look forward to sharing more of Dante and Diablo with you. They will get their HEA...they'll just have to go to Hell and back to get it.

ACKNOWLEDGEMENTS

First, I want to thank my readers. I am forever grateful and humbled for your continued support and enthusiasm for my writing. I hope you enjoyed diving into this world and stay with me for the next chapter in Dante and Diablo's story.

I also want to thank my family for their patience and support. I'm sure hearing "I'm in the middle of something" or "let me finish this, please" or "just five more minutes" is hard to hear on repeat when the writing muse calls. But just so my boys know, I am never half-listening. I hear everything.

This story came to me at a time when I doubted myself. It hit hard and fast, and with so much passion and clarity in many ways, it was the easiest story I've written so far. Thank you to my friends in the writing community who have supported not just this story but also my work and journey. You know who you are, and I am grateful for you.

Thank you to Rebecca at RFK Designs for taking four words and creating a lush cover that is everything I wanted. I have never loved a cover so much.

Thank you to Shauna and Wildfire Marketing Solutions for being such great partners to help spread the word and help me have a fantastic launch. You've been awesome.

And to the readers and reviewers, thank you for your likes, loves, shares, and support of my work. You are why I write.

ABOUT THE AUTHOR

D.M. Simmons is an international award-winning author of adult, new adult, and young adult fiction. She creates lush, atmospheric worlds, which tell captivating stories filled with complicated but swoon-worthy relationships, characters to fall in love with, and heroes to champion. Fascinated by the indelible power of love, romance is usually at the heart of her stories and the narrator's journey. She believes in love of all kinds: new, old, young, lost, unrequited, irrevocable, forbidden, enemies to lovers, friends to lovers, star-crossed, soulmates, and everything in between. You can expect a HEA, but she makes her characters work for it. When she isn't writing, she can be found reading, binge-watching TV shows, listening to music, running her kids around, creating aesthetics, and wondering where the time goes.
For news and updates visit my website at
www.dmsreadwrite.com.

ALSO BY D.M. SIMMONS

The Lake Haven Series
Evoke
Ravel

Short Stories
"Fiver" from The New Normal, A Zombie Anthology
"Risers" from Beneath The Twin Suns, An Anthology

Printed in Great Britain
by Amazon

84094062R10192